CHRIS COLMENERO

X MEMBERS OF THE FB GROUP

This book is a work of fiction. Names, characters, locations and events are either a product of the author's imagination, fictitious, or used fictitiously. Any resemblance to any event, locale or person, living or dead, is purely coincidental.

First edition published 2023

All production designs are trademarks.

Paperback ISBN: 978-1-7339619-8-1

Author's Notes

- If you aren't offended by words like fuck and meat curtains, you might enjoy this book.
- You should just stop reading now if you have a problem with Southern phrases like "His pants were so tight I could see his religion" or Southern slang words like ain't and darlin'.
- This book is riddled with dark humor, so if cheesy scenes and laughable murders aren't your cup of tea, gift this book to that annoying neighbor of yours.
- I am an admin for a readers' Facebook group in real life, but the main character and I do not share the same beliefs, opinions, or personalities. JoDi is a fictional character. It is not me. I also want to add that I have removed myself from all blocking and suspensions in the group. The other admins oversee that portion. I now only manage book giveaways, author projects, theme days, BOTM, holiday competitions, author interviews, and group trips. (So, if you find yourself blocked or suspended from the group, please do not take it out on my books.)
- There is absolutely no harm done to animals in this book.
- Children do not get murdered in this book, nor is there any rape.
- If you are a Psychological Thriller Readers FB group member, first – you rock! Second, there is a chance your name will be in here, but again, please remember that all characters are fictional. Also, the name will most likely not live for too long.
- You may want to call in sick and quickly make yourself a cocktail at about chapter 34.
- Is this a true story? This is a true story, except for all the parts that aren't true.
- Lastly, ask me about the haunted book cover … now that's a true story. You can also ask the cinematographer who took the photo. We were both there!

Definitions

1. Admin: An admin is a person who owns a Facebook group. Also known as administrators. They have control over everything in the group and manage all settings and rules. An admin can edit the page, add apps, create and delete posts, send messages to members, ban members, and suspend members.
2. Accoutrement – I have no fucking idea.
3. ARC–Advanced Readers Copy.
4. Chichis – Boobs.
5. Dismembered – Removing limbs from naughty members, preferably with an ax.
6. DNF–Did Not Finish.
7. Fanny – Someone's butt. Oh, but yeah, it also means female genitalia.
8. FOMO – Fear Of Missing Out.
9. Getting on my tits – Annoying me.
10. Masa – Dough
11. Pantalones – Pants.
12. Shenanifucks–Lots of wild fuckery gone wrong. (My own creation … you're welcome.)
13. TBR–To Be Read.
14. DBTBRP – Death by TBR pile.

Acknowledgments

I want to thank the continuous support from my family and friends. I would also like to give a huge thank you to every reader, author, and the other admins who are part of the Psychological Thriller Readers group on Facebook. None of this would be possible without you.

Book Cover Photo

Huge thank you to Cooper Dunn who took the photo for the cover of this book! I'm delighted we were able to capture this haunted photo together. It's a story that will live on forever.

Cooper Dunn is an accomplished cinematographer with over fifty major motion pictures and television shows under his belt. Some include *My Spy: The Eternal City*, *Heels*, *The Walking Dead*, *Stranger Things*, and *Tomorrow War*.

When not filming, he enjoys spending time with his siblings, seven nieces and nephews. He is a world traveler, visiting places like Rome, Alaska, and South America. Cooper feels incredibly lucky to have collaborated creatively with people worldwide.

Formatting

This book was formatted by Melvyn Paulino, a multidisciplinary graphic designer professionally trained in typography, layout, and visual communication.

"If you want to be creative, stay in part a child, with the creativity and invention that characterizes children before they are deformed by adult society."

-Jean Piaget, Swiss Psychologist

Prologue

I am a killer. I am an admin. Murdering members is what I do. However, keep in mind that I *always* do the right thing. I take a life to save a life. There is no need for some *drawn*-out pre-story to my big story. Just DO NOT get on my naughty list. Unless you want the wolves to find your pretty little fingers nailed to the bottom of a tree.

CHAPTER I

JoDi

It is eight p.m. on a Thursday, Georgia evening. The sun is sinking fast, and a fan of bright rays stretch along the western sky like strings of a golden harp, then surrender to a shiver of yellow that halo the grand forest of Kennesaw Mountain. The night's cool air is filled with the scent of olive tea tree and blooming gardenia. The earth is speaking to me. Millions of leaves collide, casting out sounds of crashing waterfalls. Pine trees too close together shriek, much like a painful death, as the wind forces the towering trunks to rub vigorously against each other. The evening insects are singing songs of triumph. I am taking it all in. I love living surrounded by trees and wildlife.

I walk inside. At the final click of my front door shutting, the sounds break into an alarming silence. The smells instantly change. The feeling inside of me merges with my surroundings. Looking around in a quiet house, like most evenings, I'm reminded that my husband is working the night shift. I am all alone.

Much like a fishing hook buried deep in my mouth, managed by an eager angler, my laptop reels me in. A part of me tries to escape into deeper waters, but another part pulls the hook tight and swallows it until it hits my bowels, where there is no turning back. I am an admin, after all, and my members need me.

Like many things in life, I am overthinking it. Do I really need to do this now? I need to pay bills. So much needs to be done; laundry, emails, clean the dishes, cook, eat, eat, eat, let's not forget to eat again. Okay, just skim through quickly, and check if there are any repetitive posts I need to delete. Go to manage and see how much spam was caught that needs to be trashed. See how many messages are waiting in Messenger. Oh, the many, many messages. Please, God, help me.

"I need to know why I can't comment. I did nothing wrong. Why did you suspend me?"

"I am not a spammer. Why was I booted?"

"Why was my post deleted? It doesn't seem fair. It wasn't any different from the others?"

"There is a member harassing other members. I just thought you should know."

"I would like an explanation as to why you deleted my comment. I was just standing up for myself. The other lady was rude first?"

"I'm an author. Would it be okay to promote my book?"

Don't get me wrong. We *absolutely* need the members to help us. We are not super-human. We couldn't possibly catch everything. Hell, it's impossible to catch most wrong-doing. However, I don't believe the members understand that most suspensions are automatic suspensions. We don't sit around all day, fire coming out of our ears, suspending members for the fun of it. No, we have things in place to assist us. If we didn't, we'd have a group full of porn or awkward videos of people getting run over by buses somewhere like Asia or South America.

I must remind myself to be patient. Even if it takes me hours to get through all the messages, just get it done.

The rules, the rules. Too many members are breaking the rules. They may not *read* the rules. They are probably connected to ten or more reading groups. I wonder if they read all the pinned posts at the top of the group page under Featured. Those are always important.

My ankles itch. My boss has a smashing body. Fuck, I need to do laundry again. Okay, get out of this funk. Be positive. You are better than this. Just log in for a bit, do some work, check on the group, chat with the other admins, and see what they are up to. When all that is done, perhaps post something highly inappropriate and dark.

Yes, that's what I'll do … I'll make some funny comments on several threads. That should make the members laugh, right? That's what I really want to do anyway. I want to make them laugh. I want them to be happy.

I sit. I grin. I reach for the anti-bacterial serum sitting next to my keyboard and apply two pumps of liquid onto the palm of my hand. As I rub it in, I observe my hands moving in perfect swirls with each other.

Where are all the germs even going? Are they just *disappearing*? Are they just becoming *smaller* and spreading even further? This stuff is making my hands crack … so annoying. Be positive, be positive—look at this pretty screen, look at this pretty keyboard. How lucky am I? There are kids and people all over the world who don't even have a computer, so stop complaining about germs and be grateful.

I hear a bling sound coming from my computer. It's a notification. With unwavering certainty, I open up my Readers Facebook group. Back to what really matters. Back to my group full of members who, like myself, find joy in reading, sharing reviews, and hoarding books. I click on MEMBER REPORTED A COMMENT alert. I open it.

Wait … did a member just tell another member to go suck-a-dick? Yes, yes, she did. Baby Jesus, shoot me down to Hell right now because I'm having a hard time not laughing. Hold it in, hold it in. But wait, this could really hurt someone's feelings. Okay, who is the person who received this comment? Dang it, the profile picture is a cat with a Lucky-charms bandana. What if the member is elderly? That's dreadful!

What part of "respect your elders" is confusing for some people? What if she is a teenager dealing with bullying at school? This is supposed to be a safe space. We don't want to cause *suicides*. We don't want to cause pain in this group. This is unforgivable.

The frustration builds up in my ankles. The entire situation has transformed into something quite serious in my mind. This is no laughing matter ... not anymore. This is a big problem, and I must take care of it. The members are like sisters, like brothers, like ... family. Yes, they are my *family*. Family. Family. I shake my ankles loose. I inhale deeply, allowing the alcohol smell from the antibacterial serum to spread through my lungs. A calmness comes over me. But before I show this dreadful comment to the other admins, who no doubt will laugh about it like I almost did, I jot down every important detail I can find about Lony Gansmann.

With a deep voice and my lips protruding, I say, "Lony, no one speaks like that in *my* group."

I like to speak out loud. It happens quite often. As I speak the words, mild rippling sensations of disgust crawl through the deep layers of my skin. I don't know if I love it or hate it. Perhaps I should bury another crystal in my backyard. That always makes me feel calm and safe.

After requesting to be Lony's friend on my personal Facebook page, I click back to the group to search where this violence had just occurred. I now notice another exchange, and Lony has crossed the line. Her comment reads, "Seriously, you are slower than a sloth on heroin, just go hang yourself already." Beads of sweat gather in my popliteal fossa. You may have gotten away with "Go suck-a-dick," Lony, but not this. Straightening my legs briefly to air them out is just one way I attempt to cool off my body.

I move the mouse and click on her personal page. Lony has accepted my friend request. A critical decision must now be made. Studying

Lony's profile image is like being sucked into a black hole. Trash. Malevolent. Or is she? With a remnant of my rational mind, I notice the vibrant smile of Lony's daughter, whose puggy face clings tightly against her mother. It's quite obvious it's her daughter by the band circling the profile picture that reads Best Daughter Ever. Their cheeks are pressed together like masa in a tortilla smasher. Staring closely into Lony's eyes, I find myself mesmerized by their brightness. The fullness of their love for one another radiates the page. With little effort, I move my stare to the daughter—eyes just as bright but with smaller yellow specks.

Lony's daughter adores her mother. She adores her daughter. Of course, yes, of course. How can I do anything to this woman? I can't kill her … *can* I?

Naturally I pause in thought. I let the words GO SUCK A DICK, JUST GO HANG YOURSELF ALREADY pass before my eyes like a banner in the sky being pulled by a small airplane. Seconds, not minutes, go by, and the battle between good and evil fades away into meaningless thoughts. They take flight into the land of nothingness.

Perhaps I will take a strand of Lony's hair and bury it in the backyard. That way, I will feel better. With great caution and near-perfect penmanship, I write Lony's name down on my ledger under ANNIHILATE. The word *annihilate* flutters between my lips just as softly as I write it.

"Annihilate." A grand whisper.

I feel a delicious numbness come over me even as I say the word out loud, some form of last vagrant vibration. Bloodthirst and vengeance devour my every thought. Every sensation. Every cell. I close my ledger. I will go back to it soon. I will go back and take care of what *needs* to be done for my group. That's what *really* matters. It must wait, though. It must wait because my plate is currently full. It is almost *always* full.

Annihilate (naughty list)

~~Jen Kline~~ N3401'45.40140 W1170'13.38580 (California Mount.)
-Jen Kline,
may I pull out your spine?
I have a set of hungry swine
that are looking to dine,
Miss pretty little Cline.

~~Daisy Car~~ N30024'14.60460 W86039'39.53170 (Mary Esther FL)
-Miss Daisy Car, just like a star,
I'll sing your favorite song as I play my guitar.
I'll take you far, somewhere bizarre.
And when I put out my cigar
on your filthy-ass tongue,
it will surely leave a scar.

~~Joyce Tiantefilou~~ N 33058'43.05760 W84034'17.22730 (Kennesaw Mountain)
-Miss Joyce, Miss Joyce,
Imma cut out that voice.
You will have no choice.
And when your face falls flat on that mud,
I will rejoice, Miss Joyce."

Sandi Bennett?

Stephanie Telas?

~~Sahnon Cates~~ N30016'16.21670 W 97046'7.84110 (Austin, TX, Lady Bird Lake)
-Miss Sahnon Cates,
your ankles will have weights
in the middle of the lake.
You'll have a lovely face
full of mace,
Miss Sahnon Cates.

Nicky Lee?

Ashley Aballi N30030'13.74790 W84018'59.94320 (Lake Jackson Tallahassee, FL)
-Miss Ashley,
you may think you are crafty,
but I assure you, your face will appear ghastly.
Perhaps I'll use a meat grinder, Miss Ashley,
and turn you into a patty.
Miss Ashly is nasty.
Should I dump your body in Tallahassee?

~~Lony Gansmann~~ N33057'38.34190 W84035'48.700600 (Kennesaw Mountain)
-Miss Lony
you are so very scrawny.
Now that you have been naughty
your resting place will be thorny.

Maria Vella?
-Shall I send your body parts to Korea,

Miss Maria?
I’ll smash your pretty little skull like a tortilla
Miss Maria.

Nichole Hollweg N46011’27.57930 W 123051’9.59120 (Cannery Pier, Astoria, OR)
-I can’t wait to see you beg
Miss Hollweg.
I’ll tie you to a bed
unfed.
I’ll get in your head
Miss pretty little Hollweg.
And after I chop off your leg
I’ll leave you for dead.

Christa Duffin?

Holli Bender N42029’48.86160 W77049’18.164220 (Ossian State Forest, NY)
-Miss Holi Bender,
let’s hope you are slender.
Will she fit if I bend her?
Maybe I’ll put your potty-ass mouth in a blender.

Raianna Bodine?

Shanna Mannley?

Jeremi Campbell N 35 27'24.05110 W83 7'42.88130 (Maggie Valley N. Carolina)
-You won't go to jail
Mr. Jeremi Campbell,
more like hell.
No one will hear you yell
and there will be no farewell.
Will your body swell?
Perhaps in a well.

Javier Mollina?
Malissa Smith?
Jessica Fenn?
Kaci Lewis?
Vicki Rowe?

Ashlyne Ward?
-Shall I make you a necklace made of metal-cord,
Miss Ward?
With a sword
I'll slice you up and never get bored.

Robinn Harris?
Daniele Sumpman?
Wendi Miille?
Sunni Murphy?
Charly Helton?

CHAPTER 2

JoDi

It has been far too long since I've traveled for personal reasons. I'm long past due for some quality time with old friends. Overly eager to visit my special friend Holli Rylee has left me restless. Visiting Holli has been on my mind for a couple of years, and now the time has finally come. She's one of those friends who will stay in my heart forever. Our reunions are all very organic, fun, and peaceful. When we were in our twenties, we spent almost every weekend together, either bar hopping in downtown Austin, Texas, or boat hopping at Devil's Cove on Lake Travis. Now more mature, living in different states, both successful, we find ourselves only able to see each other every couple of years.

Holli's apartment is undeniably special, seeing as it's on the water's edge in the most beautiful area in Florida. The community property she lives in, for the most part, is quite unique. The owners have a grand house on the property that they live in. Its thick columns and countless windows give it an above-average luxurious look. Also on the property are two separate duplexes that the owners rent out, Holli living in one of them.

When I started making plans to visit Holli, I was delighted to find out everyone on the property but the two of us were going to be gone for the holiday. It's the Fourth of July weekend when the celebration of the passage of the Declaration of Independence turns into BBQs and a drunken' blur. Here in this area of Florida, the locals dread the rampage that takes place during this particular holiday. Crab Island in Destin, Florida ... oh, Crab Island, where over a thousand boats flock to a giant sand bar out in the ocean all at once. Every first-timer is amazed; half-naked bodies, the endless earthly and natural swimming pool full of life, mischief, and gloriously bad choices. The water is waist deep, with countless people walking to other boats to mingle, water volleyball, floating bars, food boats, stereos blasting, dancing, and shade tents at every turn. It is the largest "pool party" I have ever experienced. Who knew the ocean could create such an enormous sand bar?

Anyhow, back to where I am staying. Luckily, my friend Holli lives in Mary Esther, right next to Destin, Florida. It's close enough to almost be considered part of Destin but far enough to have a comfortable level of privacy.

We have the entire U-shaped "community" village all to ourselves. My visit is timed to perfection. I can, without a doubt, carry out my plans relatively easily. This community property is on the sound, to be exact. If you don't know what "the sound" means, it's a body of water that connects a larger part of the sea. If you exit Holli's apartment, walk about one hundred and twenty steps, you will find yourself at two well-maintained boat docks, enough for at least four boats. If you drive a boat straight out, you will reach a small uninhabited island. If you go right or left, eventually, you will find a passthrough that leads you out into the open sea. What a glorious place to spend a few days with a friend. What a glorious final resting place this would be for someone.

It is late, and I am on an air mattress in the living room. My friend Holli is asleep in the bedroom, no doubt next to her white domesticated carnivore Maine Coon named Monkey. After the high-concentrate

THC hemp gummies Holli chomped on earlier, there's no doubt she will sleep soundly all through the night. I lift my body off the air mattress. Not a sound comes from my movements as the air shifts accordingly beneath my body's weight. The dehumidifier is running smoothly, providing a white noise bouncing gently off the rose-colored walls. With just the right amount of light beaming in between the large wooden window blinds, I can see geometric shadows and hints of gold surrounding various objects—an Egyptian art book resting on a small end-table, seashell picture frames with photos of friends and family, the edge of a white leather mid-century modern sofa. There is a soft glow from a night light highlighting the sofa's brushed silver Italian triangle feet, clearly indicating where the floor is. It's the perfect amount of light. I will maneuver easily.

I'm already in my Lululemon shorts and a Boat-With-Me tank top. After slipping on my running shoes and grabbing my bag, I exit the apartment. The sound of cicada mating calls relaxes my mind. Yes, cicada mating calls. Can't leave out the cicadas. The air is hot, thick, moist, and a tad bit smelly. It's like stepping into someone's mouth. Walking to my car, I feel that undeniable urge to speak to myself.

"Miss Daisy Car, just like a star." My voice is now an octave lower, as it should be. "I'll sing your favorite song as I play my guitar." I pull the rubber band from my wrist and wrap my hair tightly behind my neck. "I'll take you far, somewhere bizarre." As I move my large hips in grand strides, I feel my ass bouncing with the rhythm of each step. "And when I put out my cigar on your filthy-ass tongue, it will surely leave a scar."

I pause, slightly squat, and move my hips in circles, then up and down, then around again; my ass cheeks jiggling playfully or seductively, depending on one's point of view.

"Would you like me to at least save your heart in a jar, Miss Daisy Car?" I can only imagine that my grin is gleaming in the moonlight.

It is, after all, our heavenly night light. "This couldn't have worked out more perfectly, Daisy. Damn, will you just look at that star-filled sky! You will never hurt another member again, Daisy. I am very pleased that I saved some of your hair. I have some pillows to fill. My antique dolls love their pillows. Some of them are quite valuable, you know. I'm sure you understand by now what needed to be done. I now I am giving you a glorious resting place, Daisy. You can at least appreciate that, can't you? Your view will be amazing. Fuck, it's humid here. Did I remember my headset? God, I hope so."

My car is parked at the last parking space, closest to the water. In my pocket, I find my headset. "Perfect." I swipe my hand along the trunk of the car. I release a sneeze I didn't realize I was holding, hunching over and sneezing into my elbow like any civilized person would do. "Bless me."

"What's that?" I cup one ear. "Did I hear you say, 'Bless you'? Why, that's mighty kind of you, Daisy, mighty kind indeed."

The large hatchback trunk glides open. Daisy Car is there in several pieces, but she is there. I study her in dignified silence. The look of contempt and boredom has vanished from my face. I make a gesture of dismissal along with a kind smile. Everything is working out smoothly.

"You ready, you tiny little thing you?" The body parts have already been tightly wrapped and in small enough bags for me to maneuver. After much practice, I have almost perfected the technique. Cutting up body parts and wrapping them often reminds me of Christmas gifts. Lots of work, with the wrapping, the taping, the stacking ... but in the end, it's all for good reason.

Unfolding my sports collapsible folding wagon, I stretch my gaze as far as possible, followed by a stern look into my trunk. Daisy Car was indeed a tiny little thing, no more than 111 lbs. This will be a piece of cake. I study my surroundings again. No one is around. Not a sound except for nature's melody.

After transferring the body pieces from my trunk to the wagon, I close my trunk and again look in every direction. The sky calls out to me in silent waves. With my head raised high, I relax my shoulders and let them drop as I inhale deeply. The clouds spread out, revealing the moon as it smiles upon me.

"Wow, Daisy, just look at the enormity of it all, the darkness hugging every curve of every star … so full of unanswered questions." The stars call for me. "Have I done the right thing, stars in the sky? Is that a yes? Of course, it is. I *always* do the right thing. I know what's best for my members. Daisy Car had taken it too far and ended up in the back of my car."

Walking in smooth strides without an ounce of worry, I reach the end of the dock, slightly winded yet still transfixed. A well-needed mini-break is in order. After stretching my neck and lower back, I pop in my wireless headset and press play on "Smooth Criminal" by Michael Jackson. The music is loud in my ears. A jolt of excitement tickles my pickle, and my inner child is awake. I spin. I kick swiftly with my right leg, grab my crotch, and thrust my pelvic region forward. I thrust forward again, this time squeezing harder on my crotch. I stretch out my arms, throw my head back, then throw my head forward and begin to sing along.

Body parts are tossed in the dinghy. I'm off. Its small motor is quiet. I continue to hum along with the music … nothing but the salty air against my face and lustrously blue and gold moonlight guiding my path.

Fun facts about sociopaths and psychopaths: Their brain is their most deadly weapon. Often, they are highly intelligent. Most can captivate an audience with their astonishing vocabulary and sentence structure. Salespersons and CEOs often fit the bill.

CHAPTER 3

JoDi

I am a half-Indigenous-American half-British unicorn. That's right. My father, a bad-ass combination of Apache Native American with Spanish blood and even Mexican Aztec blood, is a complete Southern gentleman. That's because even though he and my ancestors were born in the New Mexico/Arizona area, my father was raised in Georgia from the tender age of three. The sweet South.

My mother is as British as they come, lovely as can be. And about the unicorn, yes, I am a unicorn in my field. Meaning I have touched all major parts of the business, which is extremely rare, especially in the tea business. I was co-owner of a start-up company and have moved on to a bigger company where I can spread my wings even further. I had found myself in a position I could only dream of, an offer I simply could not refuse. The VP of sales is my title. A title I worked my ass off to get. It's for a tea company called Southern Steep, a company just north of Atlanta, Georgia. I'm in a beautiful small city called Marietta that's springing with life. From its weekend farmers markets, majestic hiking trails in the Kennesaw mountains, to all-you-can-drink festivals in the town square.

Regardless of my busy work life, I still find time to enjoy my city, read, and help run the best Facebook reading group. In the winter of

2021, the admins of a readers Facebook group asked me to become a moderator. Shortly after, they asked me to become an admin. To this day, I can still remember the feeling I got when I received the invitation; the heat that rose from the base of my neck and traveled up, over, and across my eyelids. The wondrous sensation was, without a doubt, in the same category as orgasmic. In fact, that day was not only remarkable, it was transformative. Why, just moments before I had received the invitation to become an admin, I had fifteen people in my living room. The Bible study I had just hosted went off with a bang, and not one but three people turned their life over to Jesus that evening. I was making the world a better place for my local community. Now, thanks to all my hard work, I have the power to extend my necessary good deeds even further. That, my dear friends, is remarkable. But let's talk about how transformative this special day would truly become. Let's talk about how it paved the way that led to order, redemption, and justice.

Here's some information about this lively Facebook group I am so fond of. It's large. So large that it reaches every curve of the planet; America, Mexico, UK, India, the Philippines, Australia, China, Germany … the list goes on and on. It's 95% women and 5% men. The top five countries in order are the United States, the United Kingdom, the Philippines, Canada, and Australia. The top five cities in order are Dhaka-Bangladesh, New York-US, San Antonio-US, Melbourne-AU, and Houston-US. Members use interesting, various appropriate, and inappropriate words to express their emotions. Their discussions may consist of deep, meaningful subjects, or they may sometimes dive into humor that can eventually set the mood for the day.

Do they fight? Why yes, yes, they do. For the most part, they don't. But when they do … they do it so very well. You see, with a group this large, you have members with all different skill levels, education levels, social levels, age gaps, and of course, language barriers.

Let's face it, someone with a degree in literature bumping heads with someone with inordinate and exceptional street-smarts, might be cause for some entertainment and grand conflict. But in the end, it's mostly filled with people who love to read and have a profound connection with books. Books that consist of mild murders, cruel murders, murders leaving trails of tears and shivering teeth; books that dive deep into the minds of characters, characters with dark mental disorders, mental disorders that could quite possibly make one laugh soon after crying. Books with twists that make them say, "What the actual fuck," maybe toss a thing or two across the room, maybe toss the book itself, jump up and walk off the tension, immediately text a fellow reader. Books with the types of cleverness and con-like behavior that leave a person with one eye open at night, with someone no longer willing to meet up with a new friend in a dark and private place. Books with levels of suspense that cause irregular heartbeats, anxiety, and knots between their shoulder blades. Books that follow them into their dreams and manipulate the dark creatures in their heads. Books that make them cry, laugh, curse, rage, and conjure up their own clever ways to get away with murder.

Members fight, members, share, but most of all, they bond. It is beautiful. One of the things I love the most is when they laugh together.

However, what I despise the most is when members break the rules. Now that I am an admin, I can ensure that peace and order will prevail, and this beautiful thing that has taken over much of my free time will be preserved.

One of the brilliant things about social media is the ability to weasel your way in, and with enough determination, you can find yourself literally face-to-face with almost anyone. With the combination of my job that allows me to travel, access to people's activity as an admin, and social media, my astonishing journey had begun. Most of my traveling is in the United States, so it isn't too difficult to find myself face-to-face with Americans. Members in my reading group who "take it too far" live in countries and cities I don't visit, so they don't experience my true wrath; they simply get booted out of the group. They may only get booted, but they are never forgotten, thanks to my ledger, where I keep extensive notes. Those members are the lucky ones.

JOURNAL/LEDGER

There are people who think my reading Facebook group is some kind of joke. I'm here to set it straight. If I don't get this down on paper, how will anyone know the effort I have put into this? It's dangerous work. I've been an admin for a long time now. I've been taking huge risks, but at least people will pay for what they've done. This group is like family to me, and no one messes with my family. Too many rules are being broken, and way too many bullies are hurting members' feelings. Members that I care deeply about. Members that I would die for. Members that I will kill for. Members that I have killed for. What can I say, I hate bullies, and they all need to die.

I have quite the setup here. On one screen, I have the group loaded and ready to be analyzed in depth. On another screen, I have Facebook open to my main personal page. And lastly, I have my ledger. I use it for notes and to purge. I write in it sometimes daily and sometimes weekly. But most importantly, I keep a list on it. It has four categories; BLOCK, SUSPEND, OBSERVE, and ANNIHILATE (my naughty list).

Some people might make fun of me for having an actual ledger that I handwrite in, but I enjoy the musk smell of the semi-textured pages. That's right, call me old-fashioned if you must. I don't care. I also prefer physical books. I even enjoy older ones with smells that connect me to history and older times. I envision where that book must have been before me. What kind of stories does it keep secret within the stained and battered pages? I could talk about books all day. But that's not what this is for. This is for the members, my members, my friends, and my second family. Naughty members must be dismembered.

So, back to the group.

Ladies, ladies, let's clean up this mess. I would say ladies and gentlemen, but there is such a higher percentage of ladies in this group ... and boy, do they cause trouble. These ladies want to be ghetto. I'll give them ghetto. Let's see what today brings us. Until next time.

After I close my journal, I click on the FB group. For reasons that are unclear to me, I experience something special almost every time I log in. A brief and pleasurable sensation between my legs pays a visit. I squirm in my lime green well-cushioned chair, briefly close my eyes and welcome the moist vibrations. My pleasurable sensations quickly come to a halt when I encounter a woman by the name of Sara Wade, posting a most absurd question. "Should I read *Verity*? What's all the hype about?"

Well, I already know this is going to cause conflict. Sara Wade must know this thriller has been extremely popular for so very long. It's been discussed day and night for no normal amount of time. What did I start calling this book? Oh yes, a "porniller"—with all the dick-sucking, bed-biting, shenanigans that go on and on in this book. To be fair, I did actually enjoy reading *Verity*. It's not one of my top five, but it was, without a doubt, entertaining. Dang it, Sara must know the members that have been basically grandfathered in are tired of it. They are worn down to the bone. Discussions about *Verity* can find themselves on a chopping block, burned to ashes, then buried fifteen feet under. I don't know, perhaps she is a new member, maybe a new reader of thrillers in general. If that's the case, she should definitely read *Verity*. This conversation will bring out the rule-breakers. I guess I'll dive in.

I am scrolling down now, carefully reading every comment. They are getting fussier by the second.

"Wait, what do we have here?" I spot something. I can already feel the blood boiling in my chest.

Susan A: Oh please, child, not this again. For the love of everything good, shut it. We are done with *Verity*. Just go read it and talk to your neighbor about it. We are done here.

Sara Wade: You don't have to be a complete bitch about it, you cunt. Why don't you go troll somebody else, you old hag?

"Ohhhhh, Sara Wade, you disappoint me," I say again out loud with a deep voice as I prepare my ledger. "You got me over here sharpening my blade, Miss Wade. Your green eyes are like Jade, Miss Wade. Imma-go cut them out with my dirty ass blade, Miss Sara Wade." I bite my lip as I remove my fingers from the mouse.

I pull open my ledger to the appropriate page. Carefully I write Sara Wade's name under the category BLOCK. I hear a clicking sound behind me and quickly close my ledger.

"Sweetheart, is the TV on in here?" My husband is poking his head through the doorway. "It sounded like you had some kind of thug in here." He chuckles.

"Oh, hey darling, no, it must have been TikTok or something. I was messing with my phone." Still, to this day, I have no idea why I start to talk like a straight-up thug when I police the group. It just comes out naturally. I live in the South, but for the most part, I am quite proper. Perhaps it's because I am a half-breed. It's always so difficult to explain to people about my brown side. So many labels in this world. It's exhausting. Hispanic. Latin. Native American. Indigenous. Blah, Blah, Blah. I'm half proper, half spicy ... let's stick with that. And let me tell you, the half proper/half spicy comes from both my mother and father. My mother might be a proper British lady, but she can throw down with the best of them.

"Yeah, TikTok, that shit's garbage." He bites into a crisp apple and slurps the juice. "You've been so busy lately. Are you going to stay up late again? I miss you. Come to bed." His lower lip quickly extends and drops, exposing a part of his inner lip that should remain unseen. His pouting seems so elementary, so innocent. As for me, there came a flood of compassion and then another wave of intelligent fear. Will the dark side of me embrace the innocence of this man forever? Or will it take over in a heap of blood thirst?

I love him with every fiber of my being. I could never hurt him … he is family. I don't know why those thoughts enter my brain like that. He is my husband, my partner, my protector. Family is everything.

"I'm busier than a one-eyed cat watching two rat holes." I tilt my head slightly to the right. His smile lights up the room. I need to be extra nice to him. "But I'll be up in about an hour, sugar plum." I move strands of hair behind my ear, wondering if I should just get up now, rip off my husband's police uniform, and sit on his thick dick. It was his girth that kept me seeing him at the beginning of our relationship. It was such a rarity to find a man that could fill me like a properly stuffed Thanksgiving turkey.

"Okay, sweet pea," he says with a gentle grin. "Oh, and you can rest your hands when you get to bed. Mine have plenty of steam left in them." Yusuff McCray winks and wiggles one hand through the door while he shuts it, his long fingers disappearing through the crack.

I listen as he climbs the staircase. When the sounds fade, I turn my attention back to my computer.

"Yusuff, honey baby, your hand techniques are about as useless as goose shit on a pump handle."

CHAPTER 4

JoDi

Reading is probably my number one passion. I may be obsessed with many things, but reading conquers all. I collect books, and now my library is out of control. Not just that, I have piles of books in every room, including the basement. If I didn't find time to read every day, I would probably go insane. I do enjoy listening to books while I jog, walk, clean, and drive, but more than anything, I love hardcover books. I often find myself bringing the pages up to my nose to inhale *all* the smells. If it's an old book, I imagine all the secrets they hold, and those secrets join my existence. How many people have held this book? I will ask it. What is this stain? Is it tea? Is it a drop of opium? And what about this stain? Were you on a train? Was this book in London long ago? Did it make its way to America on some ship? Was this book not allowed in Germany at one point? Did you hide it and somehow sneak it in when you fled to the new world? What about this old fold? So many questions involved with really old books.

New books don't have so many stories. So many unanswered questions. But I create them ... I have secrets. The stains and bends I create have meaning, just like the rest. Books. Books. Books. That simple word is *so* very much. What about the *word*? The power of the *word* is beyond my comprehension. What would this world be without words? Words.

Words. Words. I am in awe of them. I am making myself dizzy with euphoria, exaggerated in a pathological state of mania. Literature is my elixir, my bliss … it's intoxicating.

Now that I have made it somewhat clear how much reading means to me, I think it's important to share another passion of mine, which is volunteering. Volunteering for many things, actually, but mainly at nursing homes, children's hospitals, and at dog pounds. One might question how and why a complete psychopath cares about helpless creatures, but that is an entirely wrong question. I am not a psychopath. I do the right thing … always. Almost everything I do, I do for love.

Anyhow, I have been volunteering to drive patients to their cancer treatments for so long I can no longer remember when I actually started. I'm not one of those pretentious little twats that does things for others only to expect something in return. I'm also not one of those pretentious little twats that post my volunteer work all over social media. Talking about it or bragging about it with others seems utterly repulsive to me. I want to help people, so I just fucking do it. My genuine love for animals, young children, and the elderly is a massively overbearing shit-show, to be honest. My poor husband … only he knows to what extent I love these helpless creatures. The two of us crazy cats all mixed up in saving lives and taking them. Now that, my friends, is a ball of spit-fire shenanifucks.

So, I'm volunteering today for one of my most favorite friends. I can only call her a friend because that's the proper word, even though she feels like family to me. Our love for each other has grown over these past few months. She once told me a heart-wrenching story about her grandmother, who was a slave. I'll never forget being able to look into her soul as she told me the story. My dear friend Trisha Imbambo. She is probably waiting for me near the front door, from time to time, looking through the peephole. Sure enough, before I can even knock, she opens the door. Her cane in one hand, her handbag in the other. Her smile is shot down from Heaven itself.

"Well, hello, sweet child," Trisha's Southern accent is so incredibly charming "it's so good to see your face darlin'." Fuck. I can literally feel love shooting out of this woman and making its way into my blood. How does she do this?

With shaky arms, she wraps her purse strap around her shoulder. The thinness of her skin is alarming. Each somber movement brakes me a little inside. Trisha's bony fingers grip the head of her cane. I watch steadily, and I swear I can hear cracking sounds. Scrambling, scrambling, scrambling, all in my head … it's all in my head. I know it. Her bones aren't breaking. She is fine. Fix your mind.

I pull my thoughts together. One rational thought at a time eases my anxiety. I smile. I smile because I know that's what Trisha deserves to see right now. She deserves the world.

"Mrs. Trisha Imbambo, it's so good to see you, too," I reply as she reaches for my hand. "Oh my, do you look smart today. Is that a new hat?"

"Oh, stop." Trisha's skin is too dark to blush, but no shade of pink will tell me what I already know. We embrace. The kind of hug that isn't just a routine. We hold each other firmly, taking in all the *feels* of the moment. A natural ending occurs. Our bodies know when we are full. Timing comes easily when a hug is genuine.

"I'm so sorry you are having to do this for me once again, honey." She pivots and locks her front door. "Unfortunately, my nephew rarely follows through with his promises. I don't even know why I still have hope. He will probably never change."

"This is not an inconvenience," I insist. "I absolutely love our conversations and our time together. And don't you worry about your nephew. He's still young. He'll come around."

"I don't know about that. His cornbread ain't done in the middle." With her index finger, Trisha taps her temples a couple of times.

"Oh my gosh, Mrs. Trisha, you be nice." Our playful chuckles come out as guilty as one would expect. We slowly descend the red brick stairs, passing unspoken words to each other.

On the way to the cancer clinic, I often glance at her in the rearview mirror. I'm not entirely sure why she prefers to sit in the back. I never question her on things like that. I notice she has lost more weight. Like clockwork, I dig my recently sharpened arrow-shaped fingernails into the palms of my hands to stop myself from crying. It works. This new style of fingernails is brilliant. It's like having ten little knives everywhere I go.

I'm not stupid. She is way too sick. I wonder what it would be like if I could simply take some of her pain away. Would it be a temporary moment? Or would I suffer with it until my last breath? The whole thing isn't fair. Trisha was a nurse for most of her adult life. She is incredibly intelligent and spent her healthy years on Earth caring for others. She would have it no other way, of course. She should not have to live like this.

That's it. I'm going to visit her soon. That's what I'll do. She may not have much time. I don't want her to suffer alone. Fuck, shit, fuck. I push my nails in deeper, not breaking the skin, of course. Just enough to halt the tears that have now gathered in the corners of my eye sockets.

Maybe we can bake a dish again. Mrs. Trisha is one of the best when it comes to Southern cooking. I'll take her a bottle of Jefferson's Reserve Kentucky Bourbon. It's an expensive small batch, but damn it, she deserves it. I know how much she likes her fine whiskeys. I'm going to shower her with so much love that she won't know what to do with herself. And maybe, just maybe, her last days will make up for all the suffering she has had to endure lately.

I break the destructive silence. "How have you been holding up, Mrs. Trisha?" I force a smile.

"I'm doing finer than frog's hair, my dear. My neighbor has been helping me with my garden." I listen in admiration as she shimmers her way through a story that sounds like it should be coming from someone young and healthy.

Trisha continues. "Oh, and why just the other day, I made it to bingo. One of my friends picked me up. Not really sure how we made it there alive. Why, that old SOB is blinder than a bat doing cartwheels."

I giggle and wonder how someone so ill can still find the spirit to add humor to almost every conversation. "Fantastic," I respond as I glance at my phone. There are several notifications waiting for me. The temperature in the car has gotten warmer. Or has it? Is it just me? It's the notifications, isn't it? I feel like I've been able to control my anxiety for the most part, but there are moments when I slip. I'm only human. After a few controlled deep breaths, I push back the darkness into its hiding place.

"If you ever need a ride to bingo, let me know. If I'm in town, I'll be happy to take you."

"I suppose that's better than taking me to cancer treatments."

I don't know how to respond to that. It's all too sad for me. "Nonsense." I quickly divert the conversation. "So, Mrs. Trisha, I hear you've been giving one of the nurses all kinds of hell. Is this true?"

"You must be talking about Rabecca White. She's about as useless as tits on a boar."

I laugh out loud. Louder than I probably should have, but can you blame me? This woman, my gosh. Those lingering tears rush out in a rage of glory, knowing happiness has caused their fall. Honestly, I can't begin to imagine this sweet little lady bickering with a nurse. But I sure as shit wish I could see it for myself. When I finally recuperate, it's decided that I must dig a little deeper.

"Well, I asked around, Mrs. Trisha, and it seems Mrs. Rabecca White is quite the nurse, one of the best they have, in fact."

"Puffff, surely we must be talking about two different hens."

Raindrops begin to hit the windshield. The sun is casting rays in every direction. It's as sunny as it could be, yet there they are. Large raindrops crashing on my windshield, spraying liquid light in every direction. I lean forward, searching for clouds. But no matter how far I stretch, I discover only sunshine and gusting winds.

"Would you look at that?" Trisha says.

I just know she has something clever to say. "What's that, Mrs. Trisha?"

"The Devil is beat'n his wife again."

"What in the world does that mean?"

"You young folk—my goodness. You ain't ever heard that expression?"

"No, I haven't. I thought I'd heard them all." I take the last turn and pull into the drop-off section of the cancer treatment clinic, eagerly awaiting her response.

"That's what us Southerners say when it's raining while it's bright and sunny out. Yes, mama, the Devil is beat'n his wife again."

My imagination takes a wild turn; an animated clip runs through my brain. A seated red, very long, and skinny-legged Devil pulls his large-breasted wife over his knees, face down, barely dodging his beer gut. His head and horns are much too big for his body. He licks his lips. Saliva slushes out of his mouth in an upside-down rainbow shape. She scream-giggles while her short, muscular legs kick wildly in the air. He begins to spank her, and with each blow, her bubble butt grows larger and larger, and his horns grow longer and longer. His eyes are protruding now with excitement as her ass wiggles like a large gelatin

Bundt cake. Like water faucets, her eyes spray the Earth with gushing winds of rain.

"Okay, here we are." I put it in park and walk around to open her door. The transition goes smoothly. We have done this several times. I slowly walk Trisha toward the entrance. Before we reach the door, the wind swoops up fallen leaves in front of us in a tornado-like form. I admire the dance before me. Auburn, orange, and yellow leaves twirl and twirl in a tiny tornado. The whole scene is in slow motion, as if life itself was pausing slightly just for me. I imagine my life in harmony with my husband and our future children. We are holding hands amongst the leaves, blowing round and round in unison with the warm air and gentle dust. A new aggressive wind comes through, and just like that … the leaves are taken.

Fun facts about sociopaths: They have an abundant amount of superficial charm. Their attractiveness level tends to be above average. Often, they are extremely sexual and extraordinarily clean.

CHAPTER 5

JoDi

My time to volunteer has come to a temporary halt. Work needs me. Flying around the country has its perks, but occasionally my plane experiences can be quite unpleasant. I'm flying home after a long trip.

The plane is annoyingly full. Nothing out of the ordinary, of course. Flying into Atlanta on a Friday evening is a popular time for business travelers. I can't wait to return home, fire up my 125-cc fuel-injected Genuine scooter, and head to the forest. Her name is Bella, and when her and I get out into the open road, we become *ONE* with nature. She also takes me to the farmers market every Saturday, where she gets at least one photo taken of her. She is Tiffany blue … one of my favorite colors. It's got a large black seat that's quite comfortable, much like the comfortable seat I'm currently sitting on in business class. The gentleman beside me has his face mask hovering just below his nose. He had introduced himself as Andrew Lenon during some small talk. At this point, we have both been silent for most of the flight.

His hand moves quickly to his face. It's hard not to look. It's only natural to wonder why the sudden burst of movement. He vivaciously pulls his mask down and sneezes into his hand. The light coming in from the small window allows for particles to be displayed, similar to a water hose head on the mist setting. I watch in utter disgust as the particles make their moist descent. He wipes his nose and mouth with the top of his hand, much like a child would do.

I don't understand. That is literally what the mask is for—to contain bodily fluids. Why would he pull it down and shower us with his funk? For God's sake, why wouldn't he sneeze into a tissue specifically engineered to fit over a person's face and mouth? Or why not into his elbow? Now it's all over his hand. A hand that he will be using to touch just about everything. His particles reached me. I know they did. I watched it happen. His germ-infested insides now rest on my clothes and skin, no doubt gradually seeping through my dermis. We are on a plane, for fuck's sake! Is he completely void of common sense?

I quickly reach for my pen and stab him in the leg. This is how I must cope. With a good grip, I twist the pen. I twist and twist until he apologizes for being the Devil's spawn. Until he apologizes for not sneezing into his perfectly formed mask. But it's not enough. He is a disgusting man, mask or no mask. It's not even about the mask. I can just tell he is scum. Everyone remains in their human bodies but are foxes from the neck up. Yes, we are all a batch of hybrids with oversized mouths. Their exaggerated grins and child-like giggles play well with the jolly movements of their bodies. The color of their fur is red. It stands out against the brightness of the white walls. The passengers cheer me on. "Stab him again! Stab him again!" As they smile, a star-like gleam bounces off their perfectly sharp fangs. Bling. Bling. Bling. They chant as their furry ears dance back and forth. They rise in random groups of ten as I continue to stab him in the face, his eyes, his chest. The crowd of hybrids go wild with laughter. Their high-pitched titters bounce off the walls of the confined plane. Flight attendants get closer and dance in unison with the rhythm of my blows. "I Want to Dance with Somebody" by Whitney Houston is playing in the background.

Blood is spraying like mist, just like the mist that left his foul mouth as he sneezed. I sing along, and each stab goes along with the beat of the music. Occasionally, I use the pen as a microphone. I shake my hips back and forth and back and forth. My daydream, my fantasy, my rules.

"Excuse me miss." The music in my head screeches to a hard halt. The youthful voice jolts me from my dazzling daydream. "Miss, excuse me." Again, I hear her voice. When I shift my gaze, I see a cheerful-looking flight attendant asking me to move my seat back to the upright position.

"Yes, of course. My apologies." I do as I am told.

"Oh, I almost forgot." I gently place a hand on the flight attendant's forearm. "I figured I'd see you working on this flight today. I feel like I've seen you on this particular flight many times." Leaning forward presents challenges, but I manage to wrestle my handbag out. "I've almost got it." I continue to explain as I yank on the bag from underneath the seat in front of me. "Sorry for the delay. I'm just trying to get something for you, aaaaaand …" I pull out a Barnes & Noble gift card. "Here we are." With no fuss at all, I hand it to her. "You deserve this, and I won't tell if you won't."

"Oh, well, this is very kind of you. But … why?"

"I once saw you reading a Lucinda Berry book, and another time I saw you reading a book by John Marrs. Great authors, I must say. Gosh, you clearly know that already. Anyhow, you have amazing taste in books. Those are just the types of books that have my head spinning every night in bed. Plus, I've noticed you are always so polite to everyone. I just thought you deserved a gift today. Simple as that. No big deal." I end it all with a dignified tone and a polite air of dismissal.

The flight attendant looks at the gift card and puts a hand on her chest. "Oh my gosh, you are just the sweetest person. Thank you so much. What an angel you are."

"Ahhhh, home at last." I can feel my wide ass sink lower and lower into the sofa cushion. Closing my eyes is like a kiss from the gods. I am mesmerized by the tender stillness that surrounds my butt cheeks. The ridges on the sofa feel oddly comforting as I slowly run the tips of my fingers across them. With each sway of my head, I feel the exact sore spots that have been nagging me most of the day. The discomfort seems to be coming from just about everywhere.

I'm sore from many things; sore from sitting in meetings all day in Los Angeles, from a long-ass flight, and from burying a body in the middle of the night. Yes, the body was in seven separate pieces, but cutting it up, bagging it, transporting it, blah blah, you get the point—it was difficult. The body of Jen Cline is now resting somewhere near the San Bernardino mountains of Yucaipa, California. It's a fertile valley watered by springs and creeks running off the mountains. Maybe her body will help the soil even more. Surely the Serrano Native American people will not mind. Jen had taken it too far, and now her bones and flesh belong to the earth. It was very much a rough week.

Like most nights, my husband is working, so after I shower, I can log in and have some fun on my readers' FB group. I've been looking forward to it all day. With a large goblet of wine, I stroll sloppily toward the primary suite. In one fluid motion, I swallow the remaining wine while removing my pastel pink hairband. All clothes come off.

The steam from my shower blankets the glass shower walls, resembling a blurry picture. Much like a teenager would do, I draw a large heart the size of my face on the steamed wall. Staring at it forces me to reflect on happy moments. I quickly realize how lucky I have been to have such an amazing support system.

My monthly Bible studies always end on a good note. It seems like everyone is so happy to be there. My happy hour friends are a blast; we almost always have a wonderful time. I am so very fortunate.

Questions arise like always. How did I get so lucky? Do things like this just happen? Or is it the universe? Am I directing the outcomes of my life? Do I attract what I put out? If so, the universe and I are doing swell. The universe gave me the FB group. Well, it let me be a big part of it. The other admins must feel just as lucky as I do. They love the group and also work very hard. I miss talking to the other admins. I feel like we have all been way too busy lately.

With my right index finger, I outline the heart again so it doesn't disappear. I press firmly against the wet glass.

Oh, and my husband, my hard-working, handsome, thick-dick husband, who loves me just the way I am; large and cheerful, part Southern bell/part hooligan, part angelic/part devilish, part humanitarian/part thuggish. And as Ludacris puts it, "A lady in the streets but a freak in the bed." Yes, I am truly blessed. My friends, my family, my members—all here for me whenever I need them.

I love how my husband casually reaches for my hand while watching TV. We don't even look at each other when it happens. We simply touch each other's skin, playfully moving our fingers.

As for my happy hour friends, well, they definitely bring me lots of joy. We are always patient when listening to each other's stories. None of us are ever troubled when emotions run rampant. And I can't forget about my members, how they laugh at all my corny jokes and sometimes inappropriate posts and comments.

Suddenly, without a hint of hesitation, my mind's sphere swirls into murky waters. The steam becomes a thick fog. A milky shadow forms over my skin, too quickly for me to truly read into it. The haze over my eyes seems like it has been there forever. I am in a state of normalcy, yet I am not. It is me, and it is not me. My surroundings are now a darker shade of red. It guides my fingers gradually to the center of the steamed heart on the glass wall. Deep sensations in my belly rise, creating a moan that exits my lips in a beast-like rhythm. The vibration is metamorphic. With the flat of my fingertips, I swipe the heart violently in a downward motion. Like a deer hypnotized by the brightness of headlights, I stare deep into it. The heart comes alive, beating, but very slowly. I envision luminous blood gorgeously swimming off the edges of the heart. My own hands are carving the heart into tiny pieces while blood sprays all over my face. Several fingers are now inside of me. I follow the path of darkness until I explode with pleasure.

Back into the light, back into the now, back to where my brain washes clean—I shake it off. I scrub vigorously to wash away the filth. And like I do during most showers that start like this, I question how and why I can carry out this extraordinary second life of mine.

Am I really going to put myself through these thoughts *again*? I feel like a pep talk is needed way too often. *Just enjoy your shower, for fuck's sake.* But where does it come from? How am I strong enough to stomach so much blood and filth? And to be turned on? Clearly, I can take a life without a moment of hesitation. But why? I seem to care deeply about certain things. Fuck, I'm so tired of this. Oh well, what should I make for dinner tomorrow? God, are my *thighs* getting bigger?

I finish my shower with questions still ringing in my head. The thing is, after years of research, I still don't have any answers. Is it dissociative identity disorder? Schizophrenia? Could I be possessed? Am I just straight-up evil? These questions must be answered. For most of my life, I have felt lost, having no one to talk to about my acts of rage. Utterly helpless and alone is how I feel during really dark times. I had once asked a pastor how the Lord truly views murder. After all, "good" people in the Bible murder. His answer is not worth repeating. One day I will find some answers. I know I will. I have to. But at least I know that I *always* do the right thing.

I run my fingers excitedly across the keyboard, thanking it for being a gateway to so much happiness. After logging in, I immediately notice a notification from Messenger. It's a conversation going on amongst the admins. Scrolling way up is the only way I will be able to catch up on the whole conversation. Apparently, someone had not only posted about another group similar to ours, but this person had been recommending it to several people inside several threads. The admins are all still discussing it. I search for the name and jot it down in my ledger under BLOCK. I click on manage, click on people, click on active members, and type Wendi Golding in the search section. I let out a fart I didn't realize I was holding. That probably isn't very healthy, I know.

Ah, here it is. I find the name. I click the manage button and click on block member.

I go back to the FB group. As I scroll, I find a conversation with 321 responses. It's about a trending book written by an independent author, AKA indie author. An author who is also part of the group.

For some reason, this was a popular topic, and many conversations have been overly heated.

Everything seems okay until I find a conversation between two women basically cursing at each other. Cursing in itself isn't a big deal unless it's actually calling someone a bitch, cunt, etc. "Play nice and be kind" is the main rule. But here we have a lady named Maria Vella who has crossed the line.

"What do we have here?" I take a break from my lollipop. "Are you kidding me with this right now, Miss Maria Vella?"

I see that Maria wrote this message to Jordan Abramss: "You must be the dumbest bitch on the planet. Do you even read? You should leave this group."

Well, this is disturbing. *Do you even read?* Really? What if this is a person in a country where teaching young women is forbidden? What if this person is extremely poor and living in a small town with horrible teachers who do nothing to elevate her, to teach her proper English, to get her ready for the world? What if this person feels so dumb that she doesn't feel like she provides any value and is better off dead? No, this is unacceptable.

"Shall I send your body parts to Korea, Miss Maria?" I very neatly write down Maria Vella under ANNIHILATE. "I'll smash your pretty little skull like a tortilla, Miss Maria." She has taken it too far. "No one is going to get away with bullying in my group."

Here are my basic plans for Maria Vella:

Step one: Become friends with her on FB.

Step two: Exchange books or simply offer to mail her a free book—the perfect way to get her address.

Step three: Find a client in her city and turn it into a work trip.

Step four: Plan out how and where she is to be annihilated.

Closing my ledger, I watch as the pages kiss each other. The need to hold it against my warm body is overwhelming. Pressing it into my chest relieves me, but it's not enough. With a tight embrace, I speak to it. "Am I doing the right thing?" In small circular movements, I caress its outer surface. "Sometimes it feels like it must be done, but other times it seems absurd." Unable to contain myself, I open it up again and decide to review some of the details. This little act of obsession occurs too often; a slight hiccup in the world of insanity, I suppose. I skip over sections BLOCK, SUSPEND, and OBSERVE. When I reach the ANNIHILATE section, I pause. My mouth waters. The liquid makes its presence known instantly. It travels through the deep canals of my cheeks and over my tongue. I swallow hard. The vibrations also begin. I must go over this section again. I must.

Oh, I recognize this name. I remember you.

"Miss Ashlyne Ward! Shall I make you a necklace made of metal-cord, Miss Ward?" She had taken it too far. "With a sword I'll slice you up and never get bored."

I reach for my glass of wine. Shivers run down my spine as my finger outlines Ashlyne's name. I'm imagining pulling a shiny cord around her pale neck. As I tip the glass toward my lips, a stream of fragrant Merlot runs down my chin and onto my blouse.

"Well, for fuck's sake … I'm as worthless as gum on a boot heel!" Naturally, I remove my blouse. The kitchen has the nearest sink, so that's where I run to. The cool water washes most of the red wine off, but of course, there is still a shadowy-like mauve that has married the fibers. A noise at the front door startles me. Hearing the door open has removed any dark residue in my brain, and my thoughts are now as clear as day. The film has been lifted.

This is interesting. My husband has come home early. Good, that's very good indeed.

I quickly remove my shorts and bralette. My hands are still slightly wet from rinsing my blouse. I wipe the moistness on my breasts, hoping to give them an added glow. He is getting closer. I can hear it. The sound of his boots is incredibly recognizable. As I lean, I can feel my full hips press up against the kitchen island.

"Hello. Anyone here?" Says Justin as he turns the corner and enters the kitchen.

"Holy hell, cat!" I cover my breasts. "What in hillbilly nation are you doing here, Justin?"

He has the same golden hair and deep-set eyes that I have always been so very fond of. I can feel my fanny getting warm. She would need to cool off. My lady parts need to stay out of this.

"Oh shit!" Not until he takes a full glance does he turn around. "Sorry Jo, I should have yelled or something as soon as I came in." He says as he makes his way back down the hallway.

The cheeky bastard took a mental picture. I saw it. I noticed the slight pause. I saw his eyes follow the inner curve of my waist and out to my thighs. Dammit, those eyes. What do I do? Seriously, get it together. He called me Jo, just like he used to in high school.

There had been an attraction between the two of us since middle school. Justin was my first boyfriend. We dated all through middle school and high school, in fact. Not in my wildest dreams did I think I would end up marrying his brother. While Justin Campena went off to the military, Yusuff McCray and I fell in love. Justin and Yusuff have two different fathers, but they were always incredibly close, inseparable all through school. Even now, they keep in contact quite regularly.

"Dammit, Justin, you pain in the ass. I thought you weren't coming until tomorrow?" I pick up my bralette.

"Geeez, who licked the red off your candy?" His voice is coming from deep in the hallway.

A slight panic comes over me as I wrestle with my bralette and blouse to get them back on. Only heaven knows why. This whole situation really isn't that big of a deal. They're just *boobs,* for crying out loud. It must be a combination of emotions hitting me all at once.

"Sorry, I'm just not used to someone besides Yusuff having a key to the house," I say loud enough for him to hear me. I must check my face. There is a tiny mirror just around the corner, so I run to it.

Truth be told, I never stopped thinking about him, never really stopped loving him either. I love a lot of people. Perhaps this is a little different, though. I'm not a complete moron. I understand the difference between love and being in love. The thing is, he was my first love. He was my first everything. Yes, I know, I married his brother, but that wasn't intentional. It just happened. It's honestly hard to explain. They obviously both have tremendous qualities. Maybe Yusuff was what I needed at the time.

But Justin ... my very special Justin. You know, he was the one that made me feel safe. Safe, as in, a safe space. He was my person. I don't know why he left me. How could he leave me? I felt so betrayed. We were so in love. Weren't we? Maybe I was the only one in love. He broke my heart all those years ago. He broke my heart, and he didn't come back after four years. He stayed in the military for much longer than he said he would. I was crushed. Perhaps it was because I started seeing his brother. Who knows.

Well, he's back. He's back in a big way. Walking around here, all beautiful and shit. Fuck him. Fuck me. Fuck it all. He's like a proper man now, for fuck's sake. He and his wide jaw and broad shoulders, and let's not forget his mother fucking man-smile. God, I hate that he is in my house looking the way he is looking. It is what it is.

I flatten some unruly hairs and wipe the smudged mascara off my upper cheek. Now back at the island, with my breasts safely tucked away, I can face my ex and his stupid-hot smile. "All right, creeper, get your jolly-ass back over here."

I can hear his boots make contact with the hardwood floors as he gets closer. The sound does not calm the butterflies in my stomach. At least this time, I am more prepared. Something I failed to mention is that he will be living with us for a while. He is having a house built on a piece of property he purchased just outside of Atlanta near Roswell, Georgia. He will be staying with us for the next six to nine months at least. Maybe even longer since there is such a huge shortage of labor and supplies; thank you, COVID.

He appears again, this time much slower. "Ah, there she is. Come give me a hug now that your chichis are all put away."

I taught him that word.

We hug, and of course, it's obvious to me that the military has done the body good. Just another annoying bonus I will have to deal with.

After a long embrace and half chuckle, he puts his hands on my shoulders. "I'm so excited to see you, Jo. I don't know whether to shit or go blind."

"Well, it's good to see you, too. I'm glad you are here. I'm as happy as a tick on a fat dog. I guess now that you have been reintroduced to my goods, I suppose you almost wished you were blind." I can feel my bottom lip briefly twitch. I don't know why I said that. I sound like an insecure cunt. What the fuck am I looking for? A compliment? Yuck, just yuck.

"Are you crazy right now? Jo, you are more beautiful than ever." He lets his arms drop and quickly changes the conversation. "So, where are those boxes I dropped off at your front door a few weeks ago? I've got some clothes and things I'll be needing."

"Oh yes, they're in my office. I didn't have your room ready and was moving things around. Follow me."

We walk to my office in no particular hurry. I am hoping the heat between us subsides, and it does. We spend a little bit of time going over some of the many books taking over my desk. They are piled high and take up most of its surface. It's not at all embarrassing because I've always been this way with books. He used to hide some of my books back in high school just to watch me panic. What can I say? I have a thing for books. More books, always and forever, more books.

He admires the yellow smiley face neon sign that is also sitting on my desk. He makes a slight insinuation that it's a little creepy, which makes me love it even more.

Our conversations are now organic. It's like we were never apart. We are no longer blushing or acting strange, that's for sure. If anything, it's like I found a long-lost soulmate.

As he reaches down for the first box, his boot catches the edge of my desk, and my ledger falls to the floor. I watch in horror as it lands open and exposed. He quickly picks it up. It naturally opens up to the page I often read, the page I left off on.

"Annihilate?" He runs his finger down the page.

"Justin, don't read that. It's private!" Lunging for the ledger does me no good. He is too quick. He playfully lifts it in the air as he reads, one hand holding the ledger, the other over my forehead, holding me back. "Jen Kline, Daisy Car, Joyce Tiantefilou, Stephanie Telas ..." He chuckles, trying to get through the whole list but finding it hard to. "What are these names, crazy lady, and why are they under annihilate?"

"Give that to me!" I punch him in the gut, not surprised to discover it's hard as a freak'n rock. I have to do something because here is the kicker; one of the most attractive things about Justin is his memory. He doesn't quite remember everything he reads or sees, but certainly more than the average person. He had once explained to me that his eidetic memory is transferred to his short-term memory bank for storage, and this allows it to be recalled much later.

Why, of all people, did he have to read my ledger? I fucking love this man. I don't want to hurt him. I don't want to end his life. Oh, what am I saying ... I can't hurt this man. Stop it. Stop it right fucking now.

I punch him again, but this time much harder. He hunches over, trying to recover.

"Damn, girl, calm down. You're madder than a wet hen." He laughs while handing it over. "And by the way," he continues as his eyes move down to my lower half, "you forgot to put the lid on the Tupperware."

I am mortified when I look down and see that I am standing there in my purple polka-dot panties. "Fuckity, fuck, fuck ... Justin, why didn't you tell me sooner, you ass crack?"

I reach for the water gun that's perched on top of one of his boxes. I remember that it still has water in it. I lift one eyebrow as I hold it firmly in my hands.

As Justin sprints out of the room, he yells, "What kind of person forgets to put on pants?" His voice fades as he speeds down the hallway.

CHAPTER 6

JoDi

Nicky Lee has been on my ANNIHILATE list for a while. I haven't acted on it because Nicky lives uncomfortably close to me. Atlanta, Georgia, to be exact, is only thirty minutes from where I live. Nicky had made quite the splash on my FB reading group. She had created a post with my profile picture along with another admin and placed a poop emoji on top of our heads. I was completely stunned before it actually made me laugh out loud. We all got past it fairly quickly. In fact, we admins had a great big laugh about it. However, things changed for Nicky. The real reason she made it on my naughty list was because she personally insulted one of the authors in the group.

"Listen, not everyone should be a writer, certainly not this one. It's like she took a couple hits of acid, put on a clown suit, and just started typing words. And after a long day of regurgitating words, coming up with twists that had gaping holes, she went to her full-time job as a fat clown at a children's birthday party." That was the comment she had made on someone's post asking about the author.

You see, this reading group is not just readers. It has hundreds of authors that are members as well. Many are independent authors. We also have well-known authors, such as John Marrs, Kiersten Modglin, Liv Constantine, Heather Gudenkauf, Jonas Saul, Freida McFadden,

Jeneva Rose, and Lucinda Berry. The one Nicky insulted was an up-and-coming indie author that was showing lots of potential.

The time had come for me to make my move.

It's not a dreary night. No, it's a sunny-ass morning. Birds are chirping, and every woman walking their dogs is grinning from ear to ear as if they had all just gotten eaten out by the hot Scottish guy from the Outlander series. I wave and mirror each smile like any civilized woman would do. However, my mind is enormously occupied with thoughts of Nicky Lee.

As I move farther from my neighborhood park, I notice I'm entering a more remote area. The lots are much larger, and the streets are much quieter. I don't see anyone around. It's just me and my pit bull having a good time.

"Miss Nicky Lee, I bet you wish you could flee," I mutter out loud. "I foresee your body beneath a tree or dumped at sea. Will you beg and plea, Miss Nicky Lee? I'll bend you over my knee, Miss Lee, and my sting is much worse than a bee. You will surely agree."

I am suddenly tugged to a halt. My dog spins and hunches over the lush grass. As hot poop slides out of my pit bull's ass, I roll my eyes and reach for a bag. My poem has come to an end, but that's okay. I adore my sweet baby named Blake Shelton. Well, he's really not a baby. I rescued him shortly after the artist Pitbull collaborated with Blake Shelton to create a song called "Get Ready." It was one of my favorite songs that year. Blake is blind and deaf and incredibly intelligent. He quickly learns tricks and is well-mannered. I never relocate a single piece of furniture in the house because of Blake. And because of this, he is like a madman in the house. He has memorized every curve, edge, and texture on the floor.

Even though my daydream had been interrupted by this courageous and brilliant creature, my longing to track Nicky down is still burning inside of me. I know that Nicky Lee spends a lot of time at A Cappella Books in central Atlanta. It's one of those bookstores that has maintained an amazing reputation. One that you could spend hours in.

I don't have a work trip for a while, and my husband Yusuff will be working nights this whole week. It's a perfect time to get rid of Nicky Lee once and for all.

The walk back home is invigorating. There is a spring in my step. I have 100% decided it's time to get rid of Nicky. There is no turning back now.

After washing my hands, I make a cup of ginger-turmeric tea and sit in front of my laptop. The tea is still too hot to drink, so I let it steep while I log in to Facebook. I click on the Messenger icon at the top and type in Nicky Lee in the search section. It's been a while since we've communicated on Messenger. Her bad behavior in the group is water under the bridge. At least that's what I had told her. This is something that always had to be said to a member on the ANNIHILATE list … how else would the communication continue?

JoDi: Hi Nicky, how have you been? It's been so long since we have chatted. I still very much want to meet up and exchange some books. I still have *The Drowning* by Jonas Saul, and *She is Me Too* by T.M. Shivener. I can meet you anytime this week. You are going to love these books. 😊 They are soooo good, LOL!

Nicky Lee: Oh, hey JoDi, it's good to hear from you. I hope you and the other admins are doing okay after that big glitch that came through not too long ago. There were so many members pissed off at you all … as if it was your fault!

She is dodging the question. This gal is smart or perhaps paranoid—not really sure. Last year she wasn't interested in sharing her address when I wanted to mail her some books. This may take some finesse. The conversation simply fell flat for a little while. Instead, Nicky suggested meeting in a public place—at or near a bookstore in Atlanta. She mentioned to me that she went there as often as twice a week. That seemed a little excessive. I wondered if Nicky was possessed with a violent crush on one of the employees or, perhaps more daringly, a deep obsession with one of them. An obsession in which she could no longer control her urges and must be near this person or else she would explode. I could relate if that were the case. I'd been there before.

A long oval bubble with three dots appears. It's the typing awareness indicator. It's beaming with life. I am anxiously waiting. The bubble goes off, then nothingness.

I find myself being extremely impatient. What is taking so long? Either she wants to meet up or not. After all the love and support I have shown to the members, surely she feels like she can trust me. Only a fool would think otherwise. I've always wanted what is best for the members.

The indicator is on again. The bubble with little dots dances on the screen. They go off again. After rolling my eyes, I reach for my tea. It's now the perfect temperature. And boom, there it is.

Nicky Lee–That would be lovely. I'm free pretty much anytime this week as well. Let me know what day and time works for you, and we can meet up. I also still have the books you are interested in. *Saving Noah* by Lucinda Berry and *Woom* by Duncan Ralston.

Too much time has passed, and I've already read both of those books, but it doesn't matter. The point is to meet up with her.

JoDi: Great, how about Thursday at 6 p.m.? Let's meet inside that lovely bookstore you mentioned. I think you said it was called A Capella Books.

Nicky Lee: Yes! Perfect, I'll see you then.

I decide to go to the bookstore a day early, just to see if Nicky is there. I want to observe her. Study her patterns. If I'm lucky, Nicky will lead me back to her home. After all, a little spying never hurt anyone.

Today I have chosen to wear a light-yellow dress, with a single large black rose at the bottom. Most days I choose a dress. This dress is one of my favorite casual dresses. It's mostly cotton, so it breathes well. My hair clips are plain, silver, with a single blue stripe. Aware of all the walking I may be doing, I have decided to wear my light blue and white Converse.

Before I pack up my things, I click on the readers' Facebook group. The first thing I see is a post from Kim Brousard, one of my favorite members. She doesn't cause any trouble and always recommends great books. I once asked her how many thrillers she had read, and the answer was in the hundreds … something I couldn't quite wrap my head around. I have most certainly read hundreds of books, but not from the same genre. Kim's current post is about her list of books read for the month. It was always a big day near the end of every month. Members love to share their list of books read for the month. Some members have impressive digital artwork along with reviews. I always pay close attention to Kim's list. Her list right now is *The First Day of Spring* by Nancy Tucker, *The Kind Worth Killing* by Peter Swanson, *One of Us is Dead* by Jeneva Rose, *The Book Swap* by JE Rowney, *The Family Tree* by S.K. Grice, *Wrecked* by Nick Stephens, *Delusional in Darkness* by Bella Nox, *Barefoot In The Parking* Lot by Vineet Verma, *The Apostle's Fury* by Quinn Noll, *Bittersweet Empathy* by Nicky DeKeuster. *There She Lies* by Michelle Young and *The Book of Cold Cases* by Simon St. James. I LIKE it, and move on. A post from Torri Bailey, asking what everyone is reading. She is reading *The Liar's Wife* by Kiersten Modglin. She gets three hundred and eleven comments. It's a good post. I also LIKE that one, and quickly move on. Michelle Lockwood is asking how we keep track of our books. Excel spreadsheet? She has fallen into the trap, and now she has books stashed all over her house. This group will do this to just about anyone. Most members seem to double the number of books they buy and read after joining this group. Everything looks fine in the group. I shut my laptop and head out to A Capella Books in Atlanta, Georgia.

I peer through the large glass window of the bookstore. The scent, the existence, the live flesh of innocent meat in my view is driving me crazy, that and my untamed desire to close the gap between us, either by murder or embrace. A fellow passionate reader I want to love. A fellow reader that has betrayed me and must pay for what she has done. There, standing cheerfully with a face full of glorious life, is Nicky Lee. She is tall with large, tasty curves, wearing a well-chosen moss-colored felt hat. Harmoniously sitting at a small oval table, she organizes a small pile of books. Contemplating, perhaps, if she should make such a large purchase. One by one, she lifts them and turns them around, but only for a few seconds. Clearly, she is not ruining the entire book by reading the back; she simply takes her glances, willfully pulling her eyes away. These books were probably talked about in my group, so there is no need to read the synopsis. A synopsis can often be much too revealing.

Setting the last one down carefully on top of her pile, she pauses, stands with an unwavering gaze to nowhere, and turns too quickly. Her movements are entirely too fast!

"Dammit," I gasp.

I make myself small, hoping Nicky has not caught me in the shameful act of spying. Nicky Lee returns to the bookshelves respectfully, removing nothing, only gracefully pointing with her delicate finger. A part of me wishes absolutely no harm to be done to this innocent-looking woman. But like always, somewhere deep in the coils of my being, there is a darkness that attaches to every red blood cell in my body. It is not a voice. It is not another person. It is me. I know it. I feel the bio-connection. I feel the two, the twoness that is oneness. This awareness of my double existence only fuels the flame. An excellent excuse for my wretched and irrational acts of horror.

Nicky Lee lets her arm drop to her side. She stares intently at the beautifully colored books before her. Perhaps reality has settled in because she quickly pivots once again and walks to her pile of books as though she needs to move swiftly before her impulsiveness takes dominion over her.

The store clerk picks at the edge of his nose as he watches her. He rubs his fingers together and flicks whatever nonsense he holds between his fingertips onto the floor before Nicky can see him. She walks toward him. He straightens his back. They exchange words. They laugh. They blush. They touch fingers as he hands her a receipt. The clerk's midsection sways slightly forward as if his dick could reach through the wooden structure between them. His bulge slightly presses against the counter. Reluctantly they say their goodbyes.

Nicky is moving toward the exit with a dynamic edge to each step, still blushing, still wanting. Her galvanic presence brought the bookstore to life ... and now it is over. The whole scene was indicative of pleasure with a hint of pain. I turn and face the opposite direction.

With the flat of her forearm, she pushes the door open and walks right past me. Her gentle breeze wafts the aromas of rosemary and cedar scents into my nostrils. I inhale deeply.

Is a part of her inside of me now? Yes, yes, it is. I can taste the aromas. I can taste her.

The two of us are walking now. No, only one of us is walking. One of us is stalking. Drooling. Admiring. I have no shame in this particular game.

Even though Nicky is significantly taller than me, I have no problem keeping up with her. This woman is in no hurry, and even if she were, she wouldn't bother. The world is hers. Nicky is the master of her time. The master of her long, long legs.

There is only a mild breeze. So insignificant that one would have to pause and close their eyes to enhance their sense of sound and touch. The breeze is so mild that it appears Nicky's hat is staying in place just fine. Not once has Nicky glanced back, that and her steady pace is profound proof of her trusting nature. She makes a left on Dekalb Ave. Then another left on Moreland Ave. It's been about six minutes since we have been walking, passing various gas stations, Findley Pizza, and other non-excitable structures. When finally, about eleven minutes into our walk, she slows to a near stop, moves her bag to the other shoulder, and adjusts her speed to a snail-like stroll. She enters the Little Five Points district. It's a district on the east side of Atlanta that was established in the early 20th century. It's famous for its alternative culture.

Nicky enters Village Coffee House with confidence and delight. This is yet another place she visits often. It's quite obvious by her constant flow. There is no real pause. No unsteady movements. Upon finding a cozy little two-seater table near a window, her body relaxes, her eyelids shut slowly as if she has just taken a very satisfying hit from a joint. I wish I could relax this way. Maybe I do sometimes when the world isn't spinning when my mind isn't in a battle.

I tuck myself in a corner booth, the perfect angle to watch Nicky in her element, in her safe space. Something about the way Nicky moves is fascinating to me. She glides. She doesn't shift. She flows. She doesn't turn. The way her elegant hands caress the cover of one of her new books is enchanting. There is, without a doubt, an orchestra occurring, a form of seductive foreplay.

Nicky places her green hat on the table, and lifts one of her newly purchased books to her mouth. No, that's wrong. She is lifting it to her nose. A slight elevation in her shoulders is noticeable as Nicky inhales deeply, sensually. I brush a hand over my face.

I can't kill this woman. That's absurd. I must … I must make love to her. Make love to her? What? But … yes, that is what I feel. I must preserve this one. This one must continue to add value to this world. What am I thinking? I can't kill her. Oh my gosh, this life, this breathing, walking gem, should live. She has to live.

No … the rebuttal that was surely to come. No, she must go. She must die. She must BE no more.

I open up my phone and press on the messenger app.

JoDi: I'm so sorry, Nicky, something has come up. I won't be able to meet this week. Let's keep in touch.

I wait to see if Nicky picks up her phone, but she doesn't. She's too much into her new books at the moment. After darkening my phone, I stash it away. I scooch out of the booth. With a heavy heart, I send out an apology telepathically, as if it could possibly reach Nicky's guiding mechanism that sits above her perfectly aligned vertebrae. Walking to the door unimpressively and entirely insignificantly, I cringe at my thoughts. I send her another telepathic message.

The choice is beyond my better parts. The parts that allow me to rest. The next time we meet, my flower, woman of beauty, elegance, and class, you will be nothing but flesh beneath the sharpness of my knife.

I take one last look before walking out—Nicky's hair a golden glow. The vailing light from the overhead antique fixture is merciless or marvelous, depending entirely on one's point of view.

"The human mind is not a terribly logical or consistent place."

-Jim Butcher

CHAPTER 7

Madame Fontenot

The emerald-green velvety window drapes have been pulled shut. Not a hint of the outside world can seep through. With the indoor lights off, a sense of ancient times is the overall essence of the dedicated spirit room. Cream-colored candles of all sizes are lit, casting out golden rays of light at each corner, accentuating the presence of imperfections on the withered Venetian-plastered walls. Deep harbor-blue paint layers the plaster, giving the room an elegant yet sinister look and feel. Moss, waterfall plants, and forest-like trinkets are displayed on every wall.

Glowing crystals support by offering emotional and spiritual balance. The energy in the room can only be described as mild pulsating thunder, a tremor sending out periodic motion of a rigid force. It is as if a wave or voltage is being passed by an alternating current.

In the middle of the spirit room is a round hand-carved wooden antique Celtic table that was passed down to Madame Fontenot. Each person in the room is sitting motionless with their eyes closed as they hold each other's hands. As they meditate, they take deep calm breaths, just as they have been instructed to do so. Madame Fontenot is careful not to startle the spirit. It's a harmless yet very disruptive spirit that seems to be following a set of twins. It has been occurring since childhood. Something they have been managing tirelessly for far too long.

She speaks to the spirit softly and with great pride. Her chin is held up high, waiting for the spirit to communicate with her.

The sudden tightness in her shoulders is jarring, but it lets her know the spirit is now present. The fluctuation between pressure and oscillating movements consumes her.

"The spirit is here," she says softly to her paying clients.

Madame Fontenot actually hates that she has psychic abilities. To be clear, it's a slight form of psychic abilities. This is no fantasy world. This is no magical kingdom with goblins and wizards. No, this is simply a woman who was born with a strange and uncommon ability. Her abilities aren't overpowering, nor do the visions and feelings come to her often. Her hopes of them one day simply disappearing will most likely never come. Spirits and energy of all forms seem to gravitate toward her as well. This isn't so bad now, but as a child, she was mortified, to say the least. Again, they are mild, so she can live a semi-normal life. She also receives messages from living people. They are mainly thoughts that others are having. Short and, most times, insignificant thoughts. She is incredibly intelligent and insightful, which enables her the most to help people. She can put things together, often with facts, clues, and instincts.

So far, most of these types of messages she received either made her laugh or grossed her out. The ones that ruined her relationships are the ones she can never erase from her memory. The close relationship she had with her only sister Ashley was badly bruised. They hadn't spoken in years.

Every romantic relationship was a ticking time bomb. There was only so much she could ignore. She knew she had the same type of thoughts, but still, it was hard to digest. Just think about it. What thoughts cross your mind that you would never in a million years say out loud to a boyfriend, a partner, a sister, your children, or your closest friends? Yes, those were some of the messages she heard from them. Messages that tore into her soul. But she gathered the pieces. She recovered. Loving her sister would never end, and there is still hope. A tremendous amount of hope. One day they will mend things ... she senses it. She knows it.

As far as heartbreaks are concerned, Tyler was the big one. Tyler Montgomery, he was *the* one ... so she thought. A dirty-blond-haired bartender with a red goatee. He hated his red goatee, but she found it attractive. Woodstock, Georgia, was where he was from, but they met at a place called Hamp & Harry's on the square in Marietta. He introduced her to a drink called Café Maxim, AKA espresso martini. Its ingredients are Pierre Ferrand cognac, espresso, demerara, and jumping goat liquor.

The restaurant not only has an actual La Marzocco espresso machine behind the bar, but they also have a Wiiboox latte art digital printer that prints fancy logos or any picture you want right on the drink itself. The process blew her mind. She will never forget how the conversation with Travis started. A gentleman named Stephen Charles was sitting just two seats from her. He had heard about this extraordinary craft cocktail, but those weren't his types of drinks. He always stuck to vodka or fine bourbons. However, he was so intrigued by the digital cocktail art that he insisted on buying one for her simply to witness the flawless cocktail art for himself. Tyler jumped at the opportunity to make it for her. He had been eyeing her ever since she walked into the restaurant. They locked eyes, and it was the beginning of a long love affair ... until it wasn't.

Now, she enjoys helping others. Living every day like it's her last, trying to make a difference in people's lives is her passion. One of her favorite spots to get lost in her thoughts is the Little Five Points district in Atlanta. That's where she is now. The air seems thinner than normal. It has been at least four days since the last good rain. A perfect light breeze reminds her to breathe deeply. While inhaling, she relaxes her mind and body. It's not very busy, so the sounds are calming. There is plenty of room on the sidewalk for her to close her eyes briefly without running into anyone. But, of *course*, she intercepts a message:

Even the way you walk gives me chills. My beautiful Nicky.

Madame Fontenot tries to ignore it. It's coming from a short, curvy woman in a cute dress that's heading straight toward her. She moves her head slightly and tries to make herself invisible. Relaxation is what she craves, no nonsense today … not today.

It's not because you are stunning, no, you are more than that. You are full of life, full of knowledge, full of mystery. How could I possibly kill you? Do not let me kill you, Nicky.

Madame Fontenot immediately opens her senses. There is a sudden thrust of emotions in her chest as the words ring in her ears. *Do not let me kill you, Nicky.* It repeats in her mind. There is no ignoring this one. She finds herself changing her face, focusing her energy on this adorable-looking woman that could be mistaken for a young girl with her hairpins and summer dress. Her hair is dark and long, but her eyes are somewhere in between blue and green. It's hard to tell.

Madame Fontenot moves in closer, closing the gap. She brushes up against her shoulder to create a physical connection.

It's another voice now. It's a man's voice. A deep, deep, male voice. This has just become even more alarming. The male voice is as clear as day.

This one will die.

But how can a man's voice come from her? she wonders. It's not a demon. She can tell. Demonic voices have a different sound. They are fluid-like. This clear voice is coming from this woman. But how? It is her, but it is not her.

"Pardon me. I wasn't looking where I was going." Madame Fontenot says as she reaches back with her hand. The tips of her fingers softly catch the edge of the woman's shoulder. Their physical contact was brief but thrilling.

"Oh, it's okay," the woman in the cute dress replies.

Her large shocking smile instantly sends shivers up her spine. The moment was brief, a second or two. Madame Fontenot continues to walk a few feet more before she turns around. She *must* turn around. The hunter must now be hunted. It's obvious who this woman is trailing. The tall, full-figured woman with the green felt hat—that's who. The tall woman enters a place called Village Coffee House. The shorter woman in the cute dress follows her in. Madame Fontenot re-adjusts her hoody as she enters the coffee shop. At this point, the most natural thing to do is to stand in line. So that's what she does. Even with an exceptional amount of concentration, the messages have come to a stop. This happens often. When she desires them the most, they abandon her, leaving her helpless and anxious. She is committed, though.

She's curious why the lady being stalked didn't go to the counter herself. Perhaps she is waiting for someone. The stalker in the cute dress is busying herself with her cell phone, but she is no professional. Her long-fixated gazes are quite obvious. If she were a professional, her movements and stares would be *way* less obvious.

There are several people in line, so spying on the spy has been quite easy for Madame Fontenot so far. She will stay as long as it takes. There is no rush. As soon as she heard the word "kill," she knew this would be a long and treacherous journey. Madame Fontenot will be ready at her every move. This is what she does. She helps people. She must use her gifts for good.

There is only one person in front of her now. Despite the negative situation, she's actually looking forward to her latte. A latte that would have to wait because the woman in the cute dress is making a move. That was fast. Perhaps the woman in the dress had been following the woman with the felt hat for a while already. Perhaps the woman in the dress has an emergency. Madame Fontenot is watching her closely. Watching to see if she pulls out a gun or a knife. But she doesn't. She is simply gathering her things. The stalker seems sad now. It's all very confusing. Her movements are timed well, calm, smooth, but desperate.

Madame Fontenot is ready, though. She is ready for plan A. She will follow her *all* the way home. There can be no plan B. One way or the other, Madame Fontenot will track her. She will help her. This man, this thing, will be removed from her … if possible. If not, if she cannot remove this man, this evil passenger, then there will be other ways to deal with this situation, and who knows how many dreadful steps *that* would take.

The woman in the dress slides out of her booth slowly and shyly, like one would ease out of a long bath. She's attracting no attention; the pot remains unstirred. As she passes Madame Fontenot, a message comes in quite clearly. It's a female voice this time. The message is chilling, yet so beautiful that it doesn't surprise her, no, it saddens her.

The choice is beyond my better parts. The parts that allow me to rest. The next time we meet, my flower, woman of beauty, elegance, and class … you will be nothing but flesh beneath the sharpness of my knife.

The woman in the dress walks out of the coffee shop and is no longer visible. Madame Fontenot quickly approaches the taller woman with the felt hat. She casually places a card on the table. It is solid black, with only a phone number in white.

"You are being followed. Call me if you want some help." Not waiting for a response, she quickly moves toward the door. Walking away is a must. Catching the hunter is a must, and that's exactly what she does.

CHAPTER 8

The Captive

"What the fuck is happening?"

Why does my head weigh a thousand pounds? My neck, oh my neck, what the actual fuck is happening? Why can't I open my eyes?

The faint sound of crunching, no doubt coming from a nearby animal, *slowly* becomes louder and louder. Crunch, crunch, the nearby animal takes a few steps. She can tell. She knows that sound. Birds chirping. Other birds chirping. The sound of running water, like a creek, is far from soothing.

Where the fuck am I?

She is face down. Half her face is embedded in mud, the other half encrusted with dried blood. A beam of light is seeping through the trees, blinding the only eye she is able to open. She attempts to move her head up, and a sharp pain *rips* through her spine. Pounding sensations in her temples give her a nudge.

I have to get up. Am I dying here? I can't die here. Am I already dead? Why am I here?

More sounds around her, this time leaves wildly being trampled on. This time it's a squirrel. It must be. The sound is fast and annoying.

Get up. Get the fuck up!

She pulls her arms up as if to do a push-up. Adrenaline has not yet set in. Her movements are slow, pitiful. The skin on her cheek stretches as she attempts to remove it from the earth. The mud has its fangs embedded into the dermis, cradling the swollen curve of it. She can feel her inner cheek separating from her teeth as the substances beneath attempt to claim her as their own. But no, the ground doesn't own her, not yet. She is alive, barely, but she is alive. This world would not take her now.

She manages to pull away. Crawling to a creek is her next attempt. All three *hands,* all three *creeks,* all three *squirrels, all* the dozens of trees dance before her.

Which one is my hand?

She topples over from the dizziness that consumes her.

Two rolls, and I should be able to reach the creek.

She does. Her body rolls over. It rolls over again, each time more painful. Her hands, *several* hands, multiple, too many to count, reach for the water. She misses her face the first time; the water falls to the ground under her chin. Again, she tries. This time, water washes over her right eye. Debris seeps into her eye and stings it even further. Whimpers escape her mouth. More water. More water. The sting in her eyes is no minimal thing, yet it is. It's *nothing* compared to all the painful thoughts and fears running through her mind.

Did I fall? Did someone try to *kill* me? Are they still *here*, watching me as I struggle to see, to move, to survive? Am I going to *die* here? Is someone standing right—fucking—behind me, about to tear my clothes off and *rape* me?

The water has now allowed her to fully open her right eye. Struggling to sit up on her knees, she notices wet blood, dried blood, dark blood, light blood, blood of all shades living amongst the freckles on her arms. She reaches behind her head, where most of the pain is coming from.

Her hand returns with warm burgundy fluid. Looking every which way, she sees no one, nothing. Only the sounds of seclusion. A desolate place without a soul in sight. With both hands raised in front of her as if holding a baby, she screams. She screams. She screams.

CHAPTER 9

JoDi

Ping is one of my favorite sounds. A few notifications from my phone makes me smile. I click on Messenger on my phone and see that the admins-group-text is in full force. Laughing emojis flood the conversation along with laughing GIFs and a few eggplant emojis being tossed around. I scroll up to investigate further. One thing I love immensely is laughter, so I need to find out what is so funny. There is a long discussion thread over some spam that was caught before it reached the members. A woman on her knees with her mouth open, tongue sticking out, a man holding her by the jaw. Another one of a woman taking a close-up picture of her meat curtains being crushed by sheer light-blue panties. The headline reads, "Teal Tricycle, all greased up and ready to ride." I wonder if the members would think we are a bunch of pervs, laughing at this stuff. Well, we are not. Most of our conversations are about problem-solving and how to make the group more enjoyable for our members. I talk to the other admins more than anyone else, really. We are a tight group.

I have to admit; it's quite a struggle sometimes being an admin for a group so large. It's time-consuming, and some private messages we get can be demanding in nature. I have actually been harassed several times. I've also been called cunt, bitch, retard, fucktard, asshole, twat, fucktwat, double twat, and my favorite bitchcunt … seems quite redundant to me. Threats and insults I have managed to turn a blind eye to. I would prefer not to be insulted, but we all have our bad days, don't we?

The thing is, *we* decided to become admins. *We* decided to volunteer our time for the love of books. *We* decided to work our asses off every day. And even through all the struggles, not once have I given up. It has crossed my mind, of course, but it was short-lived.

Even though some of us have full-time jobs, families, hobbies, friends, etc., we still manage to dedicate our extra time to the group and members. It's really like juggling, at least for me it is, and that's because I do those things simultaneously. I check on the group consistently on my phone throughout the day and night. I use my computer as well, of course, but when I'm on the run, my phone is always a lovely tool to use. This much effort has its purpose, and it's to keep it the best reading group in existence. I am so grateful to have such a good team. The other admins work hard, and they all have their own special gifts to contribute. It works, and it works well. I am also so grateful for the many wonderful members.

The point is that getting more complaints than "thank yous" is sometimes hard to stomach, and sometimes a good laugh is all we admins need to carry on. If you really think about it, it all makes sense. It's not like we will get a ton of private messages that simply say, "thank you." That would be too much, anyway. We already get too many messages as it is. What *is* normal is to receive messages from concerned members about a problem. In the end, we know that most members appreciate us. It takes a village, and without the members, there would be no group. Without the admins, there would be no group. So there you have it in a nutshell—we are all in it together.

Anyhow, the admins and I are now discussing planning a big trip and inviting all the members. Making it a "first come, first serve" approach.

We are thinking of an all-inclusive resort. I communicate with authors on a regular basis since I host weekly giveaways and pick the BOTM. I hope some of the authors would be interested in joining us. Author readings and signings would be spectacular. But even if we couldn't get a famous author to join us, we would still have a blast. Creating a murder mystery event at the hotel would be a must. There are plenty of authors to collaborate with for that event, and I'm sure several members would volunteer to participate. At some point, don't we all want to be either the monster or the prey? *Of course,* we do. We thriller readers are a *special* kind of breed. We are already in the process of starting a merch website. Our logo is kick-ass. We will have T-shirts, tumblers, bags, bookmarkers, and even Christmas ornaments.

The conversation with the other admins continues, and I find myself dangerously close to peeing my pantalones. Laughter will do that to me sometimes. Today is a good day.

Something interesting about the admins is that I often feel like we could be related somehow. Perhaps it's because we literally communicate every single day. It's like a group of strangers came together and created this rather odd bond. Some days it's all work. Other days it's a time for personal sharing, which is everything from discussing our daily struggles to disclosing embarrassing moments. It's a family I hope I never lose. I simply can't lose them. I often wonder what the other admins would do or say if they knew the lengths I've gone for them and the members. I mean, *I* know I'm making the right choices, but *they* may see things differently. They may not truly understand that it's all for love. And what could *possibly* be more important than love?

These past few months, I've been spending too much time following Nicky Lee. My regular routine has been disturbed. Luckily, traveling has slowed down, so I've been able to do most of my work remotely from home or really from anywhere. As long as I get my work done, that's all that matters to my boss.

It's fall, and Halloween is just around the corner. Many of the neighbors have already inflated their giant yard decorations; goblins, pumpkins, black cats, witches, and ghosts. Glover Park at the square is filled with scarecrows and bales of hay. Restaurants, law firms, bars, boutique clothing stores, ice cream shops, banks, etc., have already changed the art on their windows to spooky themes. There are fake spiderwebs and real pumpkins in almost every entryway. Green and purple lights are hanging in various bars. Some restaurants are already serving their seasonal pumpkin spiced and apple cinnamon cocktails. And let's not forget bars. They, too, have their special blue and green cocktails available. Halloween parties are being planned. Conversations about costumes are already a big hit. I myself have purchased several pumpkins and placed them in my front yard. I have the entire house decorated inside and out. This year I am throwing a karaoke Halloween party, so I need to get the ball rolling.

Since my routine is out-of-whack, I need to bring some normality back. The amount of time I typically spend volunteering has decreased substantially. It is time to get things straight again. Something I love to do is to encourage people to sing and dance. I have already volunteered at children's hospitals in and around Atlanta many times. Seeing children dance and laugh are some of my most fond memories ... especially children suffering from deadly illnesses. Illnesses that kept them confined in hospitals, lonely, suffering, with virtually no light at the end of the tunnel. My heart aches for them.

This month I decided to have that same effect on the elderly. I am going to throw a dance party at a local nursing home. I chose a nursing home that I have visited before. Last year when I found out there were residents with such poor eyesight that they could no longer read, I volunteered to read to them. It was a win-win situation, really. This time, however, my goal is to get them and the other residents to dance. I have already been in contact with the facility's physical therapy coordinator, and they came up with a simple dance routine guaranteed to make them move … even the ones in wheelchairs.

As I get ready for this event, I hear my husband Yusuff singing under his breath.

"When it is time for me to fly free, will you be with me, miss lover of bees? When I take my last breath, will you be hovering over my chest?"

He has a wonderful voice. I wrote a song called "Fly Free" many years ago—his favorite song.

"Oh, don't you cry for me. Baby, can't you see, I'm free as a bird, it's time I fly free. Oh, don't you cry for me. Baby, can't you see, I'm free as a bee, it's time I fly free."

He says there's an internal battle between it being his favorite song and an annoying song; since sometimes he can't get it out of his head, and he finds himself at its mercy. I can't help but notice that he's watching me. Like, *really* watching me. Admiring my large thighs and full breasts. I'm not what you would call a skinny woman. I'm a meaty woman, and I'm proud of it. When we make love, I often feel Yusuff swell with excitement every time my parts jiggle and bounce.

At the moment, my movements sparkle with seduction. I am moving with a purpose, bending over at various angles. He's sitting on our black velvety armchair, his black T-shirt blending in with the fabric. If he isn't in his police uniform, he's almost always in a black T-shirt and jeans. His grin, that's as big as Texas, is so overt I know he's not even trying to hide how sexually aroused he is.

"Honey, have you seen my small orange scarf, you know, the small satin one with the stripes?" I ask while vigorously thrashing through a bottom drawer, ass in the air.

"I think I saw it in the closet. Don't you hang some scarves behind the door?" He quickly stands to help me. On his way to the closet, he parks behind me. He pushes his swollen meat between my cheeks. He gives me a well-performed slap. As he wiggles my ass with his hands, I can see him through the full-length mirror biting his bottom lip. He spanks me again, this time much harder.

"Ouch," I shriek. I like it, and he knows it.

"Sorry baby, let me make it better." He kisses the red swollen hand print. "Damn, I'm a lucky man." He continues toward the closet.

"Yes, yes you *are*," I say, all the while knowing my teasing will pay off later when I get home.

"Found it." I hear him say from the closet.

"You are my sweet potato."

"I yam." He winks at me. "So, how long will you be at the nursing home today?"

"Probably only a few hours. After that, I'm going to the Marietta Wine Market in the square. I'm meeting Dreenie there." Dreenie Beeny became my best friend several years ago. We started a conversation about a psychological thriller called *Caleb* by Jeff Menopace, and ever since then, we've been like two peas in a pod.

"Well, don't drink too much. You don't want to get sloppy again. Just remember what happened the last time you were at the Wine Market with her." His chin moves down, and his eyeballs move up.

"Yeah, yeah, what can I say? Dreenie and I get mighty thirsty when we are together."

I choose a white dress with several large orange pumpkins at the hem of the dress. After pulling up my petticoat to give my dress some umph, I tie a soft belt around my waist into a bow. I'm fully aware that there are very few people who still use petticoats, but it is my signature style, and I like the way I look. I kiss my husband goodbye, knowing he will be wrestling with my petticoat later.

The nursing home has quite a few people in the lobby. Some of them are signing the guest paperwork, and others are delivering items. After a temperature check and signing in myself, they wave me on through. The music system is already set up. I kick in the charm and begin my journey into the souls of the lonely. It's an easy task for me. After gathering up the troops and telling jokes like it was going out of style, the residents are now pumped and ready for some fun. They dance, they laugh, they clap their hands. Some of the CRTs are moving residents around in wheelchairs and even popping a few wheelies. So far, it has been an all-around good time. My heart is full. We take a break and serve snacks and juice.

At this point, several of the residents appear to be sleepy and ready for a long nap. After many hugs and goodbyes, I gather my things. Walking to the exit is already heart-wrenching for me. I hurry to my car. When I close the door, tears immediately form.

"Not again. Keep it together." But no matter how hard I try, the tears will surely come. I have now been weeping for a solid fifteen minutes. This is a reoccurring event. When I volunteer, I look strong to everyone, but when I'm alone, my walls come down. Witnessing animals, the elderly, or young children suffering is difficult for me. I have learned that most of the residents don't get visitors. I also know that many of them live in their own filth because there aren't enough employees to maintain them all and give them the care they deserve. This facility is not a fancy place, it's a place that takes Medicaid, and there are never enough funds for quality food and quality care. Most of the employees do the best they can. I am hurting because I know there is nothing I can do.

After cleaning up my face, I head to downtown Marietta. It's late in the afternoon and difficult for anyone to find parking at the square. I make my usual trips around the main square to find that every spot has been taken. Refusing to give up, I take one more turn and notice a car pulling out in front of The Reading Attic. It's a super cute bookstore that recently opened up. After turning off my car, I clear my mind and focus on my friend Dreenie. I haven't seen her in a while. A wave of joy embraces my soul.

As I stroll with an ever-so-slight skip in my step, the wind plays with my hair and skirt. I greet strangers with a buoyant presence that outshines Mickey Mouse himself. My glowing cheeks and playful manner leave a trail of joviality in my wake. Outside of Marietta Pizza Company are tables arranged alongside the restaurant. They are filled with dog lovers, oversized pizzas, and pitchers of beer. Dogs of all sizes and breeds are resting at their companions' feet, each one of them no doubt longing for pizza crust. Petting each dog, leaving not a single one out, is an absolute must. I whisper in their ears that they are the cutest thing ever. Showering them with unwanted kisses and telling them I love them is another way to cope with my pain. Moving on, my blissful nature still intact, I high-five two adorable children, an act that closes the gates of sadness. My heart has fully recovered … at least for today.

As I get closer to the Wine Market, I can already hear the music. It is bouncing off the historical brick building walls. I can already tell who the performer is. It's Michael Duffee, an absolute favorite. Whenever the Wine Market has live music, they like to put a speaker outside so that the people walking by can enjoy it as well.

I push the door open and see that Dreenie is already here, glass in hand, talking amongst a group of regulars. The place is gorgeous as always—think Italy –think Chicago –think wine country. Think of all of them swimming together in harmony. The original brick walls with timeless paintings at almost every glance scream out, "Drink a glass of wine, maybe four." To the left is where the band is playing. There is a tall table right in front of the band, and behind that are three comfortable leather sofas around the fireplace. Straight ahead is the U-shaped bar, with Lana tending to every customer with grace. She has the sort of smile that is contagious. She is contagious. They are lucky to have her working here.

To the right are rows of wine racks filled with wines from all over the world, chosen by the owners themselves. There is a half wall creating a slight division. The brick archway has a historical invite to it. *Come, come through here, see what's on the other side*, speaks the archway. On the other side could be a wine tasting, there could be a book signing, there could be a private party. It is a fun place to explore. As I move my gaze over the entire market, my eyes meet with Karen, the owner, and in an instant her face lights up. I don't see her partner/husband, Randell, but I'm sure he's around somewhere. She has such wonderful energy, and tonight she seems excited to see me. Her legs shift, she says a quick word to whomever she is speaking to, and with one hand on her cheek, she heads straight for me.

"Well, hello JoDi, it's so nice to see you again."

We embrace, and the firmness is quite shocking. "Oh Karen, it's so good to see you, too." I give her an extra squeeze during our hug.

"It's been a while, but unfortunately for you, you will be seeing more of me."

"Well, that's a shame. We thought we got rid of you once and for all." She wraps her arm around my shoulder. "Come with me, darlin'. Let's get you a free glass of wine. I know someone who knows someone."

"You don't need to twist *my* arm."

"You are going to love this one. It's new. We brought in a batch from Chile. It's full-bodied with notes of chocolate and plum."

She walks me to the bar, where more hellos and hugs occur. Harrison, their gorgeous springer spaniel, brushes softly against my leg like a cat. His tail goes wild as I pet him. He's the one who really runs the place. Some customers come here just to see him, in fact. It wouldn't be the same without him.

We run into Elaine, one of the regulars. For almost an hour, we talk about her new boyfriend, Christopher, soon-to-be husband, by the sound of it. She is utterly in love. I couldn't be happier for her. She is, without a doubt, one of the nicest people I have ever met. Her smile never seems to leave her face. It's like she embodies so much positive energy that it is shared with everyone around her … it never runs out.

When Dreenie and I finally settle deep in the sofa cushions in front of the fireplace, all stress streams out of my body like water through a crack in a dam.

We are now already two glasses in, working on number three. I take a slow generous sip … the smooth flow of wine over my tongue and down my throat is transformative. Now feeling more like a woman without a care in the world, my overactive mind can rest. I twirl my oversized wineglass and watch as the burgundy liquid swims dangerously close to the edge. We talk about everything under the sun. But mostly, we talk about Dreenie's troubles at home. She is happily married to a wonderful man, but like all marriages, they have issues. It is no chore to lend an ear. I am happy to be present in Dreenie's time of need.

Soon, after the important details are shared, we find ourselves talking about the hot bartender from the Italian place around the corner, what Halloween costumes we plan on wearing, and the latest fantasy keeping us up at night. Laughter and wine spillage are on the rise.

Night catches up to us, and the glowing lights of the wine market change the mood entirely. As I set my wine glass down, I see *her* walking past the Wine Market—Nicky. *My Nicky*. Why are you here? Why are you in Marietta? This is not the time. I was just getting back to normal. Why, why, Nicky ... why did you come here? Through the front glass wall, the tall figure moves across swiftly. I recognize those hips. Those long thick legs are unmistakable. The way her arms sway by her side tells me it is her.

An instant feeling comes over me. It's abrupt, much like the closing of a door or a lamp coming on in a pitch-dark room. It takes over me. The twoness that is oneness. Something inside of me feels nothing but rage. There is a new strength and power in me. I remember the comment she made about that author. The feeling I got when I read Nicky's cruel words inched deep into my belly. My mother-bear instincts kick in. The dam breaks. *No one* treats my members that way. *No one* messes with my family and gets away with it.

"I'll be right back," I tell Dreenie without even looking at her.

I walk out with nothing but courage. I make a hard right because that's the way Nicky went. I spot her. It's dark, but I can still see the outline of her figure. Next to the old building are several broken bricks on the ground. Guessing by the amount of debris, they have been there for a while. I reach down and grab one. It's thick, heavy, and it fits perfectly in my hand. My heart is pounding. My mouth is drooling. I can hear voices in the distance, people walking in the streets. My palms are getting sweaty. At any moment, someone could come up behind me. There is no one else in the alley with us right now, but that doesn't really matter ... I can hear people all around us. I won't stop, though. I am incapable of stopping. It is dark, just like my mind. I don't care. I don't care. She must go. This one must die. She has taken it too far. This one will BE no more.

Looking around, I still don't see anyone else but Nicky. However, I do hear the voices getting louder. Again, I don't care. This must be done. Nicky's strides are long, and I am finding it slightly difficult to keep up.

The front edge of my shoe catches on the uneven surface of the ground. As I recover, I stomp loudly on the pavement. My stumbling makes a sound loud enough that it startles Nicky for just a brief moment in time. I can tell by her body language. I recover. I need to say something. I need to do something. The drive inside of me is overwhelming. I can't stop it. I won't stop it. I must do something quickly. I have a brick in my hand. I must do it now.

"Hey." It comes out like a shockwave.

Nicky, startled, no doubt, turns around. But before she can utter a word, I slam the brick against her head. Nicky falls to the ground.

CHAPTER 10

Dr. Trudi

With so many mysterious deaths and missing persons cases, Atlanta P.D. found themselves in hot water. All eyes are on them. *So* much pressure that it was imperative they bring back Dr. Trudi Rosenblun, a criminal psychologist. She had been contracted in the past for several cases, but lately, it was as if she was a full-time employee. They either called her Dr. Trudi or her nickname, "The Mentalist," from the popular TV show. She didn't mind the nickname. The Mentalist is a show she's binge-watched twice. To say she loved it would be an understatement. She is also quite ecstatic to be working with the police department. It gives her the ability to dive deep into the middle of chaos. Chaos is where troubled people end up, and she wants nothing more than to apply her skills where they are needed most.

For this reason, she spent a large portion of her life attending universities, perfecting her craft, and learning all she could about the unpredictable nature and instability of minds. The science of human behavior and the processes of a person had always fascinated her. Figuring out methods through which behavior can be modified was something she had aspired to excel in ever since early high school.

This year alone, there have been eight unsolved murders with absolutely nothing to link them together. On top of that, there are eleven missing persons cases. The theory at the moment is that they are unrelated. On the one hand, they hope it remains this way because *no one* wants a serial killer in their city. On the other, if it is just one person, perhaps that one person could be stopped.

Earlier today, she received a call asking her to come to the police station. Their request, or suggestion for that matter, is for her to once again perform hypnotherapy. To their surprise, it had proven to be quite helpful in the past. A woman who had been attacked in downtown Marietta was having trouble recalling details leading up to the event and during the assault.

Someone stumbled across her body in an alley. A visible wound on her head had encouraged a 911 call immediately. The woman attacked claims to have remembered not a single detail, yet the blood spatter, and the angle of the wound, suggest that she was facing the attacker. Their assumption at the moment is that it was entirely personal. None of her belongings were taken.

Dr. Trudi Rosenblun arrives a few minutes early, but Detective Jim Perks is already waiting for her.

"You look nice today, Dr. Trudi." Reaching out his right hand. "Well, I guess you always dress nice."

"Thank you, Detective Perks. You seem nicely put together as well."

Dr. Trudi is extremely professional anytime she works with the police department. She always shows up in a full pant suit with her hair pulled back tightly, not a single loose hair in sight. Even though she has two PhDs, this is the kind of place where she is surrounded by skeptics. She is quite the genius, but her type of work is often doubted and underappreciated by many.

Something Dr. Trudi learned long ago is that personal sharing isn't very common in this environment. In fact, she knew very little about Detective Perks and vice versa.

As expected, their small-talk ends quite abruptly, and Detective Perks rides the mental train quickly to his snarky side.

"Dr. Trudi, let me ask you something."

"Okay, I'm all ears." She already knows she won't like the question.

"There *is* no scientific proof that hypnotherapy works, or if it is even a good source of therapy." He crosses his arms over his overgrown belly.

"That *wasn't* a question, but I see where this is headed."

Dr. Trudi notices a cross hanging from his neck. Her eyes move slowly, making sure he follows them. "Well, there is no scientific proof that God exists."

"I guess that's true." He shrugs, pretending to dismiss her rude comment. Dr. Trudi knew he was fuming on the inside. There was a level of guilt there. She wasn't entirely sure why. Why should she feel guilty? Many of the police officers question her abilities.

The uncomfortable silence between them begins to catch fire, and Dr. Trudi absolutely hates when this happens.

"Listen, I don't want to get off on the wrong foot today. So, to add some numbing cream to this conversation, here's a little secret."

"Oh yeah, what's that?"

"Well, this isn't really a *secret*, but it's certainly not common knowledge."

"I'm listening."

"It is quite possible that the evidence from cosmology and physics taken with that of biology might provide further reformulation of the existence of a higher power, or God, as most people say. Undirected chemical processes may not account for the encoded information found in cells. It is possible directing intelligence has played a role in the origin of life."

"Where in the hell did you come up with that?"

"You certainly don't believe this is *my* own theory, do you? No, I read quite a bit on the matter. If I'm not mistaken, this is something Dr.

Dean Kenyon had recently suggested. He is a biophysicist. In fact, it goes against some of his earlier theories."

"I was warned you were a brainiac." He had a reassuring smile. Maybe he's coming around after all. Someone came up to him and handed him a file. "Maybe one day we can sit down, and you can explain what the hell you just said … in English … like I'm five years old. For now, you're up to bat." He grins with a form of approval, as if maybe she isn't all that bad after all.

He hands her the file. "Let's see what all the fuss is about. Nicky Lee is the victim's name. I'll send her your way soon."

Because they were needing her assistance more often lately, they cleared out a small room for her to use. Dr. Trudi insisted she needed a room far from the chaos with a window. The one they found for her has an interior and exterior window.

She had a few items delivered that she purchased on her own. Providing some form of a relaxing environment is important to her. A very large rug to cover up the cold floors and two comfortable oversized chairs fit perfectly in the space. Two pieces of artwork and a small waterfall feature tied it all together. To her, it wasn't really a proper office for psychiatric evaluations, or hypnotherapy for that matter, but it was better than what they had her using before. It wasn't too big of a concern, though. Many of these sessions were sort of a pre-examination. Some of them would end up going to her own practice where she could properly help them, especially if it were an ongoing case, which many of them were as of late.

Dr. Trudi is patiently waiting in the small office. It is a routine she's gotten used to. The police force is almost always understaffed and overworked, so running things in a timely fashion is rarely ever the case. This is a conversation she had recently with a police officer named Yusuff McCray. They have become friendly, not necessarily friends, just friendly.

They've already spoken quite a bit on each of the missing persons cases. He is working hard to soon become one of Atlanta's finest detectives.

One case he seems to show a lot of interest in is this case. He expressed his concerns immediately when finding out the attack occurred in the city that he and his wife JoDi live in. She assured him that she would do her best.

It's easy for Dr. Trudi to pass the time since she loves to read. She sees movement at the window. Nicky passes in front of it and walks up to the door frame. Her tall presence is hard to miss. Dr. Trudi is thrown aback for a short moment. She quickly checks to make sure she has her glasses on.

Nicky softly knocks on the open door. "Hello, are you Dr. Trudi Rosenblun?"

"Yes, please come in." She finally stands. "I'm sorry for hesitating. My mind was deep in this book." She briefly shows her the book before setting it down on a small end table. "But you have my full attention now." Dr. Trudi opens a small drawer and puts away her phone and headset. She extends her hand. "Feel free to call me Dr. Trudi if you'd like."

"Will do. I'm Nicky Lee, but you already know that."

"Yes, please make yourself comfortable, Miss Lee." She gestures to a chair. "That glass of water is for you, and if you need more, just let me know."

"I will, thank you, and please call me Nicky."

"Sounds good. Okay, for starters, I'd like to thank you for being here and having the courage to dig deeper. I want you to feel comfortable. Performing hypnotherapy is something I have been doing for a long time. Typically, we wouldn't jump so quickly into this type of treatment, but time is of the essence, and if you are brave enough, and if you trust me enough, this will be a successful session."

"Let's just say I'm quite eager to find out what happened to me. I don't think we will have any issues. I trust that you are good at what you do, and to be honest, I do believe that this would only help. I see no harm in hypnotherapy."

"Great, let's begin, shall we?"

"Yes, I'm ready." Nicky takes a small sip of water and leans back into her chair.

They talked for several minutes about small things like work, family, and hobbies. Dr. Trudi then asks her to describe in detail the events of the day leading up to the assault, leaving nothing out. What things smelled like. Street names. What she ate. Who she called. What landmarks she passed. The color of things. The size of things. Anything that could provide some form of connection. It was like she wanted her to sort of "re-live" the day.

"I think it's time we start with the hypnotherapy session. Is that okay with you?"

"Yes, absolutely." Nicky agrees.

"Very well. Nicky, from now on, I would like you to relax. And what I mean is I want you to relax your mind and your body. I will walk you through this. Focus on the sound of my voice. First, I want you to close your eyes. Relax your eyelids. Allow them to feel heavy and soft over your eyeballs. Now I want you to focus on the air going in and out of your nose. Examine what it feels like moving through your nostrils. Take deep breaths, but not so deep that you have to work at it. Slow and steady breaths. Now, start from the absolute top of your head and work inch by inch, relaxing every physical part of your body. When you reach your feet, I want you to imagine you are weightless. I will give you some time."

She was a good listener and a good follower. Her head glided back, and her body was now one with the super-soft chair.

"I want you to go back to the place it happened. The street that you turned on. Tell me, what did it smell like?"

"Smoked meat."

"Good, very good. Now what do you see? Is there a restaurant, a bar?"

"I just passed the Marietta Wine Market, and I can see Hawg & Ale BBQ restaurant catty-corner from me."

"Is it dark or light outside?"

"It's dark, but there are street lights."

"Good. *Now*, where are you?"

"I've made a right turn. I'm in the alley."

"What does the ground look like?"

"It's also dark, but I can see some uneven surfaces and a few potholes."

"Good, now what do you see around you?"

"It's much darker here in the alley, but I can still see where I am going. I see a dumpster to my right."

"Can you hear anything?"

"Yes, I hear some music coming from the Wine Market. I hear a car honking in the distance. I hear some footsteps."

Dr. Trudi notices the dramatic changes in Nicky's breathing. Her chest is moving up and down more rapidly. This is not uncommon, but it can be a scary place for victims that have been attacked.

"You are in a safe space right now. Tell me more about the steps you hear. Is there someone coming toward you, or is the sound coming from behind you?"

"I don't know. I can't tell. Maybe from behind. I don't like this."

"It's okay. Just slow down your breathing. No one can hurt you right now."

"Striped orange. White scarf. White fluffy dress. Pumpkins on dress." She starts naming things quickly as her chest continues to move up and down.

"Nicky, just try to relax." Dr. Trudi says as she quickly writes in her notepad. She notices that Nicky's chest is not slowing down.

"Okay, Nicky, you can wake up now. It's over. You are safe. Open your eyes on the count of three. One. Two. Three."

CHAPTER II

The Captive

"Not fucking again"

When her screams do nothing but scare the birds away, a new reality settles in. All she knows is that she is in the woods. She has been attacked. Or she has had a very bad fall but cannot recall any of it. Blood on the back of her head is one sign. Another is the amount of pain her head is feeling. Screaming has been no help at all.

No one can hear me. I still can't see straight. I still can't move my body like I should be able to. What is happening to me? Fuck. I need to get out of here. Where is here? Why can't I remember a damn thing? The blood on her body is drying. The pain in her head is intensifying. She freezes as she hears the sound of someone walking nearby. The shock, the fear, the horror has rendered her motionless. An unmistakable sense of apprehension is hanging over her. Terror has kidnapped every muscle, every joint ... she simply cannot move. Before she can scream again, an arm reaches around her. The soft cotton-like cloth covers her mouth and nose. It all goes dark.

CHAPTER 12

JoDi

I awaken with a slight hangover and a sense of irritability when I realize it's not only late in the morning, but I'm married to a wandering and importunate husband; never really knowing when I will hear from him or where he might be calling from. This new behavior of his has left me in a state of contempt. Weak and insecure are two words rarely used to describe me, but for fuck's sake, any woman would be livid at this point.

A few days ago, he hurt me, and it left an emotional scar. I remember it like it was yesterday. He had crawled into bed around four a.m. one morning. I turned the light on. "Hey, where have you been the last few days? I tried calling you, texting you, and I never received a call back."

"Can we not go through this right now."

"I'm tired of your behavior lately, what the fuck has been going on? I called your office because I thought you were dead and they couldn't tell me anything. Are you having an affair."

"Jo Di, seriously shut the fuck up. I need to sleep. I've told you this from the very beginning that there will be many things I can't talk about."

"You can't speak to me this way! Shut the fuck up? Really? That's how you are going to speak to me now?"

"And what about the credit cards you shut down without telling me? And why don't you have sex with me anymore?"

"If you don't shut up, I'll sleep in the guest bedroom."

"Fine, just go."

"Good, I don't want to hear you nag anymore anyway." He tossed the covers off of him and walked out of the room. He is like a completely different person. It's like I don't even know my own husband.

Now, I find myself lying in bed, doubting our entire relationship.

Between the sounds of the Hepa filter, which has been running for eight hours, the squirrels scattering on top of the roof, and Blake Shelton licking his paws, I know it's past time to get out of bed. Though my brain feels like it's encased in plastic Saran Wrap, I still manage to will my eyelids open as I reach for my cell phone. My eyes take a little while to reboot, so to speak. I go through my normal routine of quickly checking my text messages, Facebook, Messenger, Instagram, emails, and lastly, any missed phone calls. Nothing excitable to mention or be concerned about, so I set my phone down and take a sip of water.

The hot and moist nature of my lady garden is another reminder of just how neglected my lilies are, in such dire need of nourishment. Being forced into sexual disparity has left me longing for a proper landscaper. I'm already an open flower, and it takes nothing more than a single hand and my vivid imagination for me to enter into the realm of creator consciousness. Reaching my highest frequency, I explode into the divine space. The world's rational pieces have come together once again to complete the puzzle. Even if only for a moment, life makes sense again as I bask in the kingdom of pleasure.

After a long shower, I take my iPad down to the kitchen and have my morning coffee with toast. I open my Facebook page and click on the readers' group. My stomach growls for something more than toast.

Damn ... I could use a trip to the Big Chicken right about now.

"KFC on the brain-brain-brain, chicken legs make it rain-rain-rain. It's okay if I gain-gain-gain." I sing while scrolling through the readers' group.

It doesn't take long for me to come across a post that's getting lots of attention.

"Oh, goodie, what do we have here?"

Author of the post: "Question, forgive me, I'm a little new here, but do any of y'all ever swap? I'd totally be into that!"

"Ha! Brilliant!" I lean in closer to the screen.

I already know this is one for the books ... no pun intended, so I decide to make myself a cup of tea. Yes, I know I've already had coffee, but I'm half-British, so fuck off. Anyhow, I go back to the post, and several comments have been made, so I decide to see just how naughty the members are being. After all, this is a reading group, and I'm assuming she means swapping books. But I know my devious members. They can jump down the rabbit hole with the best of them, witty little creatures they are. It's like I have my own personal set of comedian gangsters just waiting for an opportunity like this. I'm not going to lie; I can't wait to see this unfold.

Comment: "You *are* talking about books, right?"

It gets fifty-five laughing emojis.

Author of post replies: "Ohhhh my ... laughing emoji, yes books, pineapple emoji."

It gets twenty-eight laughing emojis.

A comment from Amanda: "I mean, I'd *totally* swap my partner, I just want books in return, though."

It gets ninety-two laughing emojis and a GIF: WE HAVE A WINNER!

Next comment by Sara: "Those who do, show they're into it by displaying an upside-down pineapple."

It gets a few laughing emojis.

Amanda replies to Sara: "No idea why, but apparently swingers will put pineapples upside down in grocery carts to shop for things other than 'produce,' laughing emoji."

Tiffany replies to Amanda: "Glad I now know this. I'd hate to accidentally put a pineapple upside down in my cart!"

Next comment from Jacob: "I'll ask my wife and get back to you."

It gets seventy-three laughing emojis.

I decide to join in on the fun.

JoDi's comment: "Here I am trying to quickly see if things are running smoothly before heading out. I read this, prepared a cup of hot tea, and sat right back down ... I may get some popcorn going, too, smiley face-emoji."

More funny comments come flooding through as I sip on my Earl Grey tea. My comment is getting one laughing emoji after another. The members find it quite appealing when admins can have a sense of humor. This is another moment for me to cherish as I witness my "second family" laughing with each other. The mere knowledge of something so simple being capable of making someone's day joyous, even for a short moment, makes all the work I put into this FB group completely worth it. Venturing further into the group page gives me pleasure. I HEART and LIKE several posts. Eventually deciding to come back later. I will need to check on the "swingers" post to ensure everyone is kind to each other. After all, that is the number one rule: BE KIND. Only I know the price to pay for taking things "too far." It's for their own good. What needs to be done will be done. It is all for them. Who else is going to make the necessary sacrifices?

The sound of footsteps interrupts my thoughts. The only other person in the house is Justin. This undeniable excitement begins to worry me. There is no denying it's incredibly distasteful for me to have this type of reaction toward my brother-in-law. Not only is it appalling, but I am setting myself up for nothing but future pain.

Lord have mercy … him standing at the kitchen doorway with a mouth full of taco and one hand in his pocket. I can't decide what I would rather be, the taco in his mouth or the hand in his pocket.

"You sure do spend a lot of time online. Is it all for work? Or do you have fun, too?"

"It's all a matter of perspective, I suppose."

"Ah huh … and what do you mean by that, little lady?" He takes another bite of his taco.

"Well, most of my time spent on the computer is for work, and I do love my job. Sometimes it can be fun. But I'm sure you remember that I'm an admin for a really large FB group, which takes up a lot of my free time. It's very important to me. I've grown quite fond of the members and the other admins. They are like family. It can be a lot of fun, too, you know."

"How can managing three hundred thousand people be fun?"

"I don't really manage them. We just try to keep the peace and find new ways to make it interesting. Every day members get themselves automatically suspended for breaking the rules, and we have to deal with them one at a time, which is time consuming, so I guess, in a way, we do manage. But besides getting rid of spam, removing repetitive posts, and deleting irrelevant content, we do book giveaways, theme days, and fun projects. I'm telling you, it can be a lot of fun." I can tell he still wants to hear more.

"Look, come here," I wave him over. "Look at this." After clicking on the swingers post, I slightly angle the iPad for him. I don't want to move it too far. I want him to be close to me. I want to smell his body, his taco breath, and whatever other smells he has to offer. He places his left hand on the chair behind me and one hand bracing his weight on the table. He reads the post:

"Question, forgive me, I'm a little new here, but do any of y'all ever swap? I'd totally be into that!"

"What kind of group is this?" He laughs and begins to scroll down to read the comments. "Is she asking what I think she's asking?"

"Well, no, she's talking about swapping books, which is becoming a thing." I wink at him. "I wouldn't be surprised if she gets several messages in her PM box, though." We both laugh. His breath smells like tacos, cinnamon, and orange juice. I envision sucking the taste from his bottom lip.

"See," I point with my finger, "read this comment."

Comment from Jimmy: "I had to double-check what kind of group this was. For a second, I

thought this was a swinger's club."

It got several laughing emojis.

"I mean, come on, you *have* to respond to that one!" His face lights up as he reaches for a chair and pulls it in close.

"See, I told you this was a fun group." I click on the reply icon.

"You *are* going to reply … awesome!" He rubs his hands together.

I click on the GIF icon and search for "maybe." One pops up of Jimmy Fallon on the Late-Night show. Jimmy Fallon is shyly moving his shoulders up and down. The caption reads Maaaaaaaaybe while blinking several times. I click on it and send it.

"What?" He flings his hands over his face. "You're just as crazy as they are."

"The admins can be naughty sometimes, too, you know." I blink several times, quickly realizing that I may have created an uncomfortable moment for the two of us. There is no use in denying all the sexual tension between us ever since he moved in. There are moments I want to bring it up, and then there are moments when I decide it's a horrible idea. Maybe we shouldn't talk about it. Maybe there is no need for it. We were together for many years before he went off to the military, so it's not like our emotions were betraying anyone. Seems like this kind of reunion would dig up some old passion, no matter how deep it had been buried.

"Have I told you about Dildo Day in the group?"

"Oh hell, I don't even know if I want the details." He covers his face again.

"It started with an innocent day of women showing off their engagement rings with their current book. It moved on to *all* favorite rings. I posted a picture of the book I was currently reading, along with *my* favorite ring. The book was Wrecked, and my favorite ring was a translucent pink cock ring."

"What the hell, Jo!" He threw his hands up.

"Well, it went sideways from there. Members started posting their favorite dildos with their books—purple ones, blue ones, and some that glowed in the dark. It was a fun ride and a very active day!"

I was enjoying his laughter so much. We quickly turn our attention back to the screen. My GIF was quickly becoming a favorite. A member replied to it.

Jessica: "See, this is why I love this group, even the admins are bad-ass, laughing emoji."

We both reach for the glass of water sitting next to the iPad. Our hands touch. In unison, we quickly pull back and apologize.

"You go ahead."

"No, you go ahead."

Naturally, we both hesitate and then once again simultaneously reach for it. "Well, for fuck's sake," I say as laughter fills the room. He also laughs. Oh, his laugh. His beautiful, beautiful laugh. If it were possible to bottle joy and pour it into my ears, that's how I would describe his laugh. Its repetitive auditory effect begins to dwindle to a much-anticipated silence. Not an awkward silence as one might think. We are much too connected for that to ever happen. There is only so much eye contact I can take. Thankfully he breaks the silence.

"Hey, let's get out of the house a little later. What do you say? The Braves are playing today. Let's go to MacCracken's at the square."

There is no denying his request. I carry the delicate porcelain beauty of Justin like the jacket of some exotic rare book. The low vibrations of his voice flood my consciousness each day, subject to the tones and harmonies that arise from his lips. It is almost too much. Wait ... is it too much? No, perhaps not. Perhaps it's just what I need at the moment.

Thinking again about my husband and him being off on another "work trip" has left an unbalanced number of emotions within me. The taste of abandonment is smeared across my tongue, leaving a retched taste and a foul smell within my delicate mouth. Could intense emotions cause a physical reaction?

It is certainly odd and disappointing that all of a sudden, he has had several trips these past few months. Apparently, it concerns some leads for the "big case" he has been working on. It makes absolutely no sense whatsoever to me, partly because he is a bad liar and mostly because he is not yet a detective. Police officers didn't travel like that, right? What is really going on? I'm finding this enormous question too difficult; is he having an affair? Deep in my mind, where the rotten fruit-of-thoughts lay, were the answers I have been dreading. I took an honest inventory of my own life and did not like the results. I'd contemplated leaving him, but could I possibly find it somewhere in my twisted soul to forgive him?

Oh, please don't murder him. The act of murder is not worrisome whatsoever for me, much like a day-to-day task. It's like taking out the trash. Or, like, grating cheese—it's messy, it's smelly, but the end result is so tasty. At this very moment, I am picturing Yusuff with another woman. Picturing his hand melted over the soft tan skin between her moist legs, his fingers inching deeper toward the region of wet and sacred lands. The tall, dark-haired woman says something funny, and he laughs as his face lights up with multiple shades of bronze.

"JoDi, you there? Did I lose you?" Justin snaps his fingers in front of my face.

My head pops up. "You know what … why not?" I darken my iPad. "Let's do it! I haven't been to MacCracken's in a while."

Nothing is going to happen anyway. Justin would never betray his brother. Just because we were in love all through high school doesn't mean he was going to betray his own brother now. Justin is an amazing person with a heart of gold. He would be a perfect gentleman.

I will wear my Dirty South Comedy crop top T-shirt I purchased from my friend Mat Tamburrino. He's a very talented local comedian. He is a wise head on young shoulders, sharp as a tack, and quick off the mark.

CHAPTER 13

JoDi

It is sometime later now when the deep heat of the day has surrendered to a cooling wind from the storm that had just passed. Justin and I have agreed that a night out on the town is exactly what we need.

In the Uber, we sit wordlessly and let the primal silence of the ride translate us into no more than drifting shapes. Our minds are connected, but only by a thread. There is no lack of stimulation as we drive through the streets of the square.

We are dropped off on Atlanta Street, right in front of the famous Johnnie MacCracken's. This is a historical area. In fact, this exact part of the building used to be a firehouse back in the late 1800s. There is a tastefulness in its kindness that comes from the knowledge that MacCracken's is a permanent dimple in this charming city, while the rest are merely residences. A historic building isn't something that is plainly old, oh no, it is more than that. It is something that has permanently trapped an irreversible amount of prominent value.

Johnnie MacCracken's has two exterior red doors attached to the brick wall. They are opened up like barn doors. On the brick wall straight above is an ominous lion's head, peering over its peasants, insignificant creatures that litter the streets. A tiny yet inviting outdoor foyer is splashed with antique art and street signs. Then there the main door. It's also red and very large. It has a custom door handle the size of a man's shoe in the shape of the letter J. It's aggressive and demanding. One must grasp it and enter into the realm of Irish tradition. At the very top is a large glass window with a huge antique Budweiser sign behind it. The biggest and most obvious part of this door has EMERGENCY written just below the glass window; it's really the first thing you see when approaching. On the glass door, it reads:

"Cobb's Most Authentic Public House & Oldest Firehouse! It was here before you were born!"

An Irish Blessing
(A Blessing from St. Patrick)
May the road rise to meet you.
May the wind be always at your back.
May the sun shine warm upon your face.
May the rain fall soft upon your fields.
And until we meet again,
may God hold you in the hollow of His hand.
"Where the men are men, the ladies are respected
... and the sheep are nervous!"

Justin opens the door for me. There is an instant feeling of seduction as the dim lights play with the dark mahogany wood and weathered beams. Walls full of secrets and untold stories are covered in dusty odd art, trinkets, and antiques. Weird objects come face to face with each person at every turn. One can't help but stare with caution. It's the best kind of dark bar. Johnny MacCracken's, without a doubt, has its own heartbeat. It is alive.

The bar has plenty of open seating, which won't last long. After a few steps up, I am greeted by a well-known bartender named Travis. His distinct look is unmistakable, with his long beard and controversial yet entertaining T-shirts. He's tall and thin, with a long face and large hands. Having an air of authority is attractive and notable. Managing this authority without belittling others around him takes a certain talent that many are not blessed with. His dark humor and small talk carry a lot of weight in this particular bar, where not just regulars but bartenders are also respected and appreciated. His words matter, no matter what they are.

"It's colder than a witch's tit in here." Justin protests as he pulls stools away from the bar.

"They do this on purpose, Justin." I object. "After a few whiskeys in your system, your dry armpits will be thankful."

He tilts his head in agreement.

Another bartender named Kohl appears. His feather-like brown hair often glows beneath the neon cocktail lights. He's fit and charismatic and has a relaxing form of nature that is appealing to the higher instincts of most adults. At the moment, he's not in any particular rush ... he never is. He's much too entrancing for that. He's able to perform his duties in a timely fashion without being bothered by insignificant matters of life. I find it pleasing to watch him. It's quite annoying to me to see bartenders running around like chickens with their heads cut off. No, not Kohl. He glides, he flows, as without effort or resistance, he moves from one patron to the next with smooth and timely movements. One would think, being so handsome, he would accept compliments like water to a dry sponge, but he doesn't. I have witnessed this several times and find his bashful reaction to be quite amusing. That whole cliché "cute but stupid" does not apply to this young man ... which is exactly why I admire him. I acknowledge his presence with a quick hello and smile. I rip my gaze away in a timely fashion. He's much too young for me to flirt with, too young to even fantasize about. I will be strong and look away. I do.

To my left are three regulars seated in the most advantageous spot at the bar to watch the Braves game; Nick, Douge, and Sarah. Travis is speaking to them about the game, simultaneously splashing Jack Daniel's Fire into a shot glass for me. I feel slightly special as he pours my first cocktail without me uttering a single order. The three regulars and Travis exchange tidbits of information about the game, understood only by true baseball fans.

I'm ecstatic to see that Nick is here. I consider him a good friend. He's well known for playing good music on the AMI music app. They even created a custom nameplate for him. His symmetrical and extremely handsome face lights up when he sees me. A good sign, I suppose, since I feel the same joyfulness. Time stands still as I watch the corners of his mouth rise. His beautiful smile tugs at me. I don't look away. Not with this one. I hold his gaze firm and let it soak in, much like a fine wine to the back of a dry throat.

Even though he's not particularly fond of hugs, I hug him anyway. My face is warm. Damn it, I'm blushing. The heat gathering within the thin, delicate skin just below my eyes is one sign. The other is the tingling feeling at the top of my cheekbones.

Trying desperately not to show how much it affects me, I quickly blurt out nonsense. "So, Nick, anything exciting scheduled for tonight? Is there an event going on out back in the beer garden?" Extremely irritated at my own nonsensical questions, I struggle with my purse as I try to hang it on a hook. "Don't fuss," I mumble to myself. No one can hear my low remarks as the music drowns me out.

Nick quickly answers. "I'm not too sure about outside, but the Braves are about to play, and it's Karaoke night in here. I think they are starting pretty soon." Half his attention on me and half on the TV; I'm not offended. His affection is much like a slinky. It's part of who he is. He's attached and unattached simultaneously. It will reach out then contract, but there is no harm in that.

Justin taps me on the shoulder. "Oh, did I hear something about karaoke? If so, you definitely have to sing tonight, Jo." The excitement on his face is hard to dismiss. I quickly break out of Nick's spell and divert my attention to where it's needed.

"I'm going to need more than one shot to get me on that stage."

"No problem." He signals Kohl and orders two shots of Casamigos Tequila.

The shots are delivered in a generous form, along with a mesmerizing smile.

Justin takes a smooth glance at the men around him before he reaches for the shots. He nods quickly at Kohl, thanking him for his timely service.

He takes another look around. "Damn, there are some good look'n men in here, Jo," he blurts out as he moves his hips around in circles "even I want to kiss them."

My eyes follow his gyrating crotch. "With what … your penis?"

I hear a chuckle, no doubt from Nick. I would recognize that chuckle anywhere.

I turn and rest my arm on Nick's shoulder. "I'm sorry, I have been rude. Nick, this is my brother-in-law, Justin. Justin, this is Nick … he's the unofficial DJ here."

They shake hands. Did I just see a flicker of jealousy in Justin's body language? I am sure of it. So very strange. Also, so very strange that I am currently *so* attracted to other men. Honestly, it's embarrassing. This is *not* in my nature whatsoever. This was never the case when my marriage was stable. No one in the world existed but my husband when things were right. He was like a god to me. Now, I am a mess. But perhaps for tonight, I won't care. I won't dwell on my shortcomings. I will enjoy this moment. It's tequila and karaoke time. Life goes on. It's not like I am going to betray him.

I raise my shot glass. "Cheers to naked wings and hot women. Or is it the other way around?" I wink as I extend my arm. The excitement I feel while we clink our shot glasses together reminds me of the fun my husband and I used to have. A time when he craved my presence and couldn't get enough of me. A time when he simply could not live without me. Now I find myself face-to-face with my first love. A man I could easily connect with. A forbidden fruit at its peak ripeness.

"And cheers to old friends and new beginnings," Justin replies as he stares deeply into my eyes. Damn him. Damn him and all the words those eyes are speaking to me. What are we, fucking twenty years old? It's not just an emotional pull I feel, there is a physical reaction happening in my chest. It's deep, it's familiar, it's warm, and above all, it's growing. *Oh, fuck it all.* I take my shot.

Moments later, Rob, one of Nick's best friends, walks in. His presence is like a hundred people popping confetti cannons in a small room. It's bright, cheerful, and you never want it to end. More shots were undeniably in my future.

"JoDi!" He yells and gives me a bear hug, lifting my short body off the ground; his 6'4" body somehow growing to 7'4" within a few seconds. It is a pleasant break in the mood. Cheerfulness is just what I need. After a few laughs with Rob, I make my way to Sarah. She almost always has something insightful to say, perhaps because she is always one of the smartest people in the room. We talk for quite some time, and just before I decide to walk away, Tess walks in and joins us. She is by far one of the nicest and most interesting people I have ever met; always ready to listen and respond with care and compassion.

"Okay, ladies, you two need to come with me," I tell them as I glance back to check on Justin. "Justin." I use my loud bar voice. "I'll be right back." He is comfortably talking to someone else and gives me a *whatever* wave. He's happy, I'm happy, all is good.

I lead Sarah and Tess down the first set of stairs, the ones just before you get to the restrooms. The stairs are steep, dark, and full of mystery. At some point, the walls must have been solid and painted well. Now, they're chipped with a combination of red and green paint. I'm secretly hoping that never changes ... why take out the mystery? Why take out the weathered and beaten walls? We *want* to ask questions. We *want* to imagine a world long ago. Cracks and dents speak highly of the broken memories and tall tales that have occurred here. The stairs curve and continue down even deeper. They have uneven edges and are misshapen. The small amount of light provides just enough glow to keep us from falling. *A perfect place for a murder.*

"Where the heck are you taking us?" Sarah breaks the eerie silence with what I can only describe as a loud whisper.

"Yeah, no one is going to be down in the basement tonight. Everyone is either at the outside beer garden or getting ready for karaoke." Tess chimes in.

"Just wait and see." My voice is that of a sixty-year-old woman who has spent the last forty years smoking Marlboro Reds. Manipulating my voice is a talent I have almost perfected.

"Oh man, Sarah, she's doing that voice again! She's brought us down here for one of her creepy stories, didn't she?" Tess chugs the rest of her beer. "And now I'm empty-handed."

"You called it," I reply as I fling my hair. "It's story time."

"Ah, hell," Sarah replies jokingly. "Let's hear it."

"I'm already freaked out," Tess says as she sets down her empty beer mug and puts an arm around Sarah. "This chick is dark as fuck sometimes."

I take it as the compliment it is. We get comfortable on the brown leather sofas that sit on top of unfished concrete and rock floors.

"Okay, so I was down here one day, all alone. I was in a mood, you know what I mean? Anyway, suddenly, I hear the sound of horses … like horse hooves on a hard surface. I swear they were coming from right behind me. I leap off the couch and turned my head. I don't know why I did that; I mean, I knew there was nothing but a wall there. But I swear it was like they were right fucking behind me."

"Creepy." Sarah takes a swig of her drink.

"Yes, very creepy. So, of course, I high-tail it back upstairs and go look for someone. I ended up leaving without telling anyone. But then, a few days later, I came in here, and the owners Gary and Kathy were helping set up behind the bar or taking inventory, something like that, I'm not entirely sure. I explained to them what happened, and that's when they told me."

"Oh my God, told you what?" Tess is now leaning forward, eyes wide with whiteness.

"Bones."

"Bones?" Sarah runs her fingers through her short blond hair. "Fuck this, nope. Nope."

"Yes, bones. At some point, early on, after they purchased the place, they had to do some excavating in this very basement we are sitting in. It had to be deeper in order for it to be cleared for usage … something like that. Anyway, the crew called them and said they had to stop digging because they found bones." I pointed to the ground beneath our feet.

"Oh, heeeeell, no!" Tess jumped up from the sofa. "I'm out of here."

I reach out and grab ahold of Tess's arm. "Calm down. They were horse bones."

"Damn girl," Tess wipes her forehead, "why are you trying to give me a heart attack." We all laughed.

"Why in the hell were there bones buried here?" Sarah asks.

"Apparently, this was originally a firehouse. Like, a really long time ago, when horses were used instead of automobiles. It's sad, really ... when their horses died, this is where they buried them."

"For fuck's sake, are you telling me we are sitting on top of a horse burial ground?" Tess asks.

"Yup."

"All right, crazy lady, this was totally worth the trip down here." Sarah raises her glass to me. "So why doesn't everyone know this story?"

"The owners said they haven't really told that many people. Maybe you ladies should keep it to yourselves."

"Yeah, we can do that." Tess agrees. "Now, let's get the fuck out of here."

The velocity at which they climb the stairs is much quicker than their descent was.

When we reach the top, I'm happy to see that everyone is still at the bar. The place is still pop'n. I blend right in next to Justin, and after another shot, I decide to stand. Sitting seems boring, and the bar stool has proven to be an unnecessary and inconvenient element. It's crowding my space, forcing me to stand inches away from Justin. Periodically, I'm brushing up against his leg. The alcohol has made me steamy yet comfortable. I'm in a state of high frequency and loud rhythm. I am wet ... so very wet. The self-awareness of my body and what it craves is a sensation I am quite familiar with. I sometimes hate feeling like this. Being neglected at home makes me sexually unstable around other men. I know a distraction is needed. If I allow my body to continue down this path, I could easily climax without a single touch. I would not have an orgasm, but I would climax to the point of delusional distress. My shorts would become too drenched. "Get it together," I whisper to myself.

"All right, let's do it." I gently slap Justin's cheeks with both hands and squeeze. I hold his blurry gaze. His squishy lips protrude slightly forward as I push them together. His mouth now looks like a fish.

"What do you mean by *let's*?" It comes out as a mumble since he is unable to fully open his mouth. "I'm not going up there, Jo. No fucking way."

Wanting nothing more than to suck his fish face leaves me stranded in my thoughts. I can feel my head wobble slightly. *Oh fuck.*

"I'm like … so close to your face." I can hear the slur in my own voice. *Fuckity, fuck, fuck.* "I feel like I'm going to run into you." I hiccup and release my grip. "Okay!" I say loudly. "Fine, d'accord, bene, oralle … I'll go first but sit here and think about a duet we can sing together. I'm thinking "Under Pressure" by Queen." I sway slightly backward, leaning up against Nick's body. I turn and whisper in his ear. "What should I sing, Nick?"

"Why are you whispering, weirdo?"

"I don't know," I whisper again.

He chuckles and starts to softly sing the lyrics to "Come Get Her" by Rae Sremmurd. Something about dancing, strippers, and liquor.

"That's a good fucking song, Nick!" I yell.

"Use your inside voice," Kohl says as he wipes a glass.

He's clearly joking. We're in an Irish pub, for crying out loud. Everyone in the joint is being too loud.

"Sorry, Kohl." I raise my hands. "I tried whispering, but apparently, that was no good either." I placed a hand on Nick's lap, but it didn't quite land where it should have. "Ho, hey, okay, be careful there, family jewels and all." Nick pats my hand. I smile. *Of course,* I smile. I'm on cloud fucking nine.

"Would you like some water?" Kohl responds, smiling with his vampire-like hot fucking teeth.

"Yes, but would you like to sing "Come Get Her" with me?"

Kohl laughs and hands me a glass of water. "We've missed you around here, Jo." His kindness always has such a calming effect on me. "Now go sing a song already. You know you want to."

A hint of guilt runs through me as one of my songs, called "Fly Free," plays softly in my ears. Like I've mentioned before, it's my husband's favorite song. When I wrote it, I was thinking of him. It's the one I will sing at his burial. It's the one I always sing on a night of karaoke. The instrumental version is on YouTube. A friend of mine helped me record it in his studio. Because of this, it's very easy for karaoke DJs to find it. Most karaoke DJs these days can play just about anything. They no longer rely on software with YouTube so readily available.

If I don't sing it tonight, I will wake up with yet another regret. I scan the barcode provided by Melo Blak, who is the karaoke host and talented local comedian. I enter two songs. The first one is "Fly Free," which he will already know that it's one of my songs because I've sung it a few times here in the past. The second song is "Under Pressure" for a duet. I look up from my phone with a mischievous grin. Justin's eyes shrink.

"Oh hell, what did you do, Jo?"

"Nothing," I reply innocently. "Absofucking nada, mi amigo lindo … mi amor."

"Oh, hell, you are speaking Spanish again, or should I say Spanglish?" His eyes widen.

An attractive woman passes by us. Her curves and pouty lips are to die for. Justin watches until she's all the way down the hall. I can't help but feel a tinge of jealousy, which is absurd since we aren't together. If anything, I should be his wingman.

"Did you see that?" His mouth is slightly open.

"See what?" As if I didn't know what he was referring to.

"The woman that just passed by."

"No, not really, why?"

"She had her nose so high in the air she could drown in a rainstorm."

There is a moment of relief, but still, I felt very foolish. Is it possible he's just trying to make me feel better? But why? Again, we aren't together. What is happening? Too much booze. Too much sexual tension. Too much testosterone all around me. I'm a hot fucking mess. My hips have been rubbing up against Justin's knee for far too long. I knew he could feel it, yet he kept it there, electricity gaining strength with each passing moment.

The screen on Justin's phone lights up. "Your phone is ringing."

I'm thankful for the interruption. I have a mouth full of lies and a shirt full of sweaty titties. Not sure why the "sweaty titties" falls into place here, but it's a simple observation. What can I say? I have big breasts for my size. They do match my big ass … so there's that.

He turns to look at his phone. "I'll be right back, Jo. And don't go anywhere. You are hammered, Jo Jugs."

He hasn't called me Jo Jugs since high school. He must be feeling the booze as well.

I know what it means when his phone rings. He will be a while. Justin almost always answers his phone, and he rarely ever rushes anyone. He stands, and through the narrow gap between his elbow and body, I notice Cooper Dun's wild hair shining beneath the neon Budweiser sign. I hadn't seen him come in. We met months prior at the town square, an event called Chalktoberfest. It's where artists from around the world paint giant murals on the street using chalk. I've been to it twice, and both times were incredibly entertaining. Meeting him that day was a pleasant surprise for me. I had been alone and definitely needed some company. Though there was nothing in Cooper's behavior to suggest either grand success or a famous-leaning world, I recognized the high-achievement nature of his character on the night we met.

"Hey, it's Cooper, right?"

"Hey, how are you? It's JoDi, right?"

"Good memory."

"How could I forget? You may have been my favorite new friend that day."

"Aww, that's sweet. You're a cinematographer, right?"

He nods. "That's right." Under my lavish attention, he sprouts vividly and shares uncommon news about the film world he lives in. Though I am riveted by his professional experiences with the untouchable famous world, I find myself unable to ask him about the deep dark secrets that he holds.

Before I can find something clever to say, a drunk twenty-something-year-old stumbles between us and proceeds to move Justin's bar stool. "Oh hey, sorry, that seat's taken."

"I don't see anyone here." He continues to pull it.

Cooper reaches out quickly, yet gently, and places a hand on the man's forearm. "Hey buddy, someone is sitting there. This place has three indoor bars and a beer garden outside. I'm sure you can find somewhere else to sit."

"Get your fucking hand off me, bro."

Cooper casually takes a swig of his whiskey as if without a care in the world. He stands with a swanky smile on his face, the whites in his eyes notably visible. With one leg, he shoves his bar stool back. He and the young man are about the same height, so it isn't his height that is intimidating. No, it's that smile. The smile that says, "Look fuck face, I'm going to pull out your cute little nose ring and shove it down your cute little-man throat."

I immediately fall into one of my daydreams. Cooper is no longer wearing a nice olive-green shirt. No, he is straight-up Indiana Jones. John Williams's theme song to Indiana Jones is playing in the background. There he stands with the original off-white shirt, mostly open in the front. His pinch-front fedora hat is dirty and sturdy. A cracking sound from a whip vibrates in my ears. In his left hand is his bullwhip, and in the other, a pair of pliers. He flexes his chest, alternating each side like The Rock in the movie *Journey 2*. He jerks his head toward me.

"Hit me," he demands.

I reach over the bar and grab two maraschino cherries. With precise aim, I toss them one at a time. They pop off his chest like a tennis ball to a swinging racket.

"Everything okay here?" Justin asks.

I'm jerked from my daydream.

"Yeah, it's all good. This young man was just leaving." Cooper's smile is unchanging.

"Whatever, you fuck-dorks." The young man barks as he walks away.

"Obviously, *something* happened." Justin persists. "I was only gone for like a minute." His voice an octave higher and his grin a centimeter too wide.

"Yeah, no big deal, man," Cooper replies reassuringly. "That dude was acting tough, but he's really just a giant pussy."

"Wait, wait, wait. Hold on to your dick for this one, Cooper." I interject. "We all have this completely wrong." I look at Justin to make sure he's listening. "Hear me out, boys with balls. Here is how we have it all wrong: Balls. Pussy. I repeat Balls. Pussy. One can take a beating, and one can't. So, shouldn't we say, 'You're as sensitive as a set of balls'? Also, 'Why don't you toughen up and grow a pussy?'"

I get more laughter than I was expecting.

"I have never thought of it that way." Cooper can barely keep it together.

"Well, I'm sold. I've got some new comebacks to work on." Justin raises his glass. "Well played, my friend, well played." He salutes me. A grand gesture I highly appreciate.

"I know, I know," I say jokingly as I bow my head.

I introduce Cooper to Justin. As expected, they hit it off like a couple of teenagers on crack. They talk for a little while and are soon interrupted by Melo Blak's voice.

"JoDi, it's your turn. Come on up here." Melo Blak does, in fact, have quite the mellow voice, affably relaxed at most times.

I take a long gulp of water and walk to the stage. My steps are slightly unstable, but I feel like one would have to pay close attention to notice it.

The music to my song "Fly Free" begins. I close my eyes. The melody is so familiar that I don't need the words. I know it by heart. Of course, I do. My husband's favorite song. A song I wrote for him when we first started dating. Back when I thought I was going to be some big-shot singer. It's a song that has connected us through a web of energy that is permanent and unbreakable. I begin with a clear voice.

"When it is time for me to fly free, will you be with me, miss lover of bees? When I take my last breath, will you be hovering over my chest? Oh, don't you cry for me. Baby, can't you see, I'm free as a bird, it's time I fly free. Oh, don't you cry for me. Baby, can't you see, I'm free as a bee, it's time I fly free."

I sing the entire song. The melody ends, and I open my eyes. The crowd is clapping and cheering. A clear validation of my vocal talents. Even though I like to sing, there is always a bit of embarrassment and shyness that comes after each performance. Instead of heading back to Justin, I walk to the edge of the bar.

"Good song choice," Brian, one of the regulars, says.

"Thank you. It's one of my go-to songs."

"You sang it well," Sarah says. Her gorgeous eyes seem to be glowing now. When she smiles, her eyes shrink, but in the best of ways. She is always a breath of fresh air to be around.

"Well, to be fair, I've sung it many times, so …"

"Don't sell yourself short, Jo," Nick interrupts as he crosses his arms and leans back in his chair. The seriousness on his face could be instantly washed away with a simple smile and a single act of kindness. He is a rare creature to me. Every sentence that leaves his lips is laced with a level of intelligence that could be revered yet intimidating all at once.

"Aww, that's nice of you to say, Nick. Thank you."

Travis, one of the bartenders, approaches me and tosses a napkin in front of me. "What can I get ya?"

"Two shots of tequila, and I want to pay for this, but close my tab out, please. My friend over there won't let me pay for a single drink, and I'm starting to feel bad."

"Gotcha." He pours the shots, sets them down, and I hand him my credit card. He slides it through the machine. He slides it through again and tells me it's not a working card.

"Well shit, what the hell." I take it back. "It's the only one I brought with me."

"I've got it," Nick says without a hint of hesitation.

"No, you don't need to do that, but thank you, Nick."

"He won't take no for an answer … trust me," Travis abruptly utters.

Nick nods. "And put her drinks on my tab for the rest of the night."

"What? Wow, okay. Thank you so much." I am so embarrassed over my credit card being denied that I can't stand there a moment longer. "Can you please watch these shots for me? I'm just going to call my credit card company."

"Sure, no problem." Nick pulls them in close.

I call the number on the back of the credit card only to find out that it had been canceled. My heart is crushed. It's the second credit card my husband has canceled recently, and he didn't even bother to tell me. I am so hurt. So embarrassed. So furious that I stomp over to Melo Blak and hand him a ten-dollar bill.

"Can you please change my next song to "Irreplaceable" by Beyonce?"

"Sure, no problem," he says in his deep soft voice.

"Thank you." I softly tap his shoulder.

Back at the bar, I thank Nick again for his generosity.

As I am walking back to Justin, I can sense his eyes reading me.

"What the heck is going on, Jo?" He cups my hand softly. "You, okay?"

"Is it that obvious I'm upset?"

"Yes, it is. Now tell me what's going on."

"I shouldn't." I hand him his shot of tequila. We clink our glasses together, tap them on the bar top, and take them down. I bite down on the lime and close my eyes, enjoying the sour juice performing a stinging orchestra over my fragile tongue. Perhaps it would erase the sour feeling left in my spirit.

I set down the glass harder than normal. "It's about your brother," I blurt out.

"I figured. Just tell me, I won't say anything. You can trust me, Jo. Remember, I loved you before he did." I could see the redness in his cheeks and sense the overwhelming regret that filled him.

"Okay, fine." I broke the moment. "I'm sure you have noticed that my relationship with your brother has taken a nosedive. Well, it's getting worse. I think he's having an affair, and I think he's preparing to leave me. Like, divorce me."

"Why would you say that? That's pretty drastic. Jo, he loves you. Like really, really loves you."

"Well, then, how can anyone explain what is happening?" I start to count things on my fingers. "One, he is canceling our credit cards without telling me. Two, I opened up a bill the other day, not realizing it only had his name on it, and it was a new credit card for him. There were airplane ticket charges, bar charges, and various stores in whatever city he was in. I didn't look at the dates, but I should have. I did call, and I'm not an authorized user on the account. I've always been an authorized user on our accounts. Also, he leaves for days without telling me where he's going. He often stays out late, and I think it's work, but when he crawls into bed at all hours of the night, I can sometimes smell booze on his breath. I mean ... this doesn't happen all the time, but just the fact that it is happening now scares me. He's no longer interested in having sex with me. He doesn't look at me the way he used to. And not that I even have to mention this to you because you have witnessed this for yourself, but he's been treating me like shit lately. He belittles me. He insults me. He is downright ugly toward me, and I don't know if I can take it anymore. Justin, it's verbal abuse, and I don't deserve it." I begin to cry. I absolutely hate that I am crying in public, especially at a bar. Who the fuck does that? I feel like a fragile fuck-nut. He stands up and pulls me in tight.

We remain attached for some time, and the warmth between us is like a soft blanket on my skin.

Why, why, why is this happening? Get the fuck out of here now, before all self-respect is gone.

In the Uber, I'm resting my head on Justin's lap. A tear drops from my cheek onto his pants. With his finger, he outlines my hairline above my forehead, and I hear him softly say, "How we men sit unmoving on our asses, crippled by the mighty force of tears that fall from women we have loved for so long."

CHAPTER 14

JoDi

My husband Yusuff, Justin, and I are having dinner. My husband looks quite handsome tonight. He has the ultimate dadbod. His shoulders are overly wide for his height. His large jaw is complemented by his prominent facial muscles and dark thick beard. He is a hunk of a man. He does have a bit of a beer gut, but I like it. He is strong and very masculine. By the looks of it, he has recently been groomed. His hair and beard are flawless. I stare at his large thick hands and imagine them grabbing various parts of my body. I hope he is happy right now. Things have been so rocky, and I'm desperately hoping for a fun and peaceful evening. Dinners like this don't happen often since we all have such busy lives.

Earlier, I was exhausted, but I still made my signature lasagna. It's a family favorite, and I want tonight to be special. I'm not entirely sure why, maybe because Justin is joining us. The previous night my husband and I got into an argument. It was over something so silly. It's obvious that I love music and I love to sing. At some point, we started talking about each other's funeral. It's a conversation we've had before. It's not like this was an issue. Last night we were mostly joking, but something I was serious about was what song I would sing as his casket is lowered into the ground; the song I wrote for him, "Fly Free." It's not only one of his favorite songs as I've mentioned a few times already, but he and I have sung that song together many times during Karaoke. It is *our* song, not just his, I suppose. He agreed. He thought it was a charming idea. Last night I had briefly mentioned singing this song at karaoke the night I went out with Justin. We both laughed about it. As the joyfulness filled me, I began to sing the song. He listened for a little while, and when he opened his mouth, I expected him to sing with me. Instead, he said, "That's enough."

It was like I was shoved internally in my chest. There's no other way I can describe the feeling. That was not the man I fell in love with. That was not the man I married. I began to cry, and his frustration grew even stronger. A fight began, and it ended in slammed doors and more tears. I am convinced Justin overheard us. Maybe not the details of every word we said, but definitely the loud sound of voices and a few slamming of doors. Just a few hours after the fight, we made up, though. I don't like the uncomfortableness to last long, so I am almost always the one to hug him first after a fight even if he is the one being a complete asshole, which lately has been happening quite frequently.

Apparently, Yusuff had already apologized to Justin about the noise, and so far, tonight's dinner isn't as uncomfortable as I'd thought it would be. We are sitting at the small kitchen table. It's a square solid-wood table, not the cheap flimsy kind. It's the same casual table Yusuff, and I have been using for several years now. The formal dining room table almost always sits alone and useless. For some reason, I always feel a certain level of sympathy for the formal dining room. It's as if it has been shunned, all dressed up and nowhere to go.

Anyhow, here we are at the small square table. My husband is to my right, and Justin is directly in front of me. It's the view I have been waiting for all day. It's been nice having him around since my husband has bullied me day and night. I wish I could pinpoint when it started.

Maybe I can figure out where his rage is coming from and try to fix it. He has been unwilling to talk about it. His pattern is first verbal abuse, then he simply shuts me out, leaving me to my own detrimental thoughts.

As I pass the salad dish around, I notice Justin is looking extra fresh as well. Maybe they went to the barber together.

I look up at Justin. "Did you get a haircut today?" I don't dare ask my husband. He might use it as a way to start a fight. Like maybe I'm being controlling or don't trust him.

Justin's gaze smoothly transitions from the salad bowl to my eyes … a long-drawn-out blink between his movements. The moment is full, heavy, like too many feelings rushing in a single pulse of time. He is always fucking doing this to me now.

"I did." He receives the salad bowl. "I'm surprised you noticed." His grin is all too obvious.

Yusuff doesn't pick up on his flirtatious nature. Which is surprising, considering he's a police officer. These days it's like he's in another world. Perhaps he is. Lately, he has been working with a local detective and a large team. There has been a string of murders, and it may be possible that he can no longer keep his work and home life separate. I know this is a crucial moment. He's in line for the next detective position. Seems like every case is "the most important case of his career" lately.

Before we start eating, I say a quick prayer. "Lord, we thank you for this wonderful life you have provided for us. The ability to afford such lavish meals and a lavish home. We realize that others suffer, and we pray for them now. We know you are the true provider of all things. Bless this meal, bless our hearts, and bless our guest. We are grateful for having such a wonderful family. In your holy name, we pray, Amen." I open my eyes to see that Yusuff had already started eating. He notices that I notice.

Justin's eyes quickly move from Yusuff to me, and I can tell he's hoping the conversation doesn't get awkward. So, for his sake, I say nothing. I simply shrug my shoulders and reach for my glass of wine. As I take a sip, Yusuff speaks with a mouth full of food.

"What ... you're not going to lecture me?" Pieces of half-chewed cheese and pasta linger inside his mouth as he speaks. The vision is gross as the food swims in his saliva. A small piece hurtles out of his mouth and lands on the table as he speaks.

I instantly reach into his mouth and pull out his tongue. I slice it from one side to the other. Half his tongue falls forward, looking like a large piece of sushi. Justin jumps out of his seat and begins to move his hips as the song "Under Your Spell" by Desire is playing in the background. As Yusuff runs to the sink, spilling blood everywhere, Justin and I continue to dance. We clink wine glasses while laughing. We twist our arms around each other and take a sip of wine, much like people do at weddings. We kiss ... long and hard. Yusuff picks up his tongue and yells for help. Blood is flooding the floor. Justin pulls me in with a vigorous grip. His hand is firm against the small of my back. The tips of his fingers curl slightly like he can't get enough of me.

"Hello! Anyone there? What ... no lecture?" Yusuff says in a rude tone, breaking me out of my daydream.

"No, and I don't know what you are talking about. Let's just enjoy our meal, yeah?" I can feel my face red and swollen. It's embarrassing. Justin feels sorry for me. I can read him like a book.

"Yeah, yeah," Yusuff says as he shoves another large piece of lasagna into his mouth.

He turns his attention to Justin. "Hey, I've got tickets to the Braves game next Friday. They play the Phillies, want to go?"

"Ooh, that sounds like fun!" I shriek.

"Jo, I'm talking to Justin. Can you shut the fuck up for two seconds?"

"Man, take it easy, bro," Justin interjects as he tilts his head in confusion. It seems he, too, can't quite understand why Yusuff is behaving this way.

"Take it easy? Don't tell me how to treat my wife, bro. That's between us."

"I'm just saying," Justin responds with a deflated disposition.

"It's okay. I probably can't go to the game anyway." I defend myself with dignity.

The silence is now awkward.

"This marinara sauce is amazing, Jo." Justin breaks the silence.

"There is more on the stove if you want to top off your lasagna or for your bread. Help yourself."

"Sweet." Justin reaches for his plate.

Yusuff's own uncontrollable outrage and with a stealth-like reach, he grips Justin's arm, as obvious as a bear shielding its cub, demanding that we allow him to be in charge. The urge to humiliate me in front of someone as important as Justin must be overwhelming. "Sit back down, Justin." Yusuff snarls at him just before he turns his attention to me. "Go-get-him-some-sauce." Extending the words as a preacher might do.

I am dumbfounded, and no words can escape.

"Dude, I can get it." Justin defends me.

The fingers on Yusuff's hand curl over Justin's skin. "Justin, sit down, please." His face is stern.

"He said he can get …" I plead with him. My face is now hot. Hot with both fury and shame.

He interrupts me, "Get – up – and – get – him – some – *fucking* – sauce."

Each word separated with a spectacular amount of spite.

I finally blink. I smile. I cave. "Of course." I reach for Justin's plate. My hands are shaking. By the look on his face, Justin is at a loss for words.

I stand quickly with a cheerful face that looks like it's soon going to burst into sobs. It does. It absolutely does. But not until I reach the kitchen where I can hide. A place for me to gather my thoughts before I do unspeakable harm to my husband.

Why is he treating me like garbage? This is how people end up getting divorced. How much longer should I take this type of treatment? Is verbal abuse and neglect grounds for a divorce? I don't fucking know.

In between sobs, I hear muffling sounds. They are talking. Even though they are speaking low, I can hear their conversation. I pull myself together so I can eavesdrop.

"Dude, what's been up with you lately? Every time I turn around, you're treating her like shit."

"You wouldn't understand."

"I would like to understand. Let's talk about it after dinner. I've got some good cigars and a good fucking bottle of whiskey we can break open."

"Yeah, sure, man, that sounds good. I don't want to talk about Jo, though."

"Fair enough, let's talk about anything you want. Seems like you need to decompress."

The unruly sobs have come to a halt. Muted tears continue spilling over my face for the grand finale.

Where will this journey take me? This rabbit hole of despair, where will it end?

I attempt to erase the signs of sorrow, but nothing can eradicate what I've just heard. What has become clear to me is that Justin has proven to show a large amount of concern for me. Perhaps even love. And perhaps this kind of love and concern has become lost to my husband.

CHAPTER 15

Madame Fontenot

After Madame Fontenot had experienced that odd encounter at the coffee shop, she just had to find out what was going on. Was that short, cute woman really planning on killing the tall woman with the felt hat? After all, that was the message she had received. But was it just a dark thought? Was the woman simply playing out words in her head to write a book or something? Guessing was just a game, but knowing is what she ultimately needed in order to get a good night's rest. She had decided to follow JoDi as much as her schedule would allow it. She had indeed been following JoDi for some time now. Her time was limited due to her full-time job. Apart from her work, she had practically no social life, but she spent much of that time on JoDi. JoDi's hobbies were absolutely fascinating to her. She couldn't believe how much time she spent volunteering when she wasn't traveling for work or at home. Observing from a distance for months now seemed more like an obsession at this point, considering all she discovered was a mild-mannered woman who spent much of her free time helping others. This morning, however, there was a feeling in her gut, one that she couldn't ignore.

It's six in the afternoon. The leaves are making their sad descent. Halloween decorations are displayed in almost every household yard and business in town. JoDi is sitting in her car outside the Glover Park Brewery in downtown Marietta. Madame Fontenot looks in her rearview mirror. She watches her, she waits. Is this another dead end, or will this woman show her dark side again? This question had been on her mind for so long.

JoDi exits the car and isn't in her normal doll-like attire this time. She is in what could pass for workout clothes or simply casual clothes. These days it seems like women wear workout clothes for so many occasions. It becomes quite clear she didn't park there to go for a jog when JoDi hurls her purse over her head. It's one of those popular purses that resembles a tiny backpack. As JoDi makes her way to the brewery, Madame Fontenot gathers her things. Her movements are natural, like there's no care in the world. She is there for a craft beer, not to spy on a potential murderer … at least that's what people will see.

The brewery entrance is outdoors. One-quarter of the establishment is out in the open. There is a small portable walk-up bar outside. The large outdoor fireplace is a popular gathering spot during the fall and winter. If one is too late for that, they could simply sit on one of the long tables that have custom modern firepits embedded into the tables themselves. Madame Fontenot orders a VooDoo Pils, a traditional Czech pilsner, from the walk-up bar, casually looking around to see where JoDi has gone. There is a slight panic when she is nowhere to be found. The bartender fills her glass when she notices JoDi walking out of the lady's room. It's tucked in the far back corner of the inside bar, but she can tell it's her.

She is quite familiar with how she walks, sits, drinks, eats, and even plays with her hair. JoDi sits at one of the small high-top tables facing the bar. There is a band playing, but she is not facing the band.

She's facing the bar, perhaps for the TVs. Several young and attractive people are hovering around the shuffleboard near her; the young ladies with their crop tops and high-waisted jeans, the young gentlemen with chiseled little bodies wearing Nirvana and beer T-shirts. At some point, Nirvana became very popular with young adults these days. Madame Fontenot's vivid memories of what she was doing when she received the news of Kurt Cobain's death came rushing in. It was a deep heartbreak. He passed away in April 1994. She wonders if teenagers these days even know this.

She shakes off the memories and walks toward the indoor space. It's a large establishment with lots of people, so blending in is no issue here. Under the giant roof is a large traditional bar on the right, extending almost the entire length of the wall. To the left of that is the stage. The rest of the area is filled with various tables, most of them being high-tops. Again, her movements are natural. She belongs in this place. She is confident but not too confident to attract attention.

And there she sees it. The moment she had been waiting for. The tall, elegant-looking woman is sitting at the long, large bar, sipping on a 23oz beer. It's quite obvious that her focus is on the Atlanta Braves game.

Madame Fontenot's choice of seating was undoubtedly important. She would need to be able to spy on both of them without being obvious. The tall woman is at the bar facing the wall of televisions, and JoDi is sitting at a table behind the tall woman, about two rows away. Madame Fontenot plants herself all the way in the back, sitting behind both of them. Her view is perfect.

About an hour has passed. She looks down into her mug. The golden fluid is now so shallow in her mug that the table beneath it is visible. JoDi remains transfixed as she watches without an ounce of caution. What was so entertaining about watching the back of the woman's head?

The taller woman is now closing her tab. She briefly glances over her shoulder as though she could feel someone watching her. JoDi playfully tosses her hair, moving her hand unnaturally in front of her face. Madame Fontenot is finally amused. When is JoDi going to make a move?

The taller woman stands up and stretches out her arms. Almost instantaneously, like a lion ready to pounce on its prey, JoDi straightens her back. Madame Fontenot could feel her own torso move along with them. This was becoming an out-of-body experience for Fontenot, as if she was watching the strings unravel or submerged in a video game, not knowing who had a hold of the game controller. One by one, they leave. One by one, they get into their vehicles. Could this be the moment she has been truly waiting for? Will she be saving a life today? Or is this simply another moment of unanswered questions? Would this be the day they all get caught doing ungodly things?

From the parking lot, they make a right on Cherokee Street. They drive past the square, and to her surprise, they remain on that same street until they come to some of the most historical houses in Marietta. The tall woman pulls into a driveway, and it becomes quite clear this is her home when she parks under the only covered parking space. JoDi continues on and disappears down the long ghost-like street. Madame Fontenot slows down as she studies the house. The two-story house is covered in sage green siding. The large wrap-around porch is trimmed with both white and burgundy paint. The wooden door is grand with a large antique knocker. She has known for a while where JoDi lives, and now she knows where the mysterious tall woman lives. This is a game-changer.

CHAPTER 16

The Captive

If I eat, where the fuck am I going to take a shit?

She hears the sound of a door opening. Paralyzed by fear, she cannot look up. The last thing she remembers is being in the woods. An injury to the back of her head. An arm that came around her. A soft cloth above her mouth and nose.

Right now, her face is tight against a pillow. The chains are heavy and irritating her skin. At least they are long enough for her to move around just a bit. Not long enough to reach the door, of course.

This is the first time that door has opened. At least, that's what she thinks. She isn't sure. Everything is so fuzzy. She doesn't dare look up. It's perfect timing because she has run out of water. The next sound is very clear. A tray has just been placed on the floor. The door closes. She doesn't dare make a move or a sound. *Is he in the room with me? Is there more than one?* Her limbs begin to shake. She has no idea who her captor is. She has not heard a voice. Not a single person has spoken to her since she woke up in the woods battered and beaten.

Time passes, and it seems no one else is in the room with her. With this in mind, she musters the courage to sit up. Alone again, she reaches over her head to feel her wound. While she was unconscious, they must have cleaned it. Even though there are obvious stitches in her head, she can feel that her hair has been washed. Her arms and hands are also free of dried blood. Perhaps her captor shot her up with painkillers and antibiotics as well. There is still some pain, but not like before. She walks over to the tray and can barely reach it. On the tray is a sandwich, an apple, juice, and four bottles of water. She returns to the bed and stares at the food on her tray. The bucket in the room is both alarming and disgusting. Her gaze moves from her food and back to the bucket. She puts the tray back down and grabs one of the water bottles. She drinks and drinks and drinks. One of the bottles she tucks in close to her body. The feeling of defeat comes over her.

"Please let me go. I haven't seen your face. I won't tell a soul. No harm will be done to you. I will forget this ever happened."

Even I can measure the flawless note of insincerity in my voice. What am I to do? I can only beg. I can't fight. Can I?

Her body folds back. She lays her head on the pillow. Sorrow wraps her body so tightly that she feels like she will soon shrink into nothingness.

I don't understand why he cleaned me up. What's the fucking point? Oh fuck, is he getting me prettied up so he can rape me anytime he wants? Is that sick fuck going to drop off a white dress and a long blond wig for me to put on for him? Is he going to paint my nails red and call me Veronica or Bethany? Is he going to lick my toes and brush my hair while humming a tune?

CHAPTER 17

Dr. Trudi

Dr. Trudi Rosenblun is grabbing a quick lunch at Slutty Vegan in Atlanta, where she agreed to meet up with Police Officer Yusuff McCray to talk more about how hypnotherapy works. She has still been helping with the recent missing persons cases. It was hard not to notice how much time and effort Yusuff has given this project. When someone knows very little about her profession and techniques, she is always happy to discuss details with them. It's important for others to understand how helpful various types of psychological therapy can be.

"So, what did you order?" Yusuff asks as he unwraps his burger.

"I ordered the Super Slut burger. I've had almost everything on their menu. It's all truly amazing. That looks huge! What did you order?" She giggles.

"Go big or go home. I ordered the Menage A Trois. It has a patty, bacon, shrimp, cheese, caramelized onions, lettuce, tomato, and their slut sauce." He takes a bite and chews for a short moment. "What the fuck? This *can't* be vegan." He takes a sip of his large soda. "This is insanely good. You always hear vegans say, 'It tastes like real meat,' and I always roll my eyes. This right here tastes like real meat. This is nuts." He shakes his head and takes another large bite.

"They have come a long way recently. Vegan meats used to taste like cardboard. Now it tastes so similar. Even I'm skeptical whether it's plant-based or not."

"Yeah, no shit. I'll have to bring my wife JoDi here. That's if she hasn't been here already. Who knows, we are both so busy these days."

"Speaking of busy, I'm glad you wanted to meet up. I wish more police officers were interested in what I do."

"I know I can use Google, but I think I should hear it from you. After all, you are the real deal." He takes another bite. "Hell, I think I'll come back here next week. I'll take a sloppy non-cholesterol burger any day. Anyway, why don't I let you start, and if I have any questions, I'll chime in."

"Sounds good. Let's see, where do I begin?" She sets down her burger and wipes her mouth. "Honestly, I'm not surprised you don't know much about hypnosis. Even today, more than one hundred and fifty years after the first use of the term 'hypnosis,' the practice remains a mystery to most. I think the popular form is from what people see on TV."

"Ain't that the truth."

"I guess you already know that when it's used for public entertainment, it's often frowned upon. Well, maybe you didn't know that, but it's true. Hypnosis has widely been a plot line used to make a story more dramatic, but what you see on TV isn't always very truthful. I think many people have seen it performed on things like talk shows or live entertainment. Medical professionals agree that the 'power of suggestion' is real and can help people change their habits, cope with pain, or work through difficult emotions. Even quit things like smoking, drinking alcohol, or eating meat." They both smile at this. "And no, I didn't use it to stop eating meat, but it has been done before." She eats a few french fries. "But my point is that while all that is great, the 'power of suggestion' is quite dangerous during a session."

"Hell yeah, especially if it works," Yusuff chimes in. "Can you imagine if someone convinces you to open your safe?"

"Exactly. It's messed up. And believe me, that sort of bullshit has happened before."

"That's so fucked up."

"That's one of the reasons we are oftentimes not trusted. I enjoy working with the police department. I feel like I'm trusted a little more by the clients in that environment."

"So, how far have you all come? I mean ... like, do you all have respect in the medical community?"

"That's a good question. Hypnosis has been officially endorsed as a therapeutic method by medical, psychiatric, dental, and psychological associations worldwide. It has taken a while to get here, but here we are." She smiles and takes another bite of her burger.

"This may be a dumb question, but like, what is hypnotherapy, you know, like the definition?"

"In my opinion, there are very few *dumb* questions." She uses quotation marks with her fingers. "You've probably looked up hypnosis and hypnotherapy and read multiple things, I'm sure. It's an extraordinary phenomenon, and I don't think there truly is one satisfactory definition. It's not a magical occurrence, but more a form of receptive, highly focused concentration; in which things happening outside the hypnotic state are ignored."

"Wow, somehow I actually understood that."

"Perhaps you need to give yourself more credit. It's been proven that most detectives are highly intelligent, and I hear you are inching closer to becoming one."

"I can't wait. It's been my dream for way too long."

"Well, would you like me to skip over some of the boring history and facts, or should I elaborate?"

"No, let's do this. That's why we are here. If it gets to be too much, I'll let you know."

"Very well—animal magnetism." She rubs her chin. "Yes, that's what it was called. When hypnosis first claimed the attention of scientists, it was called animal magnetism or mesmerism; I believe it was both. Anyhow, it was named after Franz Anton Mesmer of Vienna. He was from Austria. In the late or early … no, it was in the late 18th century; Mesmer used it to heal certain nervous ailments. It was magnetism that he transferred from him to his patients … so he thought. To him, it moved patients' body fluids into the correct position. Sadly, despite helping people, his methods got him removed as a professor at the University of Vienna. In fact, if I remember correctly, he was banned from practicing medicine in Vienna. It wasn't until he moved to France that he was able to practice again." She took a sip of water, impressed that Yusuff was paying close attention.

"What's wild is that in the 19th century, before the discovery of anesthetics, physicians used mesmerism, which, of course, we now call hypnosis, in surgery. Can you imagine? In actual surgery? Just seems wild to me. So apparently, they discovered that the client would lie perfectly still after being hypnotized."

"So, when did we start calling it hypnotism?"

"It was either 1830 or 1840. I can't recall at the moment. There was a doctor named James Braid who first started using the terms 'hypnosis' and 'hypnotist,' and they stuck. It was after the Greek God of sleep, Hypnos. In the 1970s, hypnotherapy called 'hidden imagery' was introduced, and it helped athletes and musicians perform better."

"No freak'n way! There is so much I don't know."

"Well, as you know, now many medical professionals accept hypnosis because it's been studied extensively and, in many cases, found to benefit patients by reducing chronic pain, shrinking tumors, and even curing chronic infections. It is widely used on cancer patients to decrease nausea."

"That's amazing! So, what is all this I hear about people learning about past lives and shit while they are hypnotized? Also, things like people are scared of heights, but it turns out to be something about their childhood. Is that all bullshit?"

"Certainly not. Hypnosis works with the human mind in two parts. In the conscious mind, you think through decisions and put your ideas to work. The subconscious mind acts automatically. Subconscious mental activities may include the retention of data that cannot be recalled with an effort at a specific time, but that later may be remembered. A good example is if a person is unaware of ever having been pushed off a high ledge as a child, as an adult, they have a severe fear of heights. Suppose a hypnotist can help recall that memory and provide an answer to why this person is suffering. In that case, it makes it easier for the subject to understand that simply looking over the edge of a tall building isn't dangerous.

"And as far as past lives, there have been countless reports of people remembering past lives and details that are virtually impossible for them to have known. Young children with very little education describing Egypt in its ancient form, incredible ancient art, along with the artists' names, details of wars, and names of leaders even before Christ was born. It is fascinating."

"Wow, no offense, but I'm actually starting to believe all of this. It truly is mind-blowing."

"I have some books I want you to read. I'll email you."

"Yes, please do." He pauses to think. "So, why does it work for some and not others?"

"I remember having this same question when I first started. I've learned that evidence has shown that a 'good client' tends to be interested in new experiences. They also have an active imagination. Good subjects also tend to be highly intelligent."

"Intelligent? Interesting, for some reason, I would have thought the opposite, not sure why."

"It's all relative." She takes another bite.

"How many, like, what percentage can even be hypnotized? That's probably an off-the-wall question."

"If I remember correctly, about ten percent of adults cannot be hypnotized at all. I don't remember how they came to that conclusion." She pauses and thinks. "And of those who can be hypnotized, only about thirty percent will be."

"That math seems weird."

"Just because ninety percent *can* be hypnotized doesn't mean they will take the proper measures for it to happen. For example, there has to be a certain amount of trust. A client will tell themselves to trust the therapist, yet deep down, they don't. Also, a hypnotist should have a certain amount of authority in the eyes of the subject."

"Authority? Okay, so maybe one of the reasons you are so successful is that you have two PhDs, you have your own practice, and you occasionally work with the police. And any intelligent person would perhaps do some research to find this out, determining that you know what you are doing. So, when they're in your office, you have 'authority' over them."

"That sounds about right. We could also factor in that some subjects need lots of time with their therapist. They need to trust us. They need to feel a level of trust and compassion that oftentimes only comes with time spent together."

Just then, his phone rings. "I have to get this, sorry."

A few minutes later, he returns. "I'm sorry, Dr. Trudi, but I must go. I can't thank you enough for taking time out of your day to do this for me. Next time we meet, let's talk more about Nicky Lee."

CHAPTER 18

JoDi

Leg Day

Because my meeting ended early today, I am able to leave the office sooner than usual. It's four p.m., and I'm home alone. With no set plans, I'm looking forward to connecting with the members of my group. With my snacks and glass of pinot noir resting on my desk, I have happily opened up the readers' FB group. Wrapping my lips around an Italian cannoli is invigorating, the crispy shell crumbling at my lips, the creamy sweet filling glides smoothly in my mouth. I am rediscovering why all the great nutritionists castigate the pleasurable, sensual crime of sugar intake. The burst of flavors, when they become one, is an unbreakable marriage. I will never divorce desserts … never.

While my fingers rest on the keys, a feverish pull comes from my ledger. It has been a while since I have visited the deceased. I move my chair over and place my phone next to my ledger. The excitement is building. Visiting my victims is something I must do. I owe it to them. Even though I gave most of them a glorious death, they don't have a burial site for loved ones to visit them … I will carry this burden. Opening up my ledger to the annihilate list brings back some old memories. Even though I know I did the right thing, there is still a tinge of regret. I really wish they hadn't taken it too far. They caused so much pain and trouble for everyone. I haven't visited Miss Sahnon Cates in a while. She most certainly was given a glorious death. Her body rests in a beautiful lake in Austin, Texas.

I open my phone and go to my GPS coordinates app. I type in the coordinates I have listed under her name in my ledger. I zoom in on the exact location. Like I often do, I stare at the screen and imagine her body lying peacefully at the bottom of the lake, her arms crossed over her chest … one with the Earth. I talk to her and catch her up on the new and popular authors and books at the moment. Naturally, I tell her funny stories that have recently occurred in the group.

When I am done, I go into my backyard mini-forest and dig up her mason jar. I pull her tiny braid of hair out from the jar and give the ends a quick brush. After placing the braid back in the jar, I tuck the jar safely back in the ground and bury it once again. All is good. The squirrels have never bothered my keepsakes. They respect me, and I respect them.

After I wash my hands, I return to my office and turn on my yellow smiley face neon sign. I feel a sense of calmness come over me. I click on the FB reading group.

"What is this?"

A post has gotten an unusual number of views and shares.

A post from Keeland Grifith: My favorite reads so far. *Verity* is my favorite book of all time; jaw-dropping plot twist. *My Lovely Wife* has a really good plot twist. First half was a semi-slow burn but the last half made me anxious and dying to know what happened next. *Hostage* was also a slow start. Not a huge fan of any of the characters. Suspenseful once the plot got going with a lot of little plot twists, two POVs and I found one of them less exciting than the other. *All Good People* fantastic, so twisty and turny, insane plot twist.

I LIKE it, and move on.

A post from Niki Marie C: Finally, a new Stephen King book … *Fairy Tale* and UFH, it's fantasy boooo.

It has seventy-four comments that I might go through later because I see something that has caught my attention even more.

A post from Shane Summerfield: Whomever the admin of this group is, ya wanna PM me so we can have a chat? Thanks.

It has several comments: "I can't wait for this to end up being over the smallest, most boring thing ever."

"This thread fills my cockles with warmth. I love a warm cockle." A reply to this, "Me not googling cockle … laughing face emoji."

"I don't know what any of this is about, but I'm already on the admin's side."

"Please have a little chat in the public forum, so we may indulge. TYIA."

"You can't just drop that in a thriller readers' group and expect people to just let it go."

Countless GIFs are posted: GIF A Woman scarfing down popcorn. GIF Dave Chapelle's nose covered in white powder, scratching himself. GIF Alexis from Schitt's Creek saying "THIS IS ALL VERY SKETCHY," as she plays with her hair.

And then there it appears, the GIF is posted that provides some answers. It's Michael Cera from the movie *Juno*. He's on his knees, staring at a pair of woman's legs. The post is from Sammantha asking Shane if this is he. Now I get it. I remember seeing several posts with both legs and books in the picture. I look back and see that it's been what members are calling "Leg Day." Not to be confused with a member named Manny Iggi. We do love his leg posts. No, this is a whole day of lady legs.

I love it when the members get creative and funny. All day women have been posting pictures of the book they are currently reading with their legs in the photo. Some are quite cute. Some, I guess, have come across as offensive, at least to Shane. I go back to the post and make sure I read every single comment. It's time to be the enforcer. Surprisingly, I am not upset. In fact, I find myself laughing so hard that my cheeks are hurting.

A member to Shane: "How DARE you DD your post … I wasn't done reading the comments."

More comments continue. "Someone, please tell me what's going on!"

"Basically, a guy doesn't like all the legs and is a bit peeved his post received no comments or laughing emoji. That's as far as we've all got, lol."

GIF of a man eating beef jerky, saying, "I'VE GOT SNACKS."

"Dropped the kids at a sitter! We have new reading to do!"

"The admins are listed so YOU can message them. Stop clogging up the feed." A reply to this is a GIF with Meryl Streep yelling, "BOOOOOOO."

"Shit, there goes my work productivity." It gets twenty-one laughs.

Two replies to this comment: "Same … I had so many plans today!" and "Deadlines are merely suggestions anyway." It gets twenty-five laughs.

"It's a mystery. This post is like a psychological thriller." Reply "It sure is. I'm ALL in!" Also, "I have no life so yes … I'm all in too."

GIF with David from Schitt's Creek laying on a bed saying, "I'M OBSESSED."

GIF of Lucifer from the show *Lucifer* holding a box of tissue saying, "DON'T WORRY. THIS IS A SAFE PLACE."

"Which one of us is missing, and will the admins meet his demands for the members' return?" This one gets forty-one laughs.

GIF of Barney from *How I met your Mother*, fists clenched, yelling to the ceiling, "I GOTS TO KNOW!!"

GIF of Scar from *The Lion King*, arm over his eyes "*OH, THE DRAMA.*"

It goes on and on. It's gotten out of hand, but it's still hilarious. I click on the admins' Messenger group chat. None of us really know how to handle this situation. No one is being unkind. However, Shane may feel otherwise. One of the admins turns off the comments. I let out a hiss I didn't know I was holding.

Not a good move to turn off the comments.

Soon after the comments were turned off, someone posted this:

Dearest Admins,

I think I speak for many of us when I say I'm really disappointed that the comments have been turned off of two of the most engaging posts in a very long time. Could we work out a deal to get the comments turned back on? On the two posts in question? Let's say on each post that gets 500 laughing emoji heart emoji, the comments get turned back on to the corresponding post. Let's see how many people we can engage today! This was the most fun some people have had in a while. Thank you for listening!

Dearest group members,

You did not disappoint!

That is hard for me to read, especially since this is my second family. I want nothing more than to see my family laugh and be joyful in so many creative ways. Life is already too hard. Moments like this can help someone that is struggling … and don't most of us struggle?

The posts are then deleted. What a tragedy. I convince the other admins to reverse it, and they do. They, too, see the value of laughter.

The comments remain off, but at least members can go through the current messages and like them or laugh at them. This honestly is one of the best parts.

I know I need to address the members, so I create a post.

Post from JoDi ADMIN: "So, I just have to jump in here and say that I'm absolutely delighted you all had so much fun this morning with a few posts that took a hard but fun turn. Didn't realize we had so many comedians on here. Sometimes a good laugh can brighten up anyone's day. To be honest, we admins weren't really sure what to do, laughing emoji. Anyhow, I hope you all continue to find laughter throughout your day.

Love,

The ADMINS

(Baby Jesus, 👏 please don't let this post turn into trouble)

AND THIS IS WHEN LEG-DAY WAS CREATED IN THE GROUP. IT IS NOW AN ANNUAL EVENT.

I darken my laptop and notice something sticking out of a book called *Killer Fiction* by Rosemary Willhide. It's a great book so far, but I have been trying to finish it for some time now. With so much on my plate, it seems like I never have time to read as much as I'd like to. I can tell by the color and texture that it's not one of my bookmarkers. My lips widen as I realize it's another note from Justin. For months now, he has been leaving random notes for me.

I open my book. The note is lying over my bookmarker. It says, "But you don't even know how to read," signed with a hand-drawn smiley face poop emoji.

CHAPTER 19

JoDi

It is late in the afternoon. Long streams of light swim through tall pine trees highlighting curves of branches and falling leaves. What we know to be "typical sunsets" are not visible in these dense woods of Kennesaw Mountain. However, the sun surely does set beautifully here, in countless rows of beaming rays and casting shadows. I'm currently volunteering at the moment, sporting my oversized crew T-shirt and tan cargo pants. I've been a member of the cleanup crew for Kennesaw Mountain for many years now. Preserving nature is another one of my passions. Yes, I know I have many, but that's who I am. I could give two fucks about what others think of me. I don't do it for the attention. I do it because I'm a decent fucking human being. Also, it gives me access to all kinds of fun equipment and tools. This forest I know well, like the back of my hand, as many would say.

As I set my eyes upon a family of deer, I am reminded of how secluded one could become in these unpredictable trails deep in the northern mountains of Georgia. I am watching the mother deer with wild curiosity.

Will you approach me, mother-deer? Try to attack me? I know you must protect your children. You must protect the ones you love. Isn't that what matters? Protecting the people and things you care about the most? How easy it would be to lure someone into these majestic sounds and visions of nature. Here the possibilities are endless. Wildlife could feast on a body lying in its final resting place. This would be a favor … to let someone take their last breath surrounded by such beauty. It's better than dark alleyways near fowl dumpsters and filthy streets. This would be merciful; for one to have their last connection with this world just before passing into the next one. But who deserves this enchanting death? Someone who has gone too far. Someone who has revealed her hateful self. But it must be someone who has a kind side as well. This would need to be a person who deserves to pay for what they have done but also be good enough for these woods. Anyone who hurts or threatens one of my members must be shut down. I know what's best for my second family. The family I deeply care for. There are some members that don't know how or don't have the courage to defend themselves properly. But that's okay because I am here, zealously by their side. Watching over them, protecting them, eliminating the hate that haunts them.

I close my eyes and absorb the captivating sounds of nature. I steady myself by leaning on a nearby tree. My thoughts are meticulous. I do not have my ledger, my journal, but I have my memory.

Yes, oh yes, Joyce Tiantefilou. Yes, you are perfect. It's clear as day. You are the woman who will pay for what you've done. And I will make sure, my dear, to give you a glorious death.

I am scrolling through the FB reading group. There are 256 moderation alerts. I click on it and discover that members are still using words and phrases associated with violence. FB bots like to flag us, especially for violent phrases like "I hate the main character so much I want to punch her in the face," or "That book was so boring I just wanted to shoot myself in the foot," or "Can you please recommend a book that's mild, I don't like books with children being tortured." Several other FB groups have been shut down out of nowhere, absolutely no warning—just gone. I pray every day that we don't get shut down.

My anxiety level is not quite under control, so I take one of my Buspirone, hoping it will prevent another anxiety attack.

Countless hours a day working so hard to keep things fun and resourceful seems like it may have been a waste of time if they simply shut us down. It's slightly heartbreaking, but what can I do? I'm caught in a place between sorrow and anger.

In all honesty, it's not really the member's fault. Why does FB do this to reading groups? Don't they have some kind of software that can detect that our readers are simply talking about fiction? About books? We have warned the members countless times, but it's a big group, and they may not be getting the message ... even though it's been pinned at the top of the group page for a long time.

Don't they want the family to stay together? Don't they love me as much as I love them?

I stretch my neck from side to side. I know either a glass of wine or some whiskey will help me in this time of need. I walk to the kitchenette and am reminded that my wine shelf is empty. My husband Yusuff used to keep it stocked for me. He used to think about me. He used to love me. He used to spoil me. Now, I am staring at a blank wall. Nothing but metal rods sticking out where once bottles of wine from around the world used to sit patiently waiting for me. He had never let this happen in all the time we had been together.

At the liquor buffet, I see plenty of bottles to choose from. I grab a bottle of Gentleman Jack and a cocktail glass and walk back to my computer. It takes me three hours to go through every single alert and personally send them each a message. I absolutely hate doing this. These are grown-ass adults, and they shouldn't have to be told by me that FB is censoring their every word. This makes me seem like the bad guy when all I want to do is provide them with joy.

When I am done playing "annoying mother" to the members, I shake it off and focus on what really matters. It is time to focus on Joyce Tiantefilou. She is the one who deserves a glorious death in the mountains of Georgia. She had broken too many rules. She had gone too far. And that's why I had already become friends with her on FB ... just in case. Long ago, when I found out she was from a town called Woodstock, GA, just twenty minutes north of here, I had left it alone. It was too close to home. But it doesn't matter now. It's too late. I have already made up my mind. Joyce will BE no more.

I'm actually relieved Joyce is so close to home. I need something in my life to be simple. And again, there is no turning back because I have that deep pull from within, and if I don't get blood soon, I will burst.

"Let's see what you have been up to, Miss Joyce." I wiggle my fingers, caress the mouse, and begin the savage hunt. "Miss Joyce, Miss Joyce, Imma cut out that voice." I lick my lips. "And when your face falls flat in the mud, I will rejoice, Miss Joyce." I scroll through her page and see that Joyce is a realtor. What an easy target this is. Every realtor is eager to meet, talk, and make a sale. Creating relationships is part of their business strategy. This will be simple.

I click on messenger and send her a poke.

JoDi: Hi Joyce, it's been a while. I hope you are doing well. I noticed on your personal page

that you are a realtor, and I would love to meet with you sometime soon if you can.

Joyce: Oh, hi! Yes, it has been a while. I am a realtor. Are you in the market for a new

home?

JoDi: Just in the early stages.

I keep it simple. I want it to be Joyce's idea to meet in person.

Joyce: Well, I am so very happy to help. Would you like to meet for some coffee or tea?

JoDi: I don't really drink caffeine, it makes me jittery.

Joyce: My sister is the same way. Why don't you pick the place?

JoDi: I love to walk Kennesaw Mountain. I go about twice a week. You interested in that?

Joyce: I absolutely love to hike, but I never have any time. It's been so long! I would love to do that. I seem to remember there being like fifteen different places to park, and like fifty trails. Why don't you pick a spot, and I'll meet you there.

JoDi: Oh yes, it can get very confusing. Why don't we park at the Pigeon Hill parking lot? It's not as busy as the Kennesaw Mountain guest center.

Joyce: Perfect, I'll look up the address. When would you like to meet? I'm available

tomorrow, Thursday, or Friday. If none of those work, I'm available the following Saturday.

JoDi: How about Friday? I'm working from home that day, so I'm super flexible. Actually, any time between 2 pm – 4 pm would work great.

I am well aware that during those times on Friday it's like a ghost town on those trails. It's also a time when realtors aren't very busy.

Joyce: That's perfect! And thanks again for thinking of me. You are so sweet! I'll touch base with you that morning to confirm.

JoDi: Sounds great. I look forward to picking your brain.

It does sound very great, indeed. The images slide in instantly like a hot knife through soft butter. The setting is in the early 1800s when presidents like Abraham Lincoln and James Garfield were assassinated and when hundreds of thousands of men rushed to California for the gold rush. It's a thousand shades of gray. I am singing "Love on The

Brain" by Rihanna. I have a rabbit costume on. The mask is large and simple. I am knee-deep in mud as I pull out worm-like pieces of flesh slowly out of Joyce's brain.

CHAPTER 20

JoDi

It wasn't too difficult for me to get my hands on some roofies. Rohypnol isn't necessarily a common drug sold by your average drug dealer; however, one could get their hands on just about anything with enough determination. It is all about knowing the right people. Plugging into their scene, hanging on to their every word. I had spent years playing trivia with a local drug dealer in my town. But what he sold, I didn't quite need. No, I needed something more complex. And before I knew it, I was sitting next to Raymond, also known as Ray Ray, on a poker table playing a game of Texas hold 'em. The games took place in a basement near downtown that used to be a factory in the early 1900s. Daniel, a friend I had known for a few years, mentioned Ray Ray several times during idle conversations. Of course, it piqued my interest. He mentioned playing in underground poker tournaments every two weeks. While trivia-drug-dealer happened by accident, poker-drug-dealer took some intentional actions.

To my surprise, it didn't take an incredible amount of time to gain Ray Ray's trust. Appearances can be deceiving, and with my puffy dresses and colorful hairpins, one would think I was all sunshine and butterflies. Ray Ray was phenomenal at reading people, gazing through the cracks. Peeling off the shiny coat to see what really lies underneath.

He saw something quite sinister in me. He told me this himself. We became fast friends despite our differences. In no time at all, I was submerged in the same circle as he. It was something I executed swiftly using nothing but wit and charm, cleverly expressing interest in subjects and ideas that would awaken his amusement and pleasure. I was a saleswoman, after all, and a hell of a good one. Once we were friends, he was at my disposal. Ray Ray's ability to get his hands on uncommon drugs and devices was most certainly a blessing. Call me an opportunist, call me a snake, call me whatever your little heart desires. I tend to get what I want and I *don't* have to drop my pretty panties to get it.

Being prepared is key. I must not let anything distract me. Not only is this project close to home but this annihilation will be done while there is still light out; when the sun first starts its descent. The space between its tallest point and when it kisses the tops of every tree. If the roofied fresh-squeezed juice isn't appealing to Joyce, or if she is allergic to any of the ingredients, I would have to execute plan B.

I pick up Jade and hold it gently in the palm of my left hand. With my other hand, I caress its filigree details and smooth edges. Jade, my small pocket folding knife, is something I hold dear to my heart. There is a brief smile of admiration on my face just before slipping it into my fanny pack. "There she is. You fit perfectly, Miss Jade." After zipping it closed, I give it a little tap. Naming things I admire is simply in my nature. No one had ever taught me to name objects. I name everything from my vehicles to the trees on my property. Jade got her name from the two Jade stones encrusted into the handle. A lavishly decorated knife was something I had desired to possess for many years. Long ago, when I was antique shopping with my best friend Dreenie Beeny, there it was, sitting in a dark corner as if shunned and underappreciated.

Jade, the perfect shade of smoky green, with all its smooth curves and hand-crafted qualities. Maintaining its sharpness was no issue.

I had learned how to sharpen and throw knives at an early age. Actually, I learned how to swing an ax, throw an ax, cut wood, well ... just about everything you could learn about an ax. Cleaning and shooting guns were also things I learned at a young age. I had a peculiar upbringing that left me with uncommon skills. Uncommon skills for a *woman,* that is. Or even for a *child,* for that matter.

Now in my kitchen, I am fussing with some glasses, moving them around and out of the way until I find the single-serving container used for my Ninja blender. In the cup, I add blueberries, lime, spinach, strawberries, apple juice, and water. The Ninja blender is unpleasantly loud. As the razor-sharp steel blades slice through every piece of fruit, I wonder what it would be like to blend an entire hand. I empty the juice into a small tumbler. I want to make sure Joyce drinks the entire serving. It's important that she gets the correct dosage. Ray Ray had already advised me on how much an average-sized female would need to ingest to pass out fairly quickly.

My car syncs with my cell phone as soon as I start it. My chichis are hot, so I turn on the air conditioner. Reaching over to turn up the volume, I am already dancing in my seat. One of my favorite songs, "A Real Hero" by College, is playing. After watching the movie *Drive*, I instantly purchased the soundtrack on iTunes. The music is loud, and the tempo is just what I need as I race through the curved mountain streets. Multicolored trees of all sizes dance along with me as the wind picks up. A sky full of red, yellow, and brown leaves simultaneously fall and fly all around. Raining death is okay for me because I know that next spring, life will bloom on every branch, sprouting new leaves and returning my forest back to its honorable green. Where there is death, there is room for new life.

As the leaves dance to their final resting place, I imagine how beautiful Joyce's death will be. How her warm blood will flow into rich red clay soil, an exhibit of union, giving back to mother nature; the multiple shades of red might readily amalgamate and be molded into new forms. Oh, what the sounds will be like all around Joyce as she inhales and exhales her last breath. An orchestra of nature will wrap her like a blanket, and when the final drop of blood is consumed by the earth beneath her, that's when my readers' group will have room for someone else. Someone better. Someone who will not hurt the ones I love. I am their protector. A real human being and a real hero.

Just like I had suspected, I find plenty of parking spaces. A good sign indeed. We will practically be alone between giant boulders and swaying branches. I back into a space and take a few deep breaths before turning off my car. I exit my car and walk to my trunk. My fanny pack is on tight. I have two small tumblers full of freshly blended juice in my miniature backpack that I often take hiking. They have different lids, one pastel pink and the other sky blue. I unzip my bag and pull out the blue one. I empty the crushed roofie into the juice and gently shake it up. When I return the bottle to my bag, I see Joyce coming around the corner. Just in time. I like that she's punctual. With a smile, I close my trunk and wave with delight. Joyce is a steady driver and pulls into a parking spot just two spaces over. She is fumbling with things in her front seat. Finally turning off her car, I feel a tingle in my chest. It spreads like wildfire through my torso until it reaches the tips of every limb.

"Well, hello!" I say while walking toward Joyce's vehicle.

"Hello JoDi, I'm so glad we could make this work." We half hug and continue with small talk.

"It's absolutely gorgeous out here, my gosh. I wish more clients would meet me this way. How fun!"

"Yes, well, perhaps you could start a trend." Knowing full well that Joyce will never meet with another client again.

"If you didn't pack any fluids, I brought some for you, just in case."

"Oh, you are so thoughtful. I did bring some water, but it has been a while since I have been in these mountains, and I know at times, they can get quite steep. Now I'm thinking one bottle of water won't cut it, will it?"

"I've got you covered." I try desperately to remain cheerful even though I notice Joyce didn't bring a tumbler. She actually brought a single-use plastic water bottle.

I raise one hand toward the mountain. "Shall we go?"

What in God's name are her intentions? To simply toss her nasty-ass plastic bottle into the woods when she is done with it? Is her plan to violate and disrespect these already suffering woods of ours? What a pathetic and vile human being she is. I mean, who still buys those things anyway? What is this, 2010? For this reason alone, she should die. I'm doing this planet a favor, not just my group.

As we walk toward the tree line, she brings up subjects like family, friends, hobbies, and other topics to tug at my heartstrings. She knows the game. She is in sales. She knows how this goes.

Miss nasty little critter,

I wish you didn't litter.

I'm not bitter,

I'll simply toss your ashes like glitter.

We are about an hour into our hike, almost right in the middle of it. This is the area where large boulders and cliffs start to appear. Joyce asks for a quick break and takes a few selfies. There is an unyielding urge to take pictures in a place like this.

"Here," I interrupt her. "you'll love this." I don't want her to post anything on social media. Joyce's head pops up, and she puts her phone back into her pocket. I pull out the tumbler with the blue lid. "I brought you something special. I grow my own blueberries, and I made you a smoothie. It's perfect for this hike. It will provide you with all the energy you need."

Mentioning that I grow my own blueberries will hit a love nerve. She will not be rude. She will drink it. We all know realtors cannot be rude. Anyone in sales knows what's good for them … I should know. I'm at the top of the top, the best of the best.

"Wow, you seriously are the nicest person, my goodness! That looks delicious, and if we still have an hour to go, I could really use this." She takes the bottle and drinks half of it in one gulp. She glances down at her midsection and adjusts her shirt. "Good Lord, I look like a busted can of biscuits. I really need to lose some weight, JoDi."

"You hush now. You look amazing."

"You are too kind." She takes another sip, this time a much smaller and elegant sip. "Thanks again for this." Her voice softens. "It seriously tastes so fresh, and I absolutely love blueberries. You must show me how to grow them. I hear two bushes are needed for them to produce berries."

"That's right, two bushes are necessary. It's not difficult at all. I would be happy to show you." I continue to sip on my non-problematic juice.

"Do you want to talk about the property now?"

"Actually, I'm not in any rush right now," I reply. "Why don't we sit for a while and relax? We can talk about it in a few minutes. Let's just enjoy nature for now." I want to give her a glorious death … no need to fill her head with numbers and neighborhoods.

At first, we finish our beverages wordlessly and let the primitive silence of the forest transform us into nothing more than clusters of atoms. The sounds were like a musical composition that only this planet could invent, and we watch in quiet disposition as Mother Earth lives and breathes. The heartbeat I long for.

When I had my fill of God's green Earth, I spark up a conversation that only I know will bear no fruit. "So, let's talk about what kind of property I'm looking for."

I know that a little more time is needed for the roofy to kick in. Just over the next boulder is when the descent will begin. At this point in our journey, we are literally at the highest point on the trail. On the way down is a turn-off that Joyce will not even notice. She will think we are on the same trail.

"Yes, let's do that. So, instead of me asking a million questions, why don't you tell me exactly what you are looking for, and we can go from there."

I spend about five minutes talking about what I really do want in the near future. A five-acre plot of land on the lake with a large cabin-like home with windows everywhere. A large front porch and dense trees in every direction. Floor-to-ceiling windows. A large library. A private dock is a must, and plenty of space between neighbors. I go into detail, temporally losing myself in the moment.

We go back and forth for about ten more minutes, and I insist that we return to our hike before it darkens. As we make our way down, I notice Joyce's steps are a hair unsteady. We are only a few yards from the detour needed for this plan to work. So far, we have only seen two groups of people, which was a long time ago. The turn-off is so secluded that I have never actually seen anyone else use it. It is a tight plan.

"Oh my, I am getting very sleepy. How silly. I'm quite unsteady, actually." Joyce says as she leans on a nearby tree.

"It's probably just the elevation change. Here, let's go this way. It's a shortcut. This way will only take us about twenty minutes to get back instead of an hour."

"Wonderful, let's do that." Her words came out as if she was trying to tie a cherry stem with a swollen tongue.

"There's also a place to sit down this way." The new trail becomes increasingly narrow until it becomes nothing but raw land beneath our feet.

"Are you sure we are going the right way?" she slurs.

"Oh yes, I've been here a million times. Trust me." There are sounds of branches cracking as wildlife joins us at the nearby creek. I reach out and take hold of Joyce's arm. "I've got you." I smile and wink at her. Joyce's arms are like gummy worms, and her back is slightly hunched over.

"Why don't we sit here for a moment." There's a large flat rock just a few feet away. As she untangles her hair from a branch, I tighten my grip. I can feel the heaviness in Joyce's body as it gives in to the elixir. "What is happening to me?" Her bottom lip falls loose.

"Don't you worry about a thing." She doesn't make it to the rock. Her legs give out from under her. I am not strong enough to catch her. All I can do is slow down the process.

While Joyce lies on the ground, I spring into action. This has to be done quickly. I slap Joyce in the face, and as soon as she opens her eyes, I hold up her phone so that the face recognition feature opens it. Joyce's eyes quickly close again. While Joyce's phone is open, I delete all our messages on Messenger, our text messages, emails, photos, and anything I can find. I plan on destroying the phone, but one can never be too careful. I put it in my fanny pack and pull out a pair of plastic gloves. After putting them on, I pull out Jade.

"Hello, old friend," I whisper to her.

I open the knife and look around. I hear only the sounds of nature cheering me on. I put in my earbuds and start the song "The Cherry Tree" by KT Tunstall. I sing along.

I get down on one knee. Move the hair away from her soft face and neck. I pick out a nice clean bunch of hair and make a small braid. I cut it off and put it in my pocket. With one long smooth stroke, I slice Joyce's throat from one end to the other. "Pump pud-a-rump."

I continue to sing.

"That's the last time you take it too far in my group. Bye, Falisha." I watch as streams of blood flow out from both ends of her throat. I know someone will find this body unless the wildlife consumes her flesh. But still, there will be bones. It's okay. There is no connection. We are deep in the woods. No one comes here. No one.

I continue to sing. I dance to the beat.

I reach into Joyce's pocket and pull out her car keys. I tuck them safely into my fanny pack.

"Farewell, I hope you appreciate your glorious death."

I hear a loud crack. It's unclear which direction it came from. Still crouched down on one knee, I jerk my head up. Look to my right and quickly look to my left. I don't see anything. I jump to my feet and look behind me. The sound was too loud to be a fox or a squirrel.

"If anyone is approaching, please stop. I'm peeing over here."

The same thing happens every time I get nervous. My palms get sweaty. My armpits feel like steam is building up. Beads of sweat form on my forehead and upper lip. I don't want to have to kill anyone else. This isn't part of my plan. I could just start crying and yell for help, just in case someone appears. It could look like my friend was attacked. But then, what would we be doing here off the trail? A lesbian love affair? Wait, *was* someone following us? No one ever walks this deep into the forest. This is not the type of mountain where people go hunting. No, this is a protected mountain not too far from the city, where people go hiking, walking, and meditating. No, no one goes off the beaten path, at least not this far. Unless one has to take a shit, but even then, not this far.

I hear more shuffling, and my anxiety and fear turn into a form of excitable rage. An organized rage. The kind of rage that is lifesaving. A place where fear should exist but is replaced with a sense of hunting. Yes, I want to hunt. I am not the one being hunted. I don't fear. I am the one to be feared. This person is falling into my trap, not the other way around. They are the ones in danger, not me. I move slowly toward a nearby boulder. Luckily, I am prepared. I am wearing hiking boots and long pants. The woods are not too dense, but because it's fall, almost half the leaves are on the ground. I hear the sound again, this time closer and much louder. It's a human. I know it is. I have spent a lot of time in these woods and can recognize whether a sound is coming from a small beast or a large one. And if this is a human, it is most certainly a beast. Only a beast would follow two women into the dense forest.

A second after a stretch of silence, when the only sounds are birds and dried leaves colliding, I stand tall and walk in the new, measured way of mine, not as I was—scared and anxious—but confident and fearless. Eventually, of course, I would come to know who was there or at least a certain sequence of facts. I will face this person, and perhaps there would be no need for Jade to find its glistening sharp head inside another body, at least not today.

As I move around the boulder, I see nothing. I bend slightly at the waist and open my stance as I move through the branches and poison ivy. My animalistic movements are like second nature to me. My senses are heightened. It's as if I can hear and smell everything all at once. Nothing, absolutely nothing, is present but nature. I continue to breathe normally, keeping my body steady. When I have concluded that I am alone, my shoulders relax. The sounds and smells around me once again remind me of life, not death. I fold Jade and tuck her into my fanny pack.

"There you go, you pretty girl. You can take a break now." I tap on my fanny pack.

Endorphins that had been distributed throughout my body are still lingering. It is both exhilarating and tremulous in equal measure. I am embracing it with every inch of my body. And just as they give me ultimate pleasure, they come to an abrupt halt and are replaced by adrenaline. A very loud, very near, cracking sound occurs. Just before I break through the rough terrain, a large buck, large as in a twelve-point buck, dashes in front of my path. He must have been so incredibly still for so long for me not to hear him. I was stunned. I was thrown off guard. I was, in fact, jolted to the ground as an embarrassing scream came out of me like a thirteen-year-old.

"Mother fucker!!" I yelled.

After laying still for a short moment, I take the time to observe the gorgeous creature as he makes his way to the water's edge.

"If that didn't make me shit my pants, I don't know what will."

As I brush myself off, my tummy begins to turn. "Well, isn't this ironic." It has become clear that there's no time to waste now. I begin to hike quickly. I don't want to take a crap in the woods. My strides are steady, and I get quite far, but my bowels, at this point, are screaming at me.

"Are you fucking kidding me right now? Really? Right now?" The juice must have worked some magic because I have to take a mad shit—like now. I always pack toilet paper in my backpack for this very reason. I tuck myself near some non-ivy bushes and take care of business. To my delight, it was a smooth and solid event.

Now back in the parking lot, I notice a man loading up his dog. He was no doubt playing fetch with him in the open field. He keeps looking over my way, which makes me nervous. Perhaps he's just checking me out. I'm not going to lie, having thick thighs is like kryptonite for most men.

He looks over again, and I try not to let it bother me too much. I have work to do. I divert my attention back to what needs to be done.

I need to drive Joyce's car to a different location. Then I will need to walk somewhere and call an Uber.

I hear a man's voice. "Excuse me, Miss."

"Oh hell, please don't be a creeper," I whisper to myself. I poke my head around the back of my trunk and see that he's walking my way. "Yes?" I respond, holding my knife in one hand, tucked away so he can't see it. "Are you talking to me?" Stupid question, and I know it. No one else is around.

He stops before he gets too close. "I just wanted to tell you that you have toilet paper stuck to the bottom of your shoe."

I can feel blood filling my cheeks. I look down in utter despair and began to move my feet.

"I just didn't want you walking around with that on your shoe for the rest of the evening." He gave a cute chuckle, his straight white teeth gleaming against his beautiful dark brown skin. Why are black men so beautiful? Why are their teeth so white and their hygiene so spot-on?

"Thanks a bunch." I am both mortified and tickled. "There are still good people on this earth," I say while pulling out a clean set of plastic gloves.

CHAPTER 21

JoDi

Journal/Ledger

One of the things I hate about having a therapist is that they are almost always right. Long ago, one of my therapists suggested keeping a journal. She told me to write whatever I wanted. She also encouraged me to write down both positive things and negative things about my life. To my surprise, it has helped. It's like purifying my soul. I like to tell stories of my life in this journal. It's much easier than saying them out loud to a therapist. Each time that I do, it is both difficult and relieving. I believe it helps my mind process pain. I imagine I repressed so many memories that they began to fester inside me. The story I have decided to write today is from long ago. If I had to guess, I was about five years old. Perhaps I was six. It's hard to tell. It was so long ago. I'm surprised I even remember this happening to me. Why is it that I can remember all of the bad things that happened to me as a young child, but I don't really have any fond memories of when I was that age? Who knows.

Anyway, here it is.

It is shortly after Christmas. My sister had gotten a new bike. I don't remember if it was from Santa Claus or if it was from Mom and Dad. I just remember that I was jealous. I had a bike, but it had training wheels. I wanted to be all grown up, I guess. I liked to sit outside and watch my sister get on her bike and leave. She would disappear in the distance. Sometimes I would get on my bike and follow her. She would leave me in the dust, of course. One day she said if I really wanted to join her that I could. I was so excited. I had to earn it, though. She asked me to lie down on my back and extend my limbs as far as possible. I was nervous, but I wanted to ride with her so badly I just did as I was told.

My nerves were in a bundle. My sister had a talent for bringing me into her dark and creative games. I laid down as she instructed. It was obvious that she was far away. She yelled, "Don't move!" I didn't. I turned my body into stone. "If you move an inch, you can never ride with me." I lay like death was upon me. I lifted my head and saw her cycling toward me, peddling fast as if her life depended on it. My legs were spread. Was she going to run me over? Between my legs? I didn't know. My thoughts haunted me. As she got closer, I saw she was heading straight for me. I started to cry. I was so scared, but I knew my sister, and if I moved, she would never take me riding. She got closer-and-closer-and-closer-and-closer. I could feel the urine gathering underneath me. I didn't move. I can't move. I can't move. I can't move. She was going so fast. The tire was spinning and spinning, and I could see it heading down the middle of me. *Me*. My lady parts, as Momma had put it. Where God makes babies. What if she ran over my belly and then my nose, too? Not my nose again. Why the nose? It was always painful when she would flick my nose. Flick. Flick. Flick. Or she would pull it. Pull. Pull. Pull. Or tap it over and over with a pencil. Tap. Tap. Tap. She used to give me many nose bleeds. *So* many nose bleeds. Blood. Always so much blood. Iron.

There she was, towering over me. She was going so fast. My belly was bouncing up and down as I cried. My body convulsed in my own urine. I closed my eyes. I guess at the last moment, she jerked the wheel, and ran over my right hand.

When she finally let me get up, she laughed at me when she noticed I had soiled my pants. She tied me to a fence and brought her friends to laugh at me. She said this was the last test for me. She told me that if I cried, I would fail. When no one was laughing any longer, she pulled down my pants. The laughter started again.

CHAPTER 22

The Captive

"A breath of fresh air ... how fucking nice of you."

When she wakes, she is enamored by the soft sounds and bright lights. The curtains had been pulled to the side, and the windows had been opened. Captivated by this simple pleasure left her motionless.

There must have been something in the lemonade. Seems like days have gone by. She had given in. She would eat. She would drink. She would shit in the bucket. That's what she had decided. And now, she finds herself broken. Broken with acceptance. Broken from the beginning to her end.

A soft breeze blows in. It's daytime, but she isn't sure what time, of course. Her head is pounding, and her eyesight is blurry.

I need to eat more. I need to stay strong. Why hasn't this man shown his face? What a fucking coward he is. What's his game? I don't understand what he wants from me. Just kill me already.

She glares at the fresh tray by her bed. There is something extraordinarily different. What a colossal moment. Next to the tray is a large bucket of water, soap, a small towel, and a change of clothes. Normal clothes; cotton jogger pants and a long-sleeved shirt. She sits up and splashes water on her face ... her eyes glued to the ripples in the water.

Can I drown myself?

Clearly, she was drugged again. How else could he leave *all* these things? How else could he give her hope? How else could he make her imagine her own suicide? This isn't the first time she has been drugged in this place, and she knew it wouldn't be the last.

There is no use in screaming. There is no hope. I'm dead already.

The last time she screamed, she paid a heavy price; no water for an entire day, no painkillers, and no food for three days. Her prayers begin with; *please let me die before he touches me.*

CHAPTER 23

JoDi

The First Session

Once again, I find myself alone in the house. Yusuff, my husband, didn't come home last night. He didn't even text or call me to let me know if he was okay. This isn't just about the possibility of an affair. No, this is much more. He's a police officer. His job is dangerous. He could be badly hurt … he could be dead. Yes, I know my thoughts are extreme, but according to some of the other wives, they go through this type of anxiety as well. I can't imagine how hard it must be for police wives with children. It must be a complete nightmare.

How would the children cope if their father was killed, tortured, or left for dead somewhere in the woods? There would be no closure if that happened. No, I would not have any children, not anytime soon, at least. We had gone back and forth many times. Let's have a baby now! A week later … let's wait. On and on that went. It was okay, though. It didn't seem like either of us was truly bothered by it. The only time I felt a strong pull was during Christmas. It was a lonely time. A quiet, boring, and lonely time. On Christmas Eve, other families were making cookies and hot chocolate with their children. Singing Christmas carols and watching Christmas movies. In the weeks leading to Christmas, parents are hauling their little ones to Christmas markets to take photos with Santa and to the town square to take family photos.

But it's mostly Christmas Eve, and Christmas morning that rips at my heart. The absence of tiny feet running through the hallway in the middle of the night, thinking they hear Santa. Them running to every window. Sneaking downstairs to see if the cookies, bacon, and brandy are still on Santa's plate. I would often envision myself coming out of my room in the middle of the night, trying to shuffle the children back into their rooms, giving them another kiss goodnight, telling them that if they don't sleep, Santa won't come.

Soon those thoughts and feelings will come because it's now December first, when Christmas is etched in every home, every business, and now adays some vehicles. This quaint town of Marietta has its Christmas tree lighting scheduled today from four p.m. to eight p.m. The town doesn't hesitate when it comes to Christmas. Businesses start putting up lights the weekend after Halloween. Christmas is no joke around here. By the third week after Halloween, every building at the town square is outlined with large bright lights.

Glover Park downtown has steadily been transforming into the north pole. Imagine a one-and-a-half-acre park with two gazebos, many walkways, benches, and a giant fountain right in the middle of town. It's shaped like a square, of course. It's surrounded by a metal fence and has four large open gaps at each corner. The entire square is outlined by a walkway and parking spaces. Businesses line the streets surrounding the square. Streets that feed out like vines are also sprawling with local businesses. Every year volunteers decorate the town square for special events and holidays. Several Christmas trees are brought in by various schools and decorated with their own unique theme. It is a fairly large park, after all. So large that there are free concerts throughout the year.

There is a large, and I mean large, gazebo that fits an entire band, even an orchestra. It really is more like an outdoor arena, except this one is incredibly charming with its pillars and eighteenth-century details. The enormous fountain runs all year long.

On the other side of the park is the smaller gazebo, where Santa and his helpers gather. Children line up early to get their chance to sit with Santa and tell them why they are nice and what they truly want for Christmas.

The restaurants, bars, theaters, antique shops, boutique clothing shops, dessert shops, coffee shops, the list goes on and on; all partake in the holiday spirit. Think Lifetime and Hallmark Christmas movies. Don't just think it, believe it, because Christmas and other movies are actually filmed at the square.

You get the point. Christmas threw up all over the town and in my own home, and I am loving every minute of it. I have my Christmas books piled up and ready to go; some are in the living room, and some are at my bedside. There are classics like Mary Higgins Clark's Christmas murder mysteries. I also have some Christmas horror books like *You Better Watch Out* by Matt Forgit, *NOS4A2* by Joe Hill, and *Krampus* by Brom piled up and ready to read.

My brother-in-law, Justin helped me put up the outdoor Christmas lights. Almost every inch of my yard is filled with inflatable Christmas decorations. All my trees are covered in golden lights. Like every year, I decorate the Christmas wreath with a new theme. This year the theme is The Grinch. So, everyone that comes to my front door will trigger the sensor, and green lights will begin to flicker all over the wreath, followed by a recording from The Grinch saying, "What is that stench? It's fantastic."

As I'm rolling around in bed, my thoughts bounce back and forth from Christmas to my last session with Madame Fontenot, this vibrant woman that simply appeared in my life, promising help and guidance. How odd this whole ordeal is. Not odd enough to refuse her help, though. I have been seeking answers for so very long. When this woman said to me, "I think you are carrying an unwanted visitor. You may have a man with you. Or you are also a man. It is unclear. But I can help you figure it out. Here is my card." It was like the world. The card she had handed me was a black card with white numbers.

It has been three weeks since our first session. I remember it like it was yesterday:

The room was dark. To be expected from a person who was supposed to be a psychic/medium/witch of some kind. To state the obvious, I had no clue and, of course, had doubts, but at this point in my life, I was desperate. I knew that some of my actions were driven by a strong force. I just always assumed it was of my own doing. It was after all, my mind, my thoughts, my actions. What I am truly confused about is how I can be so kind yet commit murder like it was washing a set of dishes, taking out the trash, or shopping for new clothes. Now, hurt an animal or a child … never. Those are actually my weaknesses. An adult human, yeah, no big deal, as long as it was for the right reason. So far, that's exactly what it has been. It had *all* been for the right reasons.

There I was, face to face with a woman named Madame Fontenot. Unlike what you see on TV, there wasn't a crystal ball or purple drapes scattered randomly. No satanic symbols were lingering in dark corners. They were in a sitting room. It was dark, but it was probably to keep outside stimulation to a minimum. It was warm, cozy, and a little creepy, but in a good way. It smelled of honey and sage. Madame Fontenot had her hair loose and a little disheveled. She had layers of clothing on. Tights, a long dress over that, a long thin sweater over that, a scarf, and lots of rings.

Her dress was not super low cut, but it did reveal a chest full of tattoos. Quite beautiful ones. Her long sleeves were scrunched up, revealing more gorgeous and colorful tattoos. Her shoes looked like they were made entirely of some form of cotton or perhaps bamboo. Bamboo seems to be the most humane and sustainable material these days, so I've been told. Her clothing was very colorful, with unmatching patterns. How she made it work, I will never know. It was quite impressive.

After we got through all the small talk, Madame Fontenot eased into the *good stuff.*

"So, JoDi, now that I have told you some personal things about me," which she had, "why don't we dive into this voice, this suggestion box you've got woven into your mind."

"That sounds fair." My leg bounced—clearly I was nervous.

How much should I actually reveal? What if I slip? She hasn't mentioned any kind of hypnotism or any kind of exorcism, so I guess it's up to me to reveal the truths and the half-truths.

"Ask away," I said with confidence.

"Wonderful. I will start with a series of questions. Please don't feel like I'm interrogating you. First of all, you are not in any kind of trouble. This is a safe space, and no matter what you tell me, you will not be in any kind of legal trouble or danger. I give you my word as a woman, as someone who has been taken advantage of, and as someone who truly wants nothing more than to help others that are unable to help themselves.

"We are limited spiritually, that is. The things that the government doesn't understand get thrown into legal action. That's not what this is. This is me telling you that we are in another world. A world where your fate will not be determined by a set of laws created by men who have no clue on the matters of spiritual anomalies."

With those simple words, I had found myself in an extreme state of relaxation.

"You still with me, JoDi?"

"Yes. Yes, I am. I've just never found myself in front of someone who speaks like you. Who really understands what it is that I'm seeking. For once, I feel like I won't get myself into any trouble."

"I will never force anything. And I don't ever guess when it comes to serious matters like this. I will only share things that I know to be true. And if I am not certain, I will tell you so." She closed her eyes momentarily while inhaling and exhaling long, deep, and deliberately slow breaths. With a subtle smile, she reached for one of my hands. "You may answer any question with short or long answers. It's entirely up to you. Are you ready?"

"Yes."

"At this moment JoDi, are you alone in your thoughts?"

"Yes. I am alone in my thoughts."

"Do you hear a distinct voice trying to convince you to do things?"

"No. I mean, well, it's not another voice, really. It's just me. It's me telling me not to do things. And also, me telling me to do those things. Like, I have a conversation with myself. Does that make sense?"

"I do understand. Yes. But are you the boss? Or is there a part of you that is a boss and another part, the slave?"

"I am the boss."

Madame Fontenot's face changed. It isn't the face of shock. No, it was more of a slight, subtle change, but obvious enough for me to notice.

"Okay, good. So, you are the boss. You run the show. That's good, JoDi." She paused. "This next question may startle you but remember that you are safe here. When you hurt people, we all hurt people JoDi … when you hurt people, is it to feed some form of hunger inside of you? Or is it because you feel like it's the right thing to do?"

"I don't know. I suppose it's a little of both." My answers were not entirely true, and some of the things I wanted to say, I simply didn't. Because if I do, she will surely call the police on me.

"JoDi, I can't help you unless you are completely honest with me. Is there a man that urges you to do things you don't want to do? A man inside of you?"

"No. I don't really know why you are asking me these questions. There is no man inside of me."

"Understood. There is no man inside of you. Thank you for being patient, JoDi. And please stay with me. We will get to the bottom of this. Again, I'm not here to cause you harm. I'm here to help you. I hate to ask this because I will sound like Dexter from that TV show, but do you have a dark passenger, JoDi? Before you answer that, I just want you to know why I know this. I know this because I have heard him."

I could feel heat rising to my face.

"It's okay. I'm on your side."

"Prove it," I responded, maybe a bit too harshly.

"Okay, I will. It has become clear to me that this man likes riddles. He likes to rhyme. He also likes to sing. So far, he's only threatened me once during this session, but I am not afraid of him. I am not afraid of you, I should say."

"I don't know what you mean. I should probably go." My chest was tensing up.

"Please don't. But if you do, please know that you can come back."

I stood and briskly walked to the door. Before I left, I asked, "Am I possessed?" I swallowed hard. "Like, by a demon or something?"

"No JoDi, you are not possessed."

We simply stared at each other for a little while.

"Do you want to know what I think is happening to you? If so, please come sit. We can take this to the next level."

My eyes filled with tears. I was so embarrassed. So nervous. I didn't know what to say, or what to do, so I stormed out without a response.

CHAPTER 24

Madame Fontenot

The First Session

The first session is so very important. Madame Fontenot must tread lightly. She doesn't want to scare JoDi away. So far, she seems relaxed. Madame Fontenot is desperately hoping she will hear the man's voice. She needs him to come alive if this is to work. Desperate to help this woman, she is left with knots in her stomach. The whole thing was some sort of obsession. She has been losing sleep over it, so this *has* to be done, and it *has* to be done soon. They have finally reached a place in their session where she can begin with the difficult questions.

"You may answer any question with short or long answers. It's entirely up to you. Are you ready?"

"Yes."

"Are you alone in your thoughts?"

"Yes. I am alone in my thoughts."

"Do you hear a distinct voice trying to convince you to do things?"

"No. I mean, well, it's not another voice, really. It's just me. It's me telling me not to do things. And also, me telling me to do those things. Like, I have a conversation with myself. Does that make sense?"

"I do understand. Yes. But are you the boss? Or is there a part of you that is a boss and another part, the slave?"

Madame Fontenot hears a laugh. A deep laugh riddled with sarcasm.

"I am the boss," JoDi says.

Madame Fontenot hears the deep voice again.

Must I really explain that I am the boss? What kind of questions are these? You are a fraud and completely insane. This one must die. It's not like I am someone else. I am I.

Madame Fontenot is confused because occasionally JoDi's voice speaks through as well. As if they are taking turns. At one point, the voices came through simultaneously, much like a backup singer. She has never experienced this in her entire profession.

Just because I don't agree with all the ideas that run through my brain doesn't mean this isn't me. I am not two. I am one. This is a foolish game being played by a crook. This woman is just trying to scam me.

She brushes the dark voice off for the time being. "Okay, good. So, you are the boss. You run the show. That's good JoDi."

The deep voice continues.

Madame Fontenot, you are all for show, fake and fraud, we all know. Devious like a crow, Miss Fontenot. Shall your murder be slow? Perhaps I'll be kind and leave you buried in snow with a great big bow.

Madame Fontenot interrupts the man's voice. "This next question may startle you but remember that you are safe here. When you hurt people, we all hurt people JoDi … but when *you* hurt people, is it to feed some form of hunger inside of you? Or is it because you feel like it's the right thing to do?"

"I don't know. I suppose it's a little of both."

She can tell that JoDi is nervous. However, despite her appearance, she knows this is a strong woman she is speaking to, so she presses on.

"JoDi, I can't help you unless you are completely honest with me. Is there a man that urges you to do things you don't want to do? A man inside of you?"

"No. I don't really know why you are asking me these questions. There is no man inside of me."

Let's see ... what song will I sing for you during your glorious death. Hum? Oh, I know ... "Witchy Ways" by Roger Bird.

The voice begins to sing. "No matter how charming you are, your witchy ways will never fade. Even with your gentle touch, I know you won't visit my grave.

Oh witchy May
Oh witchy May
How I love your witchy ways.
Oh witchy May
Oh witchy May
How I love your witchy ways."

"Understood. There is no man inside of you. Thank you for being patient, JoDi. And please stay with me. We will get to the bottom of this."

As Madame Fontenot continues to speak, the singing continues.

"Again, I'm not here to cause you harm. I'm here to help you. I hate to ask this because I will sound like Dexter, but do you have a dark passenger, JoDi? Before you answer that, I just want you to know why I know this. I know this because I have heard him."

It's obvious at this point that JoDi is quite bothered. Her face has a new red glow. Her hands are now fiddling with nothingness.

"It's okay. I'm on your side, JoDi."

"Prove it." JoDi blurts out.

Madame Fontenot is both stunned and excited about this new turn.

The singing oddly continues, and he is quite a good singer, in fact.

"Okay, it has become clear that this man likes riddles. He likes to rhyme. He also likes to sing. So far, he's only threatened me once, but I am not afraid of him. I am not afraid of you, I should say."

Madame Fontenot is trying to be careful. She does not want to push her away. But sadly, it is too late.

"I don't know what you mean. I should probably go." JoDi grabs her purse with a firm grip.

"Please don't go. But if you must, please know that you can come back."

JoDi stands and briskly walks to the door. Before she leaves, she asks. "Am I possessed? Like, by a demon or something?"

The singing has stopped at this point. He is now silent.

"No JoDi. You are not possessed."

They simply stare at each other for a short while.

Madame Fontenot gets a message.

I am the boss.

Surprisingly, it is not a man's voice. It is a soft voice, a female voice. It is JoDi's voice.

"Do you want to know what I think is happening to you? If so, please come sit. We can take this to the next level."

Madame Fontenot's heart breaks when she sees JoDi's eyes fill with tears.

As the door shuts behind JoDi, she quickly reaches for her notepad and writes down.

1. Likes to rhyme.
2. Likes to sing.
3. Not possessed.
4. No supernatural elements in this case.
5. No paranormal elements in this case.
6. Possibility: mental disability, but not likely.

7. One theory, but nothing is set in stone.
8. Some psychological issues.

CHAPTER 25

JoDi

Second Session

It's like I have no room for anything else these days. Thoughts of my sessions with Madame Fontenot seem to take precedence. The second session was very strange and oddly scary. I would find myself putting a lot of trust in Madame Fontenot from now on. This session was something special. I remember it like it was yesterday:

Madame Fontenot was once again in her wildly colorful clothes. This time she had her hair pinned up, as though she had just rolled out of bed. Hair was going this way and that way. She had a wide, thin, colorful headband that kept most of it off her face. Maybe she can pull off this look because it goes with her personality … who knows how she does it. Her office smelled like cedarwood and lavender this time. It was a great combination, very soothing. She had made me a fresh cup of cinnamon hibiscus tea with a touch of honey. It was one of the best herbal teas I had ever had. Who knew that combination would work so well? I was thinking that I could learn many things from this woman. My admiration began to grow as I found myself safe in her presence. Safe with my secrets. The parts of me that are dark. Parts of me that allow me to sleep. Safe with a woman I hardly even knew. It was almost like I was in some beautiful trance, one I was in no hurry to awaken from.

After small talk, we began.

"Okay, JoDi, let's begin."

"Yes, I'm eager to learn what exactly you meant by the *next level.*"

"I thought you would be." She took a sip of her tea. "Are you familiar with hypnotherapy, JoDi?"

"I know of it, but I don't know much about it."

"Has a psychiatrist or anyone else ever asked you to participate in it?"

"No, I don't think I ever stayed with one therapist long enough for them to ask me. I probably would have said no. I don't like *not* being in control. To be honest, I've always been afraid of doing it."

"There needs to be some form of bond."

"I see," I respond. "Do you feel like we share some form of bond? Do you think you know me? Understand me? Do you think I trust you?"

"This may sound absurd to you, but JoDi." Madame Fontenot hesitated. "I know you quite well. I do think we have some form of bond, even though this is only our second session. And I believe in all my heart that you do in fact trust me."

There was a small pause. A much-needed one. This was no race. This would be a marathon. The two of us sip on our tea, deep in thought. I didn't feel at all uncomfortable with the silence. Somehow, I believed it wasn't silence at all. I think we were, in fact, communicating. Communicating without words, that is. Yes, this sounds a bit outrageous, but that's how I felt.

"Okay," I said in the form of an agreement.

"Okay, what?" Madame Fontenot set her cup of tea down. "Okay, you would like me to perform hypnosis on you? Or, okay, I understand what I just communicated with you?"

"Okay, let's do it. Hypnotize me." My eyes were filling with tears again. The combination of love and fear consumed me. This woman, who I barely knew, wanted to help me with a fierce I had never felt before from any therapist, pastor, or loved one. There was a reason for that. I just knew it. I just didn't know why. This woman was, in fact, special. This woman sitting before me with her wild hair and vibrant colors was going to help me. There was no greater love than this.

This time, by agreeing to the "next level," I had decided that I would open myself up even more. This was probably a once-in-a-lifetime opportunity. When would I ever trust someone so much? If this is what I had to do to get the answers I had been seeking most of my life, then so be it.

Madame Fontenot said all the right things to get me to relax. I could feel my body become numb. Even my mind was finding a dark, warm resting place. In fact, things did get dark, very dark, and very heavy.

After some shadowy, milky, hazy time had passed … I opened my eyes. It was all very confusing. I could barely recollect anything at all. Did it even work? How much time had passed? The last thing I could remember was telling Madame Fontenot my name, how old I was, what city I lived in … after that, it was a blur.

"JoDi, how are you feeling?"

"I'm a little confused and very sleepy."

"Yes, this exercise can take a toll on the mind and body."

"Did it work? I don't really remember much." I looked at the window, and where I had once seen some sunlight peeking over the window was now darkness. "Is it dark outside?"

"Yes, but don't worry about that. I know you have many questions, and I will answer them, but for now, it's important that you get some rest." She had the most calming smile. "JoDi, you did amazing. I can't stress this enough. This is one of the best sessions I've ever had with a client. I'm so very impressed with you. Thank you for allowing me this opportunity to dive in deep. Thank you for trusting me. There is no bigger compliment in my world."

I was so exhausted, all I wanted to do was lay back down. "So, what now? Should I come back tomorrow?"

"You should come back when you are ready. When it feels right."

"You don't want to go over what we just went through?"

"I need time, and I think you need time as well. You look very tired."

"I am tired. *Very* tired. Yes, let's meet again soon."

We said our goodbyes calmly this time. Half asleep, I drove straight home, where I knew a bottle of red blend awaited me. That, and my king-size bed.

CHAPTER 26

Madame Fontenot

Second Session

It is now the second session with JoDi. She is both nervous and excited. Surprisingly, these first few minutes together seem to be going smoothly, considering how abruptly JoDi had left after the first session.

As usual, there is small talk, which always seems to calm the mood. Enough time has passed, though, so Madame Fontenot makes a move.

"Okay, JoDi, let's begin."

"Yes, I'm eager to learn what exactly you meant by the *next level.*"

"I thought you would be." She took a sip of her tea. "Are you familiar with hypnotherapy, JoDi?"

"I know of it, but I don't know much about it."

"Has a psychiatrist or anyone else ever asked you to participate in it?"

"No, I don't think I ever stayed with one therapist long enough for them to ask me. I probably would have said no. I don't like *not* being in control. To be honest, I've always been afraid of doing it."

"There needs to be some form of bond."

"I see," JoDi responds. "Do you feel like we share some form of bond? Do you think you know me? Understand me? Do you think I trust you?"

"This may sound absurd to you, but JoDi." Madame Fontenot hesitates. "I know you quite well."

JoDi had no idea how long Madame Fontenot had been following her. Studying her. Spying on her. Madame Fontenot knew her habits, her hobbies, and her personality.

"I *do* think we have some form of a bond, even though this is only our second session. And I believe in all my heart that you do in fact trust me." Madame Fontenot says this with as much sincerity as she can muster.

There was a silence as the two of us sip on our tea ... a silence met with a common friend. Then the male voice announces his presence.

This should be fun. Came the male voice. He seems much calmer this time. It was a gentle statement.

"Okay," JoDi says in a form of agreement.

"Okay, what?" The excitement is building, and it's extremely difficult for Madame Fontenot to keep her cool. "Okay, you would like me to perform hypnosis on you? Or, okay, I understand what I just communicated with you?"

"Okay, let's do it. Hypnotize me."

Madame Fontenot senses JoDi is already getting emotional. The gloss in her eyes and the sudden drop of her shoulders is a big giveaway.

Why is the male voice so quiet at this moment? Perhaps that part of JoDi is excited, too, somehow.

Madame Fontenot eases JoDi into some breathing exercises. She asks JoDi to relax her mind and body. JoDi seems to melt away. Madame Fontenot dives right into the session.

"Let's start from the beginning. Let's begin with your childhood memories. What is your first memory JoDi?"

"It's bright, so incredibly bright, and I can't breathe. Everything is loud. I'm incredibly cold. This fear is overwhelming."

Madame Fontenot let her continue without interruption.

"I feel a great pain in my chest. In my lungs. My lungs are stinging. My stomach aches as well. The blinding light feels like needles in my eyes. The coldness is making me ache in my bones. I want to complain, but I don't know how. It is so very cold. The cold on my skin feels like a million knife pricks."

Madame Fontenot cannot believe this, mainly because she had only read about this in books, nonfiction stories of people being able to remember their time of birth. This is exactly what JoDi was describing. It was her birth. She was describing the feeling, the pain, the confusion, and the misery of it all.

"Let's move to another memory. One as a child, a toddler perhaps."

JoDi licks her lips. "I'm in a dark place. The walls are gray, like a sidewalk. They are cold. The door is locked, and there are no lights on. I can smell dust and rotten fruit. I'm so very hungry. My left arm aches. My left eye is in so much pain. I have been here for a long time. I can smell old dry urine coming from my undergarments. I'm scared of this small space."

"Let's leave this place. Leave it now, JoDi. Tell me something else, something perhaps when you were a teenager."

"I've been working in the cotton fields all day, and my fingers are bloody. My mother is cleaning them with a warm towel. She is so pretty. After dinner, I still have to go to the stables and check on the horses. Father has a long trip tomorrow. He is taking the horse carriage to a faraway place to pick up supplies."

"Are you sure it's a horse carriage? Do you mean a vehicle?"

"I don't know what that is. Mom is washing my socks; I only have two pair. She is upset because they have a new hole in them that she will have to mend."

"What is your name, and what year is it?"

"My name is Sammantha Wright, and it's 1819. Father won't stop talking about the financial crisis in the new world. I guess no one can afford to purchase land. And the ones who do have land can't afford to pay for it."

"Let's move on." Before she can finish her sentence, JoDi begins with a new life. At this point, Madame Fontenot has no idea how often JoDi has been reincarnated. She will be patient, though. This was by far the most in-depth hypnosis she had ever experienced. Again, she had only read about this in books and heard it on podcasts. JoDi began to speak in a foreign language. Maybe Greek, maybe Aramaic. Madame Fontenot reaches for her recorder to make sure it is still recording. The only word that jumped out at her was "Palmyra." She had taken a few classes that covered ancient Egypt and ancient Rome in college. Palmyra sounded very familiar; it was some sort of ancient ruin from something like A.D. 250.

JoDi is violently crying now. Gushing tears fall from her cheekbones. Something has to be done.

"Let's move on, JoDi. Get out of there. You are safe. Just leave. Tell me something about your adult life."

"It's hotter than the Devil's armpit out here." Came the voice. The man's voice. The deep voice that she was so familiar with.

Madame Fontenot again checks her recorder. "What is your name?"

"My name is Mike Schlistu."

She doesn't interrupt him. It's no surprise to her that he begins to whistle. She doesn't recognize the melody. He begins to sing.

"You can't go wrong with Arthur Collins," the voice says. "He'll keep you on your toes."

Madame Fontenot quickly searches on her phone for the artist and finds a song called, "Bill Bailey, Won't You Please Come Home" (1902).

"I've got you." Madame Fontenot says under her breath.

"What's your favorite hobby, Mr. Schlistu?"

There is no answer.

JoDi is now quiet. Too quiet. Madame Fontenot begins to worry. She has to protect her.

"On the count of three, you will wake up. One … two … three."

JoDi opens her eyes.

"JoDi, how are you feeling?"

"I'm a little confused, and very sleepy."

"Yes, this exercise can take a toll on the mind and body."

"Did it work? I don't really remember much." JoDi looks at the window. "Is it dark outside?"

"Yes, but don't worry about that. I know you have many questions, and I will answer them, but for now, it's important that you get some rest."

It is so incredibly difficult to mask this new discovery she had just made. Sure, she has had many clients reveal some sort of past life. Not quite as many as JoDi had just revealed, but to discover that one of her past lives is still functioning in the same body in the present time is unheard of. It's common for some of the same traits to shine through, like a fear of flying, a fear of small spaces, a fear of men, a fear of women, a fear of dying, etc. But to have a past life be embedded so intimately is unheard of. She would have to do more research. JoDi isn't possessed. There is no demon or ghost. JoDi wants to kill. Perhaps she has already killed someone, maybe several. JoDi is, in fact, evil. JoDi is, in fact, a good person. JoDi's situation is something the reincarnation world claims to be impossible. JoDi—embodies—two—souls.

CHAPTER 27

Madame Fontenot

After utilizing several of her resources, Madame Fontenot found a translator. One of JoDi's past lives was in a language she didn't know, and it was imperative that she knew the exact words she used during her last session. It would all have to go down in her records. The language was Aramaic. Needless to say, it wasn't easy finding a translator. Utter shock and disbelief were the initial reactions from Leanne Larkin as she translated the recording. A brief silence fell in the air as Leanne revealed to Madame Fontenot who it was. The Great Queen Zenobia of Palmyra was the woman, one of the lives that JoDi had once lived. The queen of Aramean, descendant, and ancestor of Cleopatra. She took power as queen of the desert kingdom of Palmyra after her husband had passed away and was a warrior queen who conquered Egypt. At some point, she had been taken prisoner. It made sense now why JoDi had shown such intense signs of pain and suffering. This undoubtedly explained the uncontrollable tears she was shedding.

Even though this was quite fascinating, this was not the most invigorating discovery she had made during the session. It was Mike Schlistu, of course. A bad soul that is intertwined with a good one. She was astonished when she found a few newspaper articles about the serial killer known as the Poet Killer in 1945. How he got this name was quite interesting. Several bodies were found with handwritten poems. When he was caught, he announced that he had not only written poems for his victims he had also written short songs for each one of them. Apparently, Mike tried to negotiate with law enforcement. He would reveal the location of the missing victims if they agreed to let him sing his songs on the radio. During that time, about sixty percent of Americans owned radios.

Looking at his photo was creepy yet enlightening. He seemed to be a semi-handsome man, quite ordinary in fact. The article stated that he had a horrible upbringing and was eventually raised by his grandmother. He didn't have many friends, but he did have a lot of pets that he took very good care of. None of his victims were elderly, young children, or animals. When she had the time, she would have to do some more research on the Poet Killer. But for now, she would need to go home.

As she is driving home, she can't help but wonder how much more she could get out of JoDi. She plays different scenarios in her mind. The excitement builds up inside of her. She is more passionate about this client than all the rest put together.

The drive home has gone by so very quickly, and she is now pulling into her driveway. She clicks on the garage door opener and pulls in. Opening the door and smelling the scent of Mexican vegetable soup brought an instant smile to her face. Her wife Gloria is such a great cook, and on this cold winter's day, what could be better than hot, wholesome soup for dinner? It was quite the event marrying a woman. The shock waves that rippled through the country club in Gloria's polished city lent proof that the tumultuous era of the 21st century had managed to breach its city limits. Imagine a penniless woman with college debt born in anonymity could win the heart of a bride whose lineage traced back to Cesar Chavez himself. Gloria was born in a world she was unfamiliar with … wealth, status, and somewhat of a royal lineage.

"Hey love, I'm home." The sound of clanking and slamming cabinet doors was a fun sound to hear. Her wife loved and hated to cook in equal measure.

"Hi! I'm in the kitchen, babe."

She sets her things down and makes her way to the kitchen, noticing all the cleaning and organizing her wife has done today. They share the chores since they both work full time, but Gloria is a bit of a clean freak, so she makes a much larger effort.

She slows her pace and watches as her beautiful wife glides from one side of the kitchen to the other, making cooking seem easy and effortless. Gloria is a large woman with amazing curves. She had always been more attracted to larger women, not entirely sure why. She had also dated many men in her life, but Gloria is who she fell in love with. *She* is the love of her life. Madame Fontenot could not imagine a life without her.

"How was your day?" she asks.

Madame Fontenot doesn't reply. She slides up behind her and wraps her arms around her chest. "I love you, darling," she whispers in her ear.

"Ah, I gather you smelled the soup."

"At least I'm easy to please," she reminds her.

Gloria turns around and kisses Madame Fontenot, pressing her lips tight against hers. As she releases, she spins her around and spanks her bottom. "Go wash your nasty-ass day off your body and come back down to eat. It will be ready in about ten minutes."

"Why did I marry someone so bossy?"

"You mean someone with proper hygiene?" Gloria snorts.

"Yeah, yeah. I'll be back," she says in the tone and accent of Arnold Schwarzenegger.

Her shower is quick but thorough. She can't wait to tell Gloria about the recent discoveries she has made with JoDi. They had both been so busy lately that they hadn't found the time to talk much.

Now sitting on the couch with a hot bowl of soup, she reaches for the remote and pauses it.

"Okay, I have to give you an update on JoDi."

"Yes, I would love to hear it. You had another session with her recently, right?"

"Yes, I did, and you will never guess what I discovered." She took a spoonful of soup and blew on it gently. "She is also a he. He is she. She is he. JoDi is a man named Mike, and Mike is a woman named JoDi." She puts the food in her mouth.

"Wait, hold the mother fuck'n phone … what in the world are you saying?"

"Babe, you won't believe this because I'm honestly not sure this has ever happened before. Well, it probably has, but I've never heard of it before. Maybe it's been kept a secret all these years. Maybe since it goes against all the rules of reincarnation, the truth has been buried."

"Reincarnation? De que hablas? Dime," she says in Spanish.

"I'm sorry, I'm all over the place. Okay, somehow, someway, JoDi has two souls. Before you say anything, please hear me out. You know how some people carry with them their fears, habits, etc., from a previous life? Well, JoDi is not only carrying those things. It seems she is a combination of the two. In fact, what I'm trying to say is that it's not entirely JoDi's fault she is the way she is. If this Mike person is still living in her, a part of her, well, then yes, he and she are either killers or about to become a killer."

"This is insane. Something has to be done. She needs to be behind bars or in a mental facility."

"Unfortunately, you might be correct on this one. I think Mike may be a psychopath. JoDi will probably need lots of professional therapy for many years. If I don't help her, she will live a life of misery. Somehow Mike's soul needs to detach. Otherwise, I can no longer say Mike. I would have to simply say JoDi. And that would mean she would need to be in a lockdown psychiatric hospital."

"Hold on. How do you even know this? Sounds like you may have made a mistake."

Madame Fontenot explains the entire second session. She also explains all the research she did on Mike. The similarities are bewildering. Just like Mike did, JoDi cares for the elderly, cares about animals, and likes to sing. His voice and her voice came out simultaneously during the session. It didn't take too much convincing. As they sat there eating their soup and drinking their wine, a sense of adventure filled Madame Fontenot's heart. She was so heavily invested in this, both emotionally and physically. This is by far one of the most interesting conversations they have ever had.

"I know I haven't shown much interest in reincarnation before, but maybe it's time you explain it to me."

"Look, honey, I know you grew up a Christian, and it's hard to wrap your head around the idea, but maybe you need to be a little more open-minded."

"It just seems ridiculous. Our soul is reincarnated after we die? It goes to another body? That just seems silly, I'm sorry."

"Oh, and Moses dividing water in some sea or river just with the movement of a hand? Jesus rose from the dead and came back again a few days later. Noah's ark? I'm not saying these things to make fun of Christianity. You know that. All I'm saying is to be open-minded. I mean, what if reincarnation is, in fact, a part of Christianity, and we just don't know it. There has been evidence of lost scrolls. Who's to say that your God, the God, a God, has a place called Heaven and also chooses some souls to be reincarnated? Maybe all that was supposed to be in the Bible, but it got lost, just like other things got lost. I know you've heard about the scrolls that were found recently. What if there are more? Anyway, I hope I'm not offending you. I just want you to be open to the idea that it's possible. There has been so much proof of past lives that I find it hard to believe you won't even consider the possibility. Did you ever read any of the books I asked you to read?"

"I didn't, I'm sorry. What were they again?"

Madame Fontenot begins to count them off using her fingers. "*Journey of Souls*, and *Destiny of Souls* by Michael Newton, Ph.D. *Life Before Life* by Jim B. Tucker M.D., *Children Who Remember Previous Lives* by Ian Stevenson M.D., and *Many Lives Many Masters* by Brian Weiss. *The Convoluted Universe* and *Between Death and Life* by Delores Cannon. *Astral Projection and Lucid Dreaming* by Mystic Mae. *The Spirits Book* by Allan Kardec. *Signs of Reincarnation* by James G. Matlock. *There Is A River* by Edgar Cayce." She looks up and sees her wife smirking. "Yeah, okay, I'll just put them in a pile for you."

"Yes, thank you."

They continue to eat in silence. After a few minutes, Madame Fontenot can tell her wife is uneasy. "What's going on?"

"Well, I was just thinking, instead of making me read all those books, why don't you school me on reincarnation first."

Madame Fontenot's eyes light up.

"Calm down, calm down!" Gloria says with a mouth full of hot food. "Don't get all freaked out, little lady. I just want the basics. I'll stop you if you start to annoy me."

"Eeekkk! Okay, sorry if I seem so happy. I've only been trying to talk to you about this for, oh, I don't know, years!"

"I suggest you start before I change my mind."

"Got it, I'll take it down to the bones. Let's see, where do I start?" She sets down her spoon and wipes her mouth. "So, reincarnation is a philosophical and religious concept that suggests the existence of a soul or consciousness that is reborn into a new body after death. It's the belief that upon the death of the physical body, the soul or essence of an individual is reborn into another body, typically in a different time, place, or form. Okay, you probably already knew that. Let's see. I'll try to be more specific." She takes a large swig of her wine. "The cycle of birth, death, and rebirth continues indefinitely until the soul reaches a state of spiritual enlightenment or liberation. Different cultures and religions have varying interpretations of reincarnation and may refer to it by different names, such as transmigration or rebirth. The soul is the important key here."

"Is there a way you can make that even more simple? Like, give me an example. Help me understand a soul better."

"Oh, I know." Her eyes light up again. "I actually like telling this story, although I probably butcher it every time. I read it in a book a long time ago called *Soul Stories*. Let's see, how did it go." She rubs her hands together. "Okay, imagine a large fleet of ships. There is one that sets the course for all of them. No matter how many are in the fleet, that one ship is the heart. But just because it sets the course for the fleet, it doesn't mean it is in control or determines what occurs on the other ships. On some ships, the journey is pleasant, while others are not. Imagine that the heart ship is the mother ship. It is the largest ship that you could possibly imagine. Now imagine that the rest of the ships are really just tiny boats with only room for one person. The small boats don't have all the information that the mother ship has. In fact, the small boats are simply temporarily part of the mother boat's fleet. The mother ship was sailing long before the people on the small boats were even born. However, the mother boat is aware of every difficulty the small boat has encountered. It knows when the sea has put them through rough waters and when their journey has been pleasant.

"Now, the mother ship may be enormous and all-knowing, and the small boats aren't, but the small boats can communicate with it. Even perhaps gain capabilities from it. If the person in a small boat stays in touch with the mother boat, they have a better chance of gaining perspective and help through storms. There are reasons for every storm, but you just don't know why. But they must learn from every storm and try to better themselves. The small boat has to make its own decision. The mother boat will not override it.

"It makes no sense for the small boats to veer off into bad weather when you have a mother boat that you can follow closely, a boat that can assist them. A mother boat will not pull them out of their troubles but will help them see things they could not see on their own. The mother ship has its own destination. It always sails toward cooperation, sharing, and harmony. When the small boat makes the same decision, the trip is much better. If a boat sails in the wrong direction, it does not have the mother ship to help them.

"The small boats are temporary, while the mother ship is not. When the person on the small boat ends, it becomes part of the mother boat. That was where that person came from to begin with, on and on. While on the small boat, they are to learn how to travel in the same direction as the mother ship. All the while, the mother boat uses its intuition to communicate with them."

"That's a cute story, my love, and I was able to follow it. So, what about religion? Do you have to be part of a religion to believe in reincarnation?"

"Not necessarily. At least, I don't think so. I will say, though, that the concept of reincarnation is found in various religious and spiritual traditions, including Hinduism, Buddhism, Jainism, Sikhism, and some New Age philosophies. The details and interpretations differ among these traditions, but the central idea remains that the soul continues to evolve and learn through multiple lifetimes."

"Hold on, it learns and evolves?"

"Yes, it does. Fascinating right?"

"Yeah, that's pretty cool."

Madame Fontenot can tell Gloria is intrigued and trying really hard not to show it.

"Anyhow, it is often associated with the concept of karma, which suggests that the actions and choices made in one life will influence the circumstances and experiences in future lives. So, with this view, or logic, the quality of one's present life is influenced by the moral and ethical choices made in past lives."

"Get out!" Gloria lets her spoon drop into her bowl. "Are you trying to tell me that when I fuck up in this life, I will pay for it in the next?"

"Kind of."

"That's freaky." She takes a moment to think. "Okay, what else? Like, give me an example of why you think it's real. Or something that happened to someone."

"Well, I've already told you about JoDi's past lives. What about that one child I told you about? While under hypnosis, she recalled a past life. She lived in ancient Africa and talked about ancient art and structures. She told her hypnotist about an ancient burial ground that historians went looking for and found exactly what she described."

"Yeah, that sounds nuts. It's hard to believe that actually happened."

"Well, when you have a doctor documenting the therapy session, a well-known historian documenting the findings, a team of archeologists working day and night to dig them up safely, it's kind of hard not to believe. Not to mention the hypnotherapy session was all on tape."

"Eeeekkk ... okay, you win. *I'm a believer.*" She began to sing.

"Maybe you should read one of the books I recommended. You will be singing that song more often."

"I will."

Madame Fontenot raises her eyebrows at her.

"What? I will! I promise. I'll start tonight."

"I'll believe it when I see it."

"Fair enough." They continue to eat in silence. Both in deep thought.

"So, what are you going to do about JoDi?" Gloria asks.

"I'm going to help her. I'm serious. I truly think if she can just take control of her thoughts and habits, she will be able to control this dark side of her. After all, it's not like she is possessed. This is all her. She has complete control."

"I don't know, babe, this seems dangerous. I know, I know, you know all about danger, but this is different. Please be careful. Please put me and yourself above this new project of yours. It sounds like JoDi could be a very evil person. I don't care how much time she spends helping the needy and volunteering. She may be a psychopath without an ounce of empathy in her. It could all be for show."

"I'm telling you, she is a good person, and I'm going to help her." She takes a sip of wine. "I am the only person that will help her, and you know it. This is exactly why I do what I do. It's my life's mission, and I'm damn good at it. You just wait and see, my love, just wait and see. Even if it's the last thing I do on this planet, I will help this woman."

"It sounds like you are obsessed." Gloria frowned and left the room.

CHAPTER 28

The Captive

"Maybe I should dislocate my fucking thumbs."

So much time has passed. So much time that reading is the only thing keeping her sane. Yes, her captor brings her books. Sometimes her captor just quickly throws them in and slams the door. Oddly enough, her captor has given her books that she enjoys reading. Most of them are psychological thrillers. Last week she tossed in *The Housemaid* by Freida McFadden and *The Good Samaritan* by John Marrs. Which, if you think about it, is kind of fucked up.

Is he trying to make me lose my mind? He must be trying to mess with my head. Jokes on you, asshole. I love to read thrillers.

She still doesn't know what her captor looks or sounds like. A part of her wants to because maybe that's when it will all end. She has suffered long enough.

One thing about having a lot of time to think is the ability to problem-solve. Even though she is thin, weak, and struggling with brain fog, she can still come up with rational ideas on how to survive.

How many days can one live without food? I can hide my food under the mattress. I can pour my juice in different places, so it's not obvious. If he can't drug me, then the next time he comes in, I'll pretend I'm passed out. I can escape. I will escape. All I need to do now is wait for the right time to dislocate my thumbs so I can squeeze out of these handcuffs.

CHAPTER 29

Yusuff

It had been a while since Yusuff and Dr. Trudi had spoken. They had met for lunch at Slutty Vegan, where she gave him a lesson on hypnotherapy. A call from work pulled him away before she could tell him how the hypnotherapy session with Nicky Lee went. This particular attack was important to him. After all, the attack had happened in his town of Marietta. He was used to this kind of violence occurring in Atlanta, but certainly not in his town. Especially in the town square … it was almost unheard of.

He was getting calls from the mayor and his close friend Johnny Walker, a prominent figure in the community.

Dr. Trudi mentioned that she would be in the Marietta area, so why not meet at the crime scene?

Yusuff thinks he's walking at a normal pace, but he is in fact walking quite slowly. His eyes dart from one building to the next, looking for street cameras, homeless people, anything that might stand out. He turns the corner onto Anderson Street SE and is pleased to find Dr. Trudi already there. Her back is to him, but he recognizes the shape of her body and hair color. Even though this is a casual meeting of sorts, he's surprised to see her once again in a pantsuit.

"Hello again, Dr. Trudi." Yusuff reaches out his hand, and with a good grip, she shakes it. In her other hand is what looks like a medium-sized notepad. "Hello, Yusuff. I'm glad we could finally meet up again."

"Yes, likewise." His eyes are pulled vigorously toward the notepad. He cannot help it.

"Yes, this is probably what you think it is." With a certain form of tenacity, she opens it, folds it over, and flips through the pages until her lips convert into a predominant kind of grin. "I have the notes from the hypnotherapy session with Nicky Lee."

"Great, I've been pretty curious, to be honest. I'm still trying to wrap my head around that whole process. Your explanation of hypnotherapy was pretty thorough. It was incredibly helpful, Dr. Trudi. I can't thank you enough. I just wish I wasn't pulled away so abruptly the last time we met."

"Well, I hope you won't be too disappointed when I tell you I didn't really get much. She quickly turned in a bad way, so I had to pull her out of it. The only thing I really got from her were a few clothing details. Absolutely nothing about the attacker's face."

"Did you at least find out if it was a man or a woman?"

"Yes, and to my surprise, I believe it was a woman."

"What?"

"Well, I suppose it could have been a man, you know, in disguise, or a cross-dresser, but she did mention a dress with a pumpkin on it."

Memories began to flood his mind like an unexpected sandstorm. He remembers quite vividly what his wife was wearing that night. He could sense the perspiration gathering around his temples. As a police officer, training to remember as much as possible carried on into his personal life. Even the smallest of details is almost haunting. He remembers her dress so well he could paint it.

"Interesting," he says simply, trying not to show how nervous he has just become. "What else did she say?"

Dr. Trudi runs her finger across her notepad. "She blurted out something about a striped orange and white scarf. Oh, and that the dress was white and fluffy. Sounds like a child's dress, to be honest."

The pounding of his heart is so very distracting. "Yes, that is strange. Do you think she could be mixing up another memory? Like, do you think maybe she had met someone earlier that evening in that outfit? Maybe she just bundled the two images together?"

"It's certainly possible, but ..." She paused in thought.

"But what?"

"Well, I remember her naming off these details while she was quite distressed, right as she visualized the attack. Makes me think that the attacker was wearing these items."

Yusuff's memory of walking into JoDi's closet and pulling her striped orange and white scarf repeated in his mind. Her gentle smile as he reached out to hand it to her. How amazing and caring she had always been toward the sick, the poor, the needy. So much was flashing through his mind he began to feel sick.

"Officer McCray, are you okay?"

"Yes, yes, I'm okay. Please excuse me for just a bit. I'll be right back." He briskly walks around the corner and out of view. His breathing is fast, and his head is pounding. What was he going to do? What was happening? Why would she do this so close to home? This had to be a nightmare. It just had to be.

"... But the human tongue is a beast that few can master. It strains constantly to break out of its cage, and if it is not tamed, it will turn wild and cause you grief."

-Robert Greene

CHAPTER 30

JoDi

Nicky Lee is on my mind today like a song you could not stop humming, which is wonderful because earlier, I couldn't get Jeremi Campbell or Ashley Aballi off my mind.

"You won't go to jail Mr. Jeremi Campbell, more like Hell. No one will hear you yell, and there will be no farewell. Will your body swell? Perhaps in a well."

These words kept repeating in my mind. I don't even want to disclose what he had done in the group. He was a bully, and he needed to die. How could those hands type those words? His hands had to pay for what they had done. Before I rolled his lifeless body off a cliff in the mountains of North Carolina, I had chopped off both of his hands. One of them I nailed to a tree for the critters to play with. On the other hand, I had chopped off each of his fingers. I drove kabab sticks through them. I buried the sticks keeping the fingers above ground so that the ants could feast. He did not deserve a glorious death. Ashley Aballi experienced a very similar death, except I was all out of kabab sticks, so I had simply nailed her fingers to the bottom of a tree. She had the most beautiful hands. I kept one of her fingers. The mason jar would protect it well enough.

So, anyhow, I am grateful that Nicky is now on my mind. I can't believe I hit her with a brick. Will she forgive me? What was I thinking? How could I do this to someone I love? Where did this madness come from? Yes, she took it too far … but we are past that. I love her. I need her. I have to see her. I have to touch her warm skin. Fantasizing about a long embrace shot gentle pulses through my torso.

Nicky, what would your skin feel like against mine? Would there be some form of electric exchange? Once I had you, would I be able to let go? I promise I will be gentle. I really just want to be near you.

I am driving around the parking garage of The Woodruff Arts Center, searching for a parking spot. I followed her to this location. It's a visual and performing arts center with a popular museum. I lost her in the parking garage because she found a spot soon. Now I find myself eager to find one.

My guess is that she is at the High Museum of Art. Yes, she is most certainly that kind of woman, full of class and creativity. Does she crave to expand her mind and cherish the beauty that others create? I hope so because I am the same way. Again, she and I are so very similar. I need to know more.

I find a parking spot and quickly gather my things.

I am in awe of this museum, of its cylinder shape and curved walkways that outline the inner walls. The spiral walkways deliver you from one floor to the next, giving you a fluid experience … one entrancing exhibit to the next.

I have now found myself in a bit of a trance as I stare deeply into an 1874 painting by Johann Culverhouse. The artist was born in Holland but immigrated to America in the mid-1800s. Nighttime scenes with more than one light source were his hallmarks. Moonlit Market is the name of the painting. The way he manipulated the light from a full moon and candles is remarkable. How does one paint the moon? How does one paint candles? The glow, the shadows, the extension of light out into the distance, the presence of depth and detail pulled up close ... it is mesmerizing. One could step right into this painting.

There are very few voices around me, but all special in their own way. Some young, some old, some bold, some faint like a sound passing through fog. I pull away from the painting, grinning as it continues to hypnotize me. Its reach had coils unraveling around each vertebra as I walked away. I can visualize them releasing through the veins and muscles and out of my skin. I blink. I blink again. Art has a way of altering my inner power and self-control.

I hear it. The sound I had been waiting for. The voice ... much more powerful than the painting. Nicky Lee.

Each step I take is feather-like; slow, light, and smooth. There is no need to rush. Around the corner, I see her. She is standing quite erect, wearing dark jeans, a red and white striped shirt, with a navy-blue sports coat. Her hair shiny, with large golden waves. I let out a feline purr I didn't know I was holding.

Nicky, what are you staring at? What is your beautiful mind thinking this very second? Do you simply appreciate art? Or are you the type to outline every curve, trace the smile, and follow the paths of light? Do you, like myself, attempt to read the minds of every artist, try to feel their pain, their passion, their love, and sorrow? Do those parasite-like emotions gather in your chest? Can you demolish those parasite emotions as I can? Or do they fester within you and eat at your soul?

I move on to the next painting, clearing my thoughts as I do.

"I see you." Was a whisper so quiet, so gentle, that I wasn't sure if it came from Nicky or if it came from the people behind her. Maybe it came from my own mind.

Those hands. Those delicate wrists dazzled with dainty golden bracelets. What would it feel like to wrap my hands around her wrists? Are they cold and clammy? Or are they warm, pounding with blood?

Nicky turns back to the previous painting. Our eyes meet! My heart is pumping extra blood. My feet will not move. I am frozen. It was a brief moment, but it happened. The combination of love and dread fills me. Now Nicky has seen me. Truly *seen* me. Once would be okay. But not twice. Not three times. I could never let her *see* me again, or else she would know.

CHAPTER 31

JoDi

Journal/Ledger

I've had some anxiety today, so it's time for a story. It's time for me to cleanse my soul. This story is too awful for me to tell my therapist. I'm so thankful to have this journal. Sometimes it works better than medicine. Well, here it is.

I was seven. I know I was seven because it was shortly after my birthday, and Mom and Dad had bought me a bike without training wheels. My sister had told me that when I got my own grown-up bike, she would let me go visit her clubhouse. Maybe even join her club. She and her friends used to go out into the woods and play for hours. She never let me join them, no matter how much I begged. She would never let me visit, and that was that.

I was ready and excited to see what kind of clubhouse she and her friends had built. She used to talk about all the furniture and kitchen stuff she put in it. They would play house, and they even had a firepit where they would make s'mores.

Of course, there would be a test, but it wouldn't be until I was out in the woods. I followed her until nothing but pine trees surrounded us. I knew this would be tough. The clubhouse was even better than I had imagined. Her friends weren't there, though. It was just me and her. I was okay with that. I always wanted to gain her love. I begged for it. It rarely came, but maybe this time it would.

The first test wasn't so hard. She said to be a true woman of the woods that, I had to be ONE with nature. She made me take off all of my clothes except for my shoes. Not sure why she let me keep my shoes on, but I was grateful. That wasn't so bad.

During the next test, she blindfolded me. I wrapped my arms around myself. I guess it was just an instinct to do so. It's not like anyone was around. I don't know who I was hiding from. I did what I was told. She pulled me by the arm and leaned my naked body against a tree. She said in order for me to be ONE with nature that, I had to endure what nature endured. If I was to yell or cry, I failed. If I ran, I failed. If I begged her to stop, I failed. If I uttered a word, I failed. I could hear her walking around. I could hear the birds, the leaves under her feet crunching. It was soon quiet, and I wasn't sure where she was. She finally asked me if I was ready. I wasn't, but I said I was anyway. I wanted so badly to be part of her club. I wanted so badly for her to love me.

I felt a sharp pain in my shoulder as something cold and hard hit me. I couldn't complain. Another one, and then another one. It became clear to me that it was rocks that she was throwing at me. She kept saying don't cry. Don't block them. One hit my cheek, and it stung so bad that fluid instantly filled my eyes. It was a natural reaction. I was so scared she might hit me in the eye. I didn't want to lose an eye. She was getting closer and closer, and the rocks were getting bigger, and they were hitting harder. Don't cry, you little shit, she yelled at me. I didn't cry. I was in so much pain, but I stayed strong. My body was convulsing with fear, yet I stood there.

When she was done, I was relieved I didn't pee on myself again. She whispered in my ear that there was one last test. And if I told on her, I would never be able to join the club or do anything with her and her friends again. I whispered back, I promise I won't.

My body was throbbing all over from the blows I had endured. She scooted me over just a bit and lifted my left hand. She pushed my left hand against the tree. I could feel the roughness against my skin. She said to hold it still. I did as I was told. I could hear her walking somewhere, and when she came back, she told me not to make a sound. I could hear something evil in her tone, but I had gotten this far, so there was no turning back.

I felt something sharp pressed against the palm of my hand. I thought maybe she was going to write something on my hand. But she didn't. I suddenly felt the most pain I had ever felt in my life as she hammered a nail through my hand. I yelled. I cried. I pulled the blindfold off my face. I screamed as loud as I could. I was in so much pain. I had seen her help Dad build a staircase outside, but I had no idea how strong she was. She was good with a hammer and nails. As she walked to her bike, she said that I had passed, but if I told Mom and Dad, it was all over. She left me there for hours. It was pitch dark for several hours before she came for me. I had stood there, alone in the dark, naked and in pain. I prayed and begged the animals not to eat me. They didn't. They protected me. They accepted me as one of their own.

CHAPTER 32

JoDi

Every year in December, Marietta, Georgia, has a fun Christmas event called Merry Market, which takes place at the town square. Booths start to pop up as early as nine in the morning. It's everything from handmade Christmas ornaments to adult hot chocolate with enough booze in them to warm up frosty fingers and red noses. This year they have hired musicians. Around lunchtime they were blessed with five young adults who played various classical instruments: cello, violin, clarinet, timpani, and piano. Not only could they play instruments, but they could also sing. When they were done with their performance and the sun set, a man and his guitar took over, adding humor and laughter into his act.

Now that night has set in, and every inch of the place is glowing with Christmas lights, the late-night band is changing the mood. Blasting their dance music has people moving their hips and releasing their inner child. Not only is the adult hot chocolate a hit but so is the glühwein. I often find myself pulling out my phone to do research, and little did I know that glühwein is quite old. It has been around since 1420.

Yusuff, Justin, Katy Moore, and I are in line at the adult hot chocolate booth. Katy Moore, whom I am not entirely fond of, is someone Justin is currently dating. She was as boring as watching paint dry.

"Where did you all meet again?" I ask Katy, showing way too many teeth as I smile awkwardly. I know very well where and when they met, but I want Katy to think otherwise; like maybe I haven't been paying attention. Maybe Justin didn't take the time to tell me. Maybe I want Katy to think this doesn't bother the shit out of me or that deep down inside, I don't want to wrap Katy's long smooth ponytail around her neck until her face turns blue.

"We met at Mac's Raw Bar at the square."

"My butt is prettier than your Sunday face," I say under my breath as I sip on my water. The music is loud, and words are easily distorted ... so one would think.

"What's that?" Katy's eyes are wide.

"I said wow, it's pretty, this day, this place." I gave her a perfunctory smile.

"Oh." Katy's face changes from appalled to confused. "Anyhow, the story of how we met is actually very cute. At least, I think it is. I'm surprised Justin hasn't told you the story. He tells everyone that story. Don't you, pumpkin?" She grips her straw with two very feminine fingers and sucks on her vodka soda like it's going to shatter in her hands right then and there.

I did not want to hear the story again. I had, in fact, already heard it from Justin. But before I could say, "Oh yes, that's right," Katy begins her story. And with a heavy Southern accent, she tells the tale as if it's her first time. Enthusiasm shines through, even with her first word.

"I was there all alone, sitting at the bar, of course, my favorite bartender Tony was there. He has the most amazing dimples, by the way. Anyhow, there I was, like I said, by myself when this gorgeous look'n man with a jaw to die for taps me on the shoulder and asked if the seat next to me was taken. Of course, I said no. I was so embarrassed because I knew I had stuttered. I stuttered, and I blushed, and I acted like a darn fool. There was no doubt in my mind that this man who just spoke to me knew I was unequivocally smitten with him already. It was silent for a dreadfully long time, and I just couldn't bear it. Lord, please let him speak, I kept thinking to myself. Why, just then, he started up a conversation. A conversation that lasted for hours, I might add. I mean ... who talks to someone for the first time for hours? It's just unheard of, really. We ate, we drank, we laughed, and at some point, in the thick of it all, we touched. We both reached for a water glass simultaneously and when our fingers touched, there was a spark of electricity. A spark that tickled me from my ponytail down to the tips of my pinky toes. That's it, end of story. It was magical. We have been inseparable ever since. Like two peas in a pod. Have you ever heard anything so romantic in your life?" She puts a hand to her chest and looks up at the stars.

She's getting on my tits. I don't want to hear another word. I want to barf. Is this the same story Justin told me? I don't think so, Miss Katy Moore. She clearly likes to exaggerate. What a little liar she is. Nobody likes liars, right? I mean ... unless it's for good reason. But this is no good reason. This is just embarrassing, Miss Moore, the whore.

"JoDi, go get us some more beers." Yusuff interrupts her thoughts. He quickly turns around and continues to talk to Justin. He didn't say please. He didn't even really look at me. He isn't asking for a favor. No, it is an order.

I see Justin's reaction. He is disgusted to see his brother like this. Justin looks at me. I know he can see the hurt in my eyes. I wish he couldn't. I wish this were all just a dream. A very bad dream.

"I'll go with you," Justin inserts quickly. "I feel like changing it up. Yeah, I don't want another IPA. Katy, why don't you keep Yusuff company? We will be right back." He places a hand behind my shoulder and gives me a little push.

Written all over Katy's face is nothing but annoyance.

Awe, poor Katy Moore, she just isn't very independent, is she? She just wants Justin all to herself, right by her side. God forbid she has to be creative enough to start an interesting conversation. God forbid she has to pretend like she is enjoying herself without Justin.

Justin and I are now walking side by side through the Christmas-lit streets until we get to The Red Haren Brewery. Before we walk through the door, we pause. We look at each other, playfulness written all over our faces.

"Are you thinking what I'm thinking?" he asks me with a frolicsome yet mischievous look in his eyes.

"It depends. Are you thinking we should walk to Mac's Steak House and get a Pineapple dream Martini?" I respond as I playfully move my eyebrows up and down.

"You Devil you." He looks back at Yusuff and Katy. "Let's go before they see us." He grips my hand. We are jogging slowly, occasionally giggling like a couple of teenagers. When we get to the corner, we come to a complete stop. He doesn't let go of my hand. Christmas carolers are here, with their large black top hats and wool scarves. Justin releases my hand, pulls out a ten-dollar bill, drops it in their tip jar, and requests one of my favorite Christmas songs, "Winter Wonderland."

"You mean you don't want to hear "Jingle Bells"?" one of the carolers asks sarcastically.

"I take it that's been a favorite?" Justin replies with a smile as big as the moon.

"You have no idea." He chuckles and signals the others to begin.

As they sing, others gather around. I can't believe that after all this time, he remembers one of my favorite Christmas songs. I have never been able to choose just one, but this is definitely top five.

While standing there, singing along, the tip of his right pinkie touches the tip of my left pinkie. Gently and painfully slow, we caress each other ... just the edges. Just the soft outer edge of a single tiny finger. We cannot look at each other. We must not look at each other. This is wrong. This is beautiful. This is forbidden.

The song ends. Cold air fills the space between our fingers as our bodies move apart. Justin notices that I am slightly shivering. He removes his beanie and pulls it over my head. His warmth washes over my frigid ears. Anyone observing us would assume we are a couple. A new couple. A couple in love.

"How about that martini?" Justin asks as he begins to walk backward. He can't keep his eyes off of me. His playful manner is goofy and sexy, but not sexy enough. He begins to turn around. "Watch out ..." I say loudly as I throw my hands up. He spins around and walks straight into a metal pole. The sound of his head ramming into metal was both hilarious and worrisome. It took every ounce of willpower for me not to laugh. It was so hard, I ached.

"Ahhhhh ... Kelly Clarkson!" he yells. He put his hands on his forehead. "Fuck! You see Jo, this is why we can't hang out. Next time it will be a bus!"

I just can't hold back anymore. I fold over in laughter, grabbing my stomach,, praying to God I don't piss my pants.

"You *would* laugh at this. I swear, when I die, you will be the last face I see." We laugh together as we continue on with our forbidden journey.

One of the coolest things about the square is that it's legal to buy any booze you want to-go, "para llevar," and take it out of the establishment. What better way to enjoy the center park, shopping, and of course, the Merry Market. We have received our martinis to-go and are now rushing back to the brewery to get Yusuff a beer. We know we've been gone for longer than normal, but it's not a big deal. We are all grown-ass adults, right? As we enter the brewery, we see that both Yusuff and Katy are in line to order.

"For fuck's sake, guys, what took so damn long? Where did you go?" Yusuff was not asking this playfully; he was truly bothered.

"Yeah," Katy agreed, throwing her hands up in the air "Why did you just leave me, Justin?" Her voice is shaky.

"Don't worry, hun," Yusuff shot back at Katy. "Just because they used to fuck in high school doesn't mean that will happen again." Yusuff turns his gaze on me and eyes me up and down.

Did he just insinuate that I'm too fat and unfuckable? That Justin would never go for me now? Shame, embarrassment, and anger seeps in.

"Watch it, buddy, or I'm gonna cream yo' corn." I threw the keys at Yusuff. "I'll call an Uber!" I snapped at him. Even though my eyes are watery, and I want to crawl into a hole and die, I speak kindly to Katy and Justin. "So sorry for the drama, guys. I had a lovely evening." I walk briskly out of the brewery with my head held high.

"Wait." With a single finger on Justin's chin, Katy moves Justin's gaze from me to her "you and JoDi used to fuck?" She put a hand on her hip.

CHAPTER 33

JoDi

A two-tiered book chandelier hangs from the ceiling. Two square metal racks hang about eighteen inches apart, one above the other. Each metal rack holds several books, from one end to the other, not a gap in sight. The books are facing the opposite direction, so instead of seeing book titles, you see blonds, whites, beiges, creams, and tans. Standing directly underneath it, however, you can look up and read the titles from the inside. It is by far the most beautiful and creative chandelier I have ever seen. The establishment is called the Read Shop in Atlanta. It's kind of a fancy part of town, which makes complete sense. How many coffee shops/bookstores have an immense custom-made book chandelier the size of a kitchen table? The walls are lined with books. The center is a designated social area. Loveseats and very comfortable lounge chairs are in clusters to accommodate several groups. Madame Fontenot suggested we meet somewhere outside her home office, somewhere we could simply talk and get to know one another. I have been quite excited about this meet-up. I'm as nervous as a long-tailed cat in a room full of rocking chairs.

What I feel at the moment is something very notable. It's admiration. It's comfort. It's love, yes, but friendly love. I'm just so full of joy that she wants to be my friend. All women need female companions. All women want to feel like there is a female bond, something that seems to come easily for men. We have to fight for it. We have to grow it, feed it. I don't know what I did to deserve this, but I'm truly happy. Not only does she want to help me with a lifelong struggle that has haunted me forever, but now she simply likes me for me. This still doesn't feel real. Is it real? I need to order something to drink instead of staring at the menu on the back wall.

"Can I help you narrow it down? What are your preferences?" Asks the barista from behind the counter. She has a lovely look to her, not boring, not beige, no, it's blue, like the color of her hair. She is as lovely as the color of the sea.

"I'm so sorry. My mind was trailing off. Thank goodness no one is in line behind me." I look behind me, and through the front glass doors, I notice Madame Fontenot walking up the stairs.

"My friend just got here. I'll wait for her. I want to pay for the both of us." I tell the barista.

"No worries, take your time. I have nowhere else to be."

This time Madame Fontenot is not covered in bright mismatched clothes. She is wearing a long baggy boho style dress with pockets and what looks like tan Tom shoes. Her hair is loose and wild, with a few tiny braids here and there.

"Well, hello. You look super cute today!" For fuck's sake, did I really just say *super cute*? Someone kill me now.

"I'm feeling very organic today. Let's just hope I don't spill coffee all over myself."

We have ordered our fancy coffee, which is served in fancy mugs, and are now seated underneath the fancy book chandelier … the best seats in the house. Fancy. Fancy. Fancy.

"So, tell me JoDi, how is your love life?" This is no joke. Her face is still, calm and full of sincere curiosity.

"This sounds like a therapy session." I chuckle before taking a sip of my vegan maple syrup, whatever-whatever.

"Ha, okay. How are you and the hubby doing? Sex, is it good? Give me a number from one to ten. Then I'll give you some tips on how not to make a conversation between new friends awkward."

We laugh at this. But not a fake laugh. We are, in fact, friends. We are, in fact, quite comfortable around each other.

"Well, sex used to be a ten, then it moved to eight, and now it's nonexistent. He is under a lot of stress at work, I think. I'm sure it will pass. Justin has always been able to perform in bed, so I'm sure it's just a faze."

"Justin? Who is Justin? I thought your husband's name was Yusuff."

Oh shit, oh shit, I seriously just said Justin. Mother trucker!

"Well, that's embarrassing. Once again ... awkward." I take another sip. "Yusuff, of course Yusuff."

Madame Fontenot is eyeing me. The look is playful. Every part of me wants to tell her the truth, but I know I can't.

Perhaps I can confide in her. Isn't this how we build trust?

"Forget Yusuff. Tell me more about Justin. Is there a one to ten for him?"

I tell her the story in detail and leave nothing out. From our first kiss to the first time, we made love in high school, to him shipping off to the military after he graduated, to me marrying his brother, to the slamming of the head at the square after my favorite Christmas song. I left nothing out.

We then jump into all aspects of life, family, friends, and personal struggles like anxiety and fears. We laugh. We cry. We fart, faint, and flow with the beat of our proverbial drum. Like bosom buddies, we are in sync. There is no room for talk of work. We leave our careers out of the conversation and keep it personal. Sitting here talking for hours is as natural as gray hair on a middle-aged human ... they come without warning and blend in as if they are in their rightful place. They belong there. They have earned their right to be there. They flow with the same curves yet stand out at times, even in directions they shouldn't, yet they fit right in. That's what our relationship is—a gray hair.

CHAPTER 34

JoDi

As I am packing up Yusuff's food into a to-go container, I'm reminded of the days when I would visit him often at work. Not to take up his time or anything, just a quick hello. I would deliver him homemade food, sweets and sometimes takeout from his favorite restaurants. His co-workers would make fun of us, all in good cheer, though. Everyone knew we were in love. Those days seem so far away.

Now, today, I am nervous about being rejected. I'm nervous he will embarrass me, mistreat me, and instead of teasing, I would be greeted with silence or pity. The world didn't need to know that someway, somehow, my husband decided to stop respecting me. Stop desiring me. Stop protecting me. Stop loving me.

I lift my head and take in a deep breath. With it comes the aromas of the dish I had just prepared for him. He can't say no to my delicious coconut curry veggie dish. I made it from scratch using only organic ingredients. The flavors will burst in his mouth. He will not reject this dish. He will not reject me, not in front of all of his coworkers.

Before I can change my mind, I reach for my coat and head out the door. I have decided not to wear a dress today. Instead, I am in a pair of yoga pants that Yusuff had commented on a while back ... a time when he was still hot for me. "You are not allowed to wear these in public."

He had told me; just before pulling them down and pushing me up against the wall. Kissed the back of my neck while growling. Oh, how I wish I could go back in time.

The drive to the police station has gone by fairly quickly. So far, I have run eight different scenarios of how he will respond to my presence there. They all started great but inevitably turned into a disaster. It is cold outside, yet my armpits are already sweaty. Nervous sweat is always a smelly situation, full of nervous hormones and toxicity. As I pull in, I admire the Christmas decorations. They are different this year. Clearly, more effort was put into it. There are now twelve potted Christmas trees up front, decorated from top to bottom. They will be replanted somewhere in the city after Christmas.

The entire building and the surrounding trees on the property are covered in lights. It's daytime, so I have no idea what color they are, but I imagine they look magical at night.

Now in the elevator, feeling confident, at least forcing myself to feel confident, I am smiling from ear to ear. When the doors open, I want everyone to see how happy and normal I am. The elevator doors open, and no one has noticed me. It doesn't seem like much has changed. The overall feeling and vibe give me a sense of comfort. Unable to enter a room without some degree of dramaturgy, I raise my large bag of food and take a quick spin. I'm quite satisfied with myself when I notice a few raised heads with cautious smiles. I wave at a few, and they seem excited to see me.

To my delight, Yusuff is at his desk, typing away. It bothers me to see my husband leaning too far forward and hunching his back. This kind of posture is why his neck and lower back are always hurting. I'm well aware of how difficult it can be to keep good posture when severe concentration is needed. I know exactly how that feels. When I spend hours on my readers' FB group, time slips away, and my posture is the last thing I am thinking about. Nearly folded in half, I gently place a hand on his back. "Hey, sweetie."

His head pops up. It's amazing what one can read in just a matter of seconds, even microseconds. He is surprised, then pleasantly surprised, then worried, then confused. The order in which they came is comforting. They all seemed natural, considering I hadn't shown my face in this place in quite some time. Upset and annoyed had not been one of his reactions, so I'm quite pleased with my decision.

"Well, *this* is a nice surprise." He reaches out for my hand.

"I … I," I stammer. "I'm sorry … I just thought it would be nice to bring you a treat. I know it has been a while."

I don't know what the hell is going on, but I'm suddenly filled with emotions. It takes everything I have not to cry. I dig my fingernails into my palms to hold back tears. It works every time. I once had a therapist tell me that hurting myself to stop me from crying was dangerously unacceptable. That it had to stop … especially pinching myself so hard that it left bruises. Cutting myself was the worst and was the final turning point in our professional relationship when she insisted on me starting a new medication. That had been our last session together. I no longer cut myself. I have much better control now.

"It *has* been a while." He reaches for the lunch bag. "What did you bring me?"

"Hi, JoDi!" Alison Kawalski's face is like a bowl of sunshine. "Well, how the hell have you been, lady?" She walks over with open arms, and we embrace.

"I've been good, very busy, but good," I say as I lean against his desk.

"Your man here has been working his tail off, too," Alison says as she also leans over and sits on his desk. She is a short woman, so the whole thing looks natural as her tiny left cheek fit perfectly on the corner.

It is so good to feel normal. Alison always makes me smile and feel special.

Yusuff is busying himself, opening the bag. "Nice." I hear him say as he pulls out the large container full of food.

"Oh damn, please tell me you brought enough for me, too." Alison bites her bottom lip.

"There's enough for three people, so you will have to take that up with him. Who knows if he's up for sharing."

From a distance, a female voice drowns out our small talk. "Yusuff, great, I'm glad you are here." I recognize that voice right away. The way some of her words come out as a melody. The way there is a slight sexy roughness as if she used to be a smoker.

I turn my head, and we lock eyes. The moment is shadowy. Am I in dream? This, what is this? No, this can't be real. What the hell is she wearing? Does she have a twin she hasn't told me about?

"Dr. Trudi, I was just about to call you." Yusuff notices that Dr. Trudi and I have locked eyes for what seems like an unnatural amount of time.

"Dr. Trudi, this is my wife JoDi." he points with his hand. "JoDi, this is Dr. Trudi. She is the therapist I told you about that has been helping me with the missing persons cases."

My nails are digging exceedingly hard into my palm this time, but it doesn't stop the tears. I need to run to my woods, my forest. I need to feel safe.

I am staring despairingly into Madame Fontenot's eyes.

CHAPTER 35

Dr. Trudi

As JoDi runs off, Dr. Trudi puts an arm out and stops Yusuff from chasing her down. It's important that she speak with him ASAP. She will deal with JoDi later. Yusuff was the one she was desperate to speak with.

Yusuff and Dr. Trudi are now in the stairwell.

"What the hell is going on, Dr. Tudi? You know my wife? And if so, why the hell did she run out like that? Why the fuck was she crying?"

"Look, this is not the best place to discuss this."

"Yeah, no shit. I gathered this when you dragged me into the stairwell."

"We must meet somewhere private another time, but let me briefly tell you what is happening."

"Fine, you have ten minutes, then I'm going after my wife."

"Where do I start . . ." She rubs her chin. "Okay, so, apart from being a doctor, I also have another business. Fuck, how do I put this? I'm what some people call a psychic, but I honestly hate that word. This will take too long to explain. One, I'm not a fraud. Two, I only help people. I don't hurt them. I don't get involved with people unless they or someone else is in danger. Three, JoDi is not just a client. She is a friend. She is desperate for help, and we need to help her. She is involved with some dark shit, but it's not her fault. At least, I don't think it is. That's what

I'm trying to figure out. It's obvious she is a good person, better than me, that's for sure. Something inside of her is poisoning her, and if we don't help her, it will be too late."

Dr. Trudi/Madame Fontenot goes on and on. Yusuff, the good police officer that he is, lets her speak. He listens without interruption.

"Also, she trusts me. Well, at least she used to. Now, after this new development, I don't know if she will even talk to me anymore. I have to try. Sorry, okay, let me get to the point."

Dr. Trudi explains the whole situation. From the beginning to end. She leaves nothing out. At least she tries not to. He is getting increasingly agitated by the second, rocking back and forth. It's hard for Dr. Trudi to gauge if he is angry, scared, shocked, or in disbelief.

"Dr. Tudi, you can't tell anyone else about this. Do you understand?"

"Yes, I understand."

"And you can't tell JoDi I know everything you told me. No one can know that I know this. I'm a police officer, for fuck's sake."

"You have my word. I am speaking to you as Madame Fontenot, JoDi's friend. You have my word."

"I need to be the one to tell her I know," he says as he continues to pace. "I need to take her somewhere. I need to do something. And I need to do it soon."

CHAPTER 36

Months Prior

Yusuff

Police officers often write letters to leave behind just in case something happens to them. He has written many but never did give them to his brother Justin to hold. This time he would. He knows it's a big risk, but it must be done. In case something happens to him, Justin will have this letter to give to JoDi.

My dearest JoDi,

I don't know what to do anymore, my love. I've decided to write you this letter hoping that one day soon I can use it to better explain what my life has been like these past several months. Or has it been a year already? I don't even know. It's been so incredibly stressful, it's almost like a blur. The amount of sorrow, stress, and pressure I have been under has led me to break the laws which I have vowed to follow. I have lied. I have done things I never imagined I would ever do. I have started to resent and mistreat you, which is insane considering everything I have done for you.

JoDi, my darlin' JoDi, I found your ledger. I found it a while back. I wasn't even necessarily looking through your things. One day I just went into your office, which I know we both promised not to do. Your office is your space, and my work is my private work. But I couldn't help it. You spent so much time in there, and I knew it wasn't all work. I knew you were consumed with your readers' group, but I thought there was something more. What I found broke my heart.

The thing is … the thing is that I know my JoDi. My big-hearted wife who loves to help others in need. The woman that spends so much of her time volunteering and expecting absolutely nothing in return. You don't go around telling people how much of that you do. You don't do it to brag so that people can say, "Oh, she's such a good person." No, you keep it to yourself. You do it for them. You do it because you genuinely care for people, and don't like seeing them suffer. I've never met a soul like you before. A beautiful, beautiful soul. You will always be a secret angel to me. An angel that has saved me as well. You saved me from so many dark moments I thought I could never repay you until I read your ledger.

I read your ledger and the names listed. And as I read, I recognized some of the names. Some of those names under annihilate were missing. Some of those names I didn't recognize, but when I searched for them, I found they were missing in different states. The dates they went missing matched closely to the dates you were in those cities. I didn't want to believe it. There was no way, my angel, my true love, my everything, was a … I can't write it down. But I must, I must write it down. A murderer, a murderer, you are an angel and a demon. But I love you anyway.

I will go to the ends of the earth for you. Well, I did, in a way. You see, I found it interesting that you left coordinates next to some of the names. Why, why would you do this? I don't understand. But now I see that it was important that you did. It was important because that's how I was able to help you. This made it easier for me to find the bodies. Some of the coordinates I went to and didn't find a body.

I assume it's because you buried them too deep or dumped their bodies into the ocean or a lake. A couple of them you didn't bury deep enough. I had to pull them out. I actually moved the bodies to another location, just in case anyone else saw your ledger. I buried them deep, deep into the ground. I did this for you. All those trips I took were for you, my love. All those places I went, I couldn't tell you where I was going. I almost lost my job because of this. I had to explain that I was going through a family crisis. I had to say I was sick. I had to lie again and again. All those credit cards I closed were because those were the cards you used during your trips. I wanted, no, I needed you to have a fresh start. I'm sure that makes no sense, but I was desperate. I didn't know what to do. With all of my training and all of my love for you, I was still so very lost. I need you to find help, and I need us to start again.

I don't understand your ledger, though. Some of the missing persons on your list didn't have any coordinates beside their names. Maybe you got lazy. Maybe you forgot. I don't know, but every single name on your list, I either found and cleaned up after you or I didn't find because the coordinates led me to the ocean, or a river, or a lake. I assume you dumped the bodies in the water.

The other names with no coordinates are just simply missing, and I had no idea how to clean up your mess for those people. Why, just why, were their names on that list without coordinates? I need to know everything. I have to think, I have to believe, I have to hope, that those people were horrible people. Why else would they have to die?

I often wonder how you did it. I never did spend extra time with the bodies. I was in such a hurry to hide all the evidence that I didn't examine them. On one of them, I noticed her throat was sliced from one end to the other. Anyway, I did what I had to do. I did it for you. I can't believe that one of the bodies wasn't even buried. Did you want to get caught? I mean, why didn't you at least burn it, or I don't know, something, anything? You are so incredibly smart. You have to explain this to me because it's killing me on the inside. It's like you didn't even care. Did you think because you had gotten away with it several times already that, you were invincible? Obviously, you had no idea that your husband was traveling around the country destroying all the evidence. So, what was your plan? Were you just going to get caught and go to prison for the rest of your life? You were just going to leave me? Leave me all alone, without you? I can't live without you. That's why I was so angry with you. That's why sometimes I couldn't even be around you. How could you just leave me? Did you stop loving me?

We need to talk, but I just can't find a way. I'm sorry. I need to go find the bodies of the other people on your list. I need to find the evidence and get rid of it. But if you are reading this, it's too late. Damn it, why did you want to leave me in this world alone? You are my everything. I would die for you, don't you understand? Don't you get it? I need you. I love you more than life itself.

Obviously, this letter was sealed. I trust Justin not to open it. He would never betray me like that. I hope you aren't reading this. I hope I get to ask for this letter back from Justin and burn it. I hope I can talk to you … I just don't know how. I don't know the right time. I've been cleaning up your mess, but now I feel like I'm at the end. I need to know where the other bodies are. I've done all I can do on my own. I need you now. I need you to help me help us get through this. JoDi, I need you.

Love,

Your best friend, your partner, your forever soulmate,

Yusuff.

CHAPTER 37

JoDi

My phone will not stop making noise. Both calls and text messages are breaking my train of thought. I need to drive. Just keep driving. Keep thinking, processing. Madame Fontenot is Dr. Trudi. Dr. Trudi is Madame Fontenot. Why? How? Fuck.

"I was born at night, but not last night!!" I yell as my hands strangle the steering wheel.

I have borrowed a vehicle from one of my friends whom I drive to cancer treatments. This car hasn't been driven in a while. Laimae Meyers can't see very well, so her car has been sitting in the garage for some time now. Surprisingly, so far, it hasn't given me any trouble.

Problem-solving has always come naturally to me while driving.

What the fuck is going on? Dr. Trudi, a doctor that works for the police, is also a woman named Madame Fontenot who runs her own private psychic business. Or was her home office all a sham? Was her double life all a sham? Was it all for me? Was she leading a double life? Or was it really just a big show, all for me? Oh my God, Madame Fontenot and my husband must have been plotting against me this whole time. That's why he's been treating me like shit. They know something, perhaps everything. But why? Why is this happening? Why am I not in prison? If they were out to get me, why am I not in jail right fucking now? They must want to make sure they have enough evidence. They must think I'm stupid. How have I not put two and two together? My husband hates me. Now I know why.

Now I know why he has completely changed. He was waiting for the right moment. Did he hire Madame Fontenot, Dr. Trudi, whatever the fuck her name is, to follow me? To scam me? To get close to my heart and deceive me? How could he do this to me? He was my everything. I thought I was his everything. I thought he loved me no matter what. He should've given me the chance to explain. He has no idea who I am protecting. He has no idea how many lives I have saved. Imagine if I were to let bullies remain in my group. What if I let them remain in this world, bullying everyone around them? How many people would indeed go jump off a bridge because of their careless words? Their words matter. Their words influence people. They are evil, and they had to die. I know what's best for my group, my family. I guess they are all I have left. I must continue to protect them. Who else will? You can do this JoDi. Don't let your wood get wet.

I have driven back to the police station. Here I am, waiting patiently like a vulture. Several hours have passed. Finally, I see Madame Fontenot walking into the front door of the police station. As soon as I see her enter, I rush to her house. I'm already imagining it in my head how she will die. How her life will end in a moment of panic and fear.

After ensuring no one is home, I walk around to the back of her house. I break one of the small glass windows to the back door. Reaching carefully to avoid cutting myself, I unlock the door.

I've already devised a plan, so my movements are steady but fast. It's a rough plan, but it might work. I distinctly remember that whenever Madame Fontenot would make us some tea, she always had to use a match to light the burner. She has a defective stove top.

Madame Fontenot always enters the house through the garage. I have witnessed this many times. Enough times to ensure this is how she will enter her house. The kitchen door is what leads to the garage. This is the door Madame Fontenot will use to come in. I secure sandpaper on the floor at the foot of the door. With duct tape, I attach a large fireplace match securely to the bottom of the door, facing down. The red flammable tip is touching the sandpaper. This way, when Madame Fontenot opens the door, the red flammable tip will rub up against the sandpaper and ignite a flame.

I pull out my phone and notice several voice messages waiting for me. I darken my phone and put it back in my pocket. I need to disable the smoke detectors. I've got to piss so bad my eyeballs are float'n! But I don't have time. I run around the house removing all the batteries from the smoke detectors. I turn on all the knobs of the defective stove, and the gas quickly escapes. I run out the back door with both regrets and non-regrets pulling at my heartstrings. This will not be a glorious death.

CHAPTER 38

JoDi

I still haven't listened to the several voicemails that have been left on my phone. I am too busy thinking. Too busy planning. Too busy to hear excuses. I am on my way to meet my husband. I suppose now is a good time to listen to them. But to be clear, I have no desire to. Madame Fontenot will only lie to me. Fuck, that's not even her real name. Fuck. Fuck. Fuck. She will only give me excuses.

Nevertheless, I need to listen to them. And so, here it goes. I reluctantly press play.

Voicemails from Madame Fontenot:

Voicemail one: "*JoDi, listen to this carefully. We need to talk. We need to meet up. You don't understand what's happening. Your husband has absolutely no idea about my side business. He has no idea that you were coming to see me. He has no clue about the hypnotherapy. He didn't know we were friends. Your name never came up in any of our conversations. I do help a lot of people. Yes, my name is Dr. Trudi Rosenblun, and yes, I do collaborate with and assist the police in certain cases from time to time, but I also help people that the police cannot help. My side business is very private, and because of this, I go by Madame Fontenot. Please just hear me out. Please call me back.*"

Voicemail two: "*JoDi, why won't you pick up? I know somewhere inside of you, you believe me. I want to help you. I need to tell you what happened in that second session we had. It's not your fault. None of it is your fault. I can help you. You just need to do some self-help, self-awareness and rewire your thoughts. Hypnotherapy can help you. Please let me explain everything to you."* There's a quick pause which worries me. "*JoDi, you need to know what's going on with your soul."* The voicemail ends.

"My soul?" The words barely come out. I let out a breath I didn't realize I had been holding. I quickly click on the third voicemail.

Voicemail three: "*Dammit, I didn't want to put this in a voicemail, but you have left me with no choice. I don't want you to do anything stupid. I don't want Mike to do anything stupid. Do you want to know who Mike is? Yeah, well, call me.*"

Voicemail four: "*Listen and listen very carefully. During your second session, you revealed several past lives. I don't know if you have ever studied reincarnation, but it's real. There have been countless reports of true events. I have so many books with real-life events and experiences for you to read. Anyway, one of your past lives was a man named Mike Schlistu. He was a mass murderer in the 1940s. Typically, some fears and traits will carry on into the next life with the soul, but JoDi, I think someway, somehow, his soul carried on with one that was supposed to be liberated. The cycle of birth, death, and rebirth continues indefinitely until the soul reaches a state of spiritual enlightenment or liberation. I think the good side of you was a soul that was supposed to be liberated, and it didn't. Mike's soul was set for you, and it collided with the other. We can get rid of him. At least, I think we can. I have heard him. Really, really, heard him. He is attached to you. He is not a demon. He is a part of you. Which is absurd because it goes against the teachings, but I believe this is a phenomenon. The only reason I haven't reached out to others in this field is because I'm afraid they will turn on you. I am your only hope—*"

Voicemail five: "*Your phone cut me off. We need to do intense hypnotherapy to get rid of him. I know you are a good person. He is the one influencing you to do bad things. I don't know if you have already done terrible things, but we can stop it now. It's time to let the soul of Mike Schlistu separate from you if that's even possible. If not, we can at least have better control of your actions through the power of suggestion. I think I can help you stop your cravings for evil-doing.*"

Voicemail six: "*This is it, my last attempt. JoDi, I know about Nicky Lee. This is how this whole thing started. I had actually given her my card after you left the coffee shop. That's right. I offered to help her. I was there. But the crazy thing is, is that after you attacked her in Marietta near the wine market, I ended up hypnotizing her at the police station shortly after. She had holes in her memory of that night. When she saw me at the police station, I looked familiar to her, but she didn't figure it out. Fuck ... at least I don't think she did. Anyway, I was in my full pantsuit with my hair tied back and glasses, completely different than my day-to-day wear. Well, you already know that—*"

Voicemail seven: "*Dammit, I got cut off again! Anyway, I was there. The day you followed her to the coffee shop. Mike is probably the reason you are so obsessed with Nicky. I bet there is some form of sexual attraction, and now it makes total sense why. You are utterly infatuated with her. I know you have been following her. If you don't believe me, I remember the exact thoughts that ran through your head before you walked out the door of that coffee shop. They were so heart-wrenching that I remember them word for word.*

The choice is beyond my better parts. The parts that allow me to rest. The next time we meet, my flower, woman of beauty, elegance, and class ... you will be nothing but flesh beneath the sharpness of my knife."

CHAPTER 39

Dear autocorrect,
It's never duck.

I dedicate this chapter to an author many of us love and cherish.
You know who you are.

Sincerely,
All the MARRSians.

CHAPTER 40

Madame Fontenot/Dr. Trudi

Madame Fontenot is on her way home. She is mentally exhausted. JoDi has not been answering her phone or responding to her text messages. What she desperately needs is to talk to her wife. That might help with her anxiety.

When she gets to a red light, she says, "Hey Siri, call Gloria Wife." She answers right away. Just hearing her wife's voice has already made a difference. This was one of the reasons she fell so deeply in love with her. They are connected in a way that's hard to put into words. Their relationship had grown even stronger since they started the adoption process. After a long struggle, they were finally approved. They met with various children and then one hit. It hit their hearts like a ton of bricks. A three-year-old boy named Tommy. He was severely neglected and had some abuse in his background. They can't wait to get him into their home, where he will be loved and protected. In only two weeks, their life will be so different. So full of purpose and love. Yes, it will be hard, but that's okay. Her life will have a deeper purpose. In times like this, Madame Fontenot can't help but think about Tommy. She thinks about the things that really matter in her life. Her wife and her soon-to-be son. Both had agreed: "We will just know. It will happen.

The bond will reveal itself, and there will be an instant love that will wash over us." And it did.

On the phone, they carry on a conversation about everyday matters like dinner and weekend plans. This is what she needs right now. She needs normality to balance things out. As she turns onto their street, she says, "Hey love, I'm home. I'll see you here a little later."

"Okay, make sure to get some rest. Try to relax. I mean it. Chill out. Life is too short. Have a glass of wine. Read one of your books. Promise me?"

"Yes, I promise. I love you."

"I love you, too, bye."

"Bye."

CHAPTER 41

Madame Fontenot

She pushes the button on her remote, and the garage door opens. Her body is already starting to relax. Her home has always been a safe space for her. She will listen to her wife and have a glass of wine after a long shower. She had been looking forward to returning to a book called *She is Me, Too* by T.M. Shivener. She had started it weeks ago but was so consumed with JoDi that she couldn't find the time. She would, of course, leave her ringer on, just in case JoDi called. It took everything in her power not to go searching for JoDi, but she knows JoDi her space. She just hopes she doesn't do anything drastic.

She puts the car in park and shuts it off. Her head falls back against the headrest. The soft sound of Odesza is playing. Her eyelids are so very heavy. The melody puts her in a calm, sweet trance. Her body is like jelly. She swears she is so tired she could literally take a nap right this very second. It takes so much willpower to peel her head off the headrest. After rubbing her eyes, she gathers her things and walks to the door. She is about to press the garage door button on the wall next to the door but decides to leave it open. Her wife will be coming home soon anyway. She's probably only five or ten minutes behind her.

As she reaches for the door handle, she remembers her laptop is in the back seat. After getting her laptop, she heads back to the door, only to remember the trash can needs to be taken to the end of the driveway. Tomorrow is trash day. She sets her laptop bag down and swears she can smell gas. Brushing it off, she walks to the trash can and pulls on the large handle. As she pulls the trash can down her driveway, she is reminded of how quiet her neighborhood is. It has a subtle loneliness to it. It's always been a quiet and uneventful neighborhood. That's one of the things she likes most about it. The air has a distinct smell to it. It's about to start raining. She looks up and notices very dark clouds heading her way. After she places the trash can at the end of the driveway, she opens her weather app. A storm is heading in. It looks like only a small portion of this area will be in the red.

During her walk back up the driveway, she can't help but think about everything she wants to say to JoDi. She lifts her laptop bag, and again she smells gas. She contemplates calling 311 but decides she will investigate first. She opens the door witnessing the smallest of sparks at her feet. Then the brightest light she has ever seen fills the air.

CHAPTER 42

JoDi

I have been busy. Too busy to call Madame Fontenot back. But the last few hours have been so fucking stressful. I'm freaking out!

One thing at a time, JoDi! It's all going to be okay.

As I dig deep in the forest, I am beginning to regret the match, the gas, the terrible death that is about to fall upon Madame Fontenot. There is a gruesome panic that arises from the depths of my bowels.

Fuck. Why didn't I stop it earlier? Fuck, fuck, fuck, don't go home, Madame Fontenot. I can't take this stress. What did I do? Dammit!

I let go, and the shovel falls to the ground. I reach for my phone. I dial.

Come on, pick up. Pick up the bloody phone Madame Fontenot.

There is no answer.

Should I even care this much? She is a scam artist, right? But what if she is really my friend? What if she was really trying to help me? Fuck! Fuck all of you for hiding everything from me!

I dial again, but there is still no answer. There is nothing I can do now.

One thing at a time. Finish here. She's probably still at work. Yes, she's a busy woman. She's not home yet. Call her back but get this done. Get your shit together!

When I darken my phone and look up, something just snaps in my brain. I begin to admire the forest. The way the shadows cast figures of all shapes across land so innocent, so clean and pure. The space around me is filled with the most beautiful sounds. My mind relaxes, and I begin to enjoy myself. Something that often happens during a time like this.

I pop in my headset and press play. The hole is finally starting to seem big enough. It's a lot of work, but the soil in this area is a gorgeous red clay, so it's not all that difficult to dig into. The ground in places like Austin, Texas, where it's full of limestone, is a whole different story. It's impossible to bury a body there. Thankfully, they have plenty of lakes and rivers. But no, not here. Here in north Georgia, the ground is much softer, plus it rains the same amount here that it does in Seattle, Washington. Yet, it is still a workout, but I can manage. I have had plenty of practice. The hole is big enough now. I roll the body once, twice, and on the third time, the body falls in. I begin to sing along to his favorite song. This would be the last time I would ever sing this song. The song I wrote for him long ago.

"When it is time for me to fly free … will you be with me, miss lover of bees? When I take my last breath, will you be hovering over my chest? Oh, don't you cry for me. Baby, can't you see, I'm free as a bird, it's time I fly free. Oh, don't you cry for me. Baby, can't you see, I'm free as a bee, it's time I fly free.

Chapter 42: JoDi

"Even a happy life cannot be without a measure of darkness, and the word happy would lose its meaning if it were not balanced by sadness."

-Carl G. Jung, Swiss Psychiatrist

CHAPTER 43

Weeks Later

There are many reasons I am sad and regretful, but I know life goes on. Perhaps it all makes sense in the end. I need to surround myself with the people that love me the most. Justin has not left my side … well, in a matter of speaking. He has been supportive but has also given me space, you know, to grieve. He's grieving, too. His brother has gone missing.

Taking time off work is no trouble at all. I have always been good at my job, and the last account I landed made the company six million dollars. Time to process everything that has happened is very important for my well-being. How else am I to move forward? How else will I get back to protecting my members? The readers surely miss me. Surely there has been some bullying that I didn't catch, and *that* is unacceptable. The ledger had been a problem, and as much as I love it, and do not want to live without it, destroying it is the only option.

The paper turns black, then smoke, and ends with dust right before my eyes. The fire is bright orange and red. I am taking my time, one written memory at a time. With each page, I cringe just a bit. Each page feels like a part of me is burning. I hear fumbling at the front door. Justin is unlocking it. I'm sure of it. No one else has a key. I close the half-destroyed ledger and walk to my office. After placing it in a locked drawer, I look into a mirror.

I look rather pretty today.

"Hello, JoDi, you home?" I hear in the distance.

"I'm in my office." I walk out, trying not to seem too excited. I am certainly sad that my husband is several feet under the ground, but I need to appear devastated. To be honest, a part of me is devastated. I loved him. I loved him, and he betrayed me. My life will never be the same. Would I ever love another man so deeply?

He and Madame Fontenot were clearly conspiring against me. No one knew of this betrayal. All anyone knew was that my husband had gone missing, and Dr. Trudi Rosenblun, who was also working on the case, has also gone missing. Her house was on fire when her wife showed up, but Dr. Trudi, Madame Fontenot, was nowhere to be found. This is what the police are saying, at least. I am convinced that Madame Fontenot survived the fire and is currently in hiding. She knows what I am capable of, which is obviously something I would need to fix. I'm incredibly curious as to why she has not come for me. Maybe that day will come.

Absolutely. It will.

Right now, I need to mourn. At the same time, I am in a constant state of fear, living in a high-alert mode. I'm worried Madame Fontenot and the police will show up at my door at any moment and take me in. The last thing I should do right now is drool over Justin. We have become much closer, but life is too messy right now. Love, lust, and passion are tucked away for the moment.

I turn the corner to find Justin standing in the living room with yet another plant. In the dim light, I could see the magnificent radiance in his eyes and the sorrow-filled mask of his skin. He was in some form or brilliant pain. The small orchid in his hand was another sign of his struggles. Its purple and white peddles dangle dangerously close to his chest.

It is so adorable and thoughtful. Instead of bringing me fresh-cut flowers, he has been bringing me plants. Something that can live on instead of shriveling up, leaving a mess … another reminder of death.

"Is this for me?" I reach out.

"Yes, of course, it's for you, Jo."

"Thank you." I lift it up and admire the tiny peddles. "It's perfect."

"I have something else for you." He pulls an envelope from his back pocket. "I'm sorry this took so long, but honestly, I had a hard time finding it. I'm so ashamed. I should have put it somewhere safe, somewhere easy to remember, but I didn't. This right here is a code of honor." His hands tremble as he passes it to me. "I'm sorry, Jo. Please forgive me."

"It's okay. Aren't you being a little hard on yourself?"

"Jo." His eyes start to water. "It's from Yusuff."

The room goes silent. This is big. This is odd. This is perhaps trouble.

"I don't understand, Justin. What do you mean this is from Yusuff? Was he found? Is he alive?"

I have to play the part. I have to believe he is missing.

"Jesus." He wipes tears away. "I'm so sorry, Jo. No, this is a letter he gave me. I was instructed to give it to you if anything happened to him."

"Why would he do that?" I stare at the envelope in shock and disbelief. "Why would he—"

Justin interrupts me. "A lot of police officers do this. So do people in the military. I did the same thing. You know, dangers of the job and all."

"Oh, okay."

"I don't know what to do now. Please tell me what to do, Jo." He begs. Do I stay here while you read it?" He clears his throat. "Do I leave you alone and give you your space?"

"You can go, Justin." My eyes remain glued to the envelope. "Thank you. I'll call you later."

"Okay. I'm here for you. Whatever you need." He gently pats my shoulder before walking out.

I put down the purple and white orchid and sit on the sofa slowly, as if I shouldn't make a sound.

I open it carefully, one watching would think it's about to shatter in my hands, and as I unfold the letter, something inside of me expands. I begin to cry even before I can read the first word. I set it down for a few moments while I recover. My next attempt is still very slow. I owe it to him. He at least deserves that. After all, he didn't even have a proper burial with his family around.

I open the letter.

My dearest JoDi,

I don't know what to do anymore, my love. I've decided to write you this letter hoping that one day soon I can use it to better explain what my life has been like these past several months. Or has it been a year already? I don't even know. It's been so incredibly stressful, it's almost like a blur. The amount of sorrow, stress, and pressure I have been under has led me to break the laws which I have vowed to follow. I have lied. I have done things I never imagined I would ever do. I have started to resent you, and mistreat you, which is insane considering everything I have done for you.

JoDi, my darlin' JoDi, I found your ledger. I found it a while back. I wasn't even necessarily looking through your things. One day I just went into your office, which I know we both promised not to do. Your office is your space, and my work is my private work. But I couldn't help it. You spent so much time in there, and I knew it wasn't all work. I knew you were consumed with your readers' group, but I thought there was something more. What I found broke my heart.

The thing is … the thing is that I know my JoDi. My big-hearted wife who loves to help others in need. The woman that spends so much of her time volunteering and expecting absolutely nothing in return. You don't go around telling people how much of that you do. You don't do it to brag, so that people can say, "Oh, she's such a good person." No, you keep it to yourself. You do it for them. You do it because you genuinely care for people, and you don't like to see them suffer. I've never met a soul like you before. A beautiful, beautiful soul. You will always be a secret angel to me. An angel that has saved me as well. You saved me from so many dark moments, I thought I could never repay you until I read your ledger.

I read your ledger, and the names listed. And I as I read, I recognized some of the names. Some of those names under annihilate were missing. Some of those names I didn't recognize, but when I searched for them, I found they were missing in different states. The dates they went missing matched closely to the dates you were in those cities. I didn't want to believe it. There was no way, my angel, my true love, my everything was a … I can't write it down. But I must, I must write it down. A murderer, a murderer, you are an angel and a demon. But I love you anyway.

I will go to the ends of the earth for you. Well, I did, in a way. You see, I found it interesting that you left coordinates next to some of the names. Why, why would you do this? I don't understand. But now I see that it was important that you did. It was important because that's how I was able to help you. This made it easier for me to find the bodies. Some of the coordinates I went to and didn't find a body.

I assume it's because you buried them too deep or dumped their bodies into the ocean or a lake. A couple of them you didn't bury deep enough. I had to pull them out. I actually moved the bodies to another location, just in case anyone else saw your ledger. I buried them deep,

deep into the ground. I did this for you. All those trips I took were for you, my love. All those places I went, I couldn't tell you where I was going. I almost lost my job because of this. I had to explain that I was going through a family crisis. I had to say I was sick. I had to lie, again and again. All those credit cards I closed were because those were the cards you used during your trips. I wanted, no, I needed you to have a fresh start. I'm sure that makes no sense, but I was desperate. I didn't know what to do. With all of my training, and all of my love for you, I was still so very lost. I need you to find help, and I need us to start again.

I don't understand your ledger, though. Some of the missing persons on your list didn't have any coordinates beside their names. Maybe you got lazy. Maybe you forgot.

I pause from reading.

Oh my gosh, my love. What have I done? Why did I let the dark side take over? And what in the hell do you mean by missing coordinates? What are you talking about? I wrote down the coordinates for every member I killed. The ones without coordinates should not be missing. I don't understand.

I continue to read.

I don't know, but every single name on your list, I either found and cleaned up after you, or I didn't find because the coordinates led me to the ocean, or to a river, or to a lake. I assume you dumped the bodies in the water.

Yusuff, I don't know either. I don't know why members that I did not kill are missing.

The other names with no coordinates are just simply missing, and I had no idea how to clean up your mess for those people. Why, just why, were their names on that list without coordinates? I need to know everything. I have to think, I have to believe, I have to hope, that those people were horrible people. Why else would they have to die?

I often wonder how you did it. I never did spend extra time with the bodies. I was in such a hurry to hide all the evidence that I didn't examine them. On one of them, I noticed her throat was sliced from one end to the other. Anyway, I did what I had to do. I did it for you. I can't believe that one of the bodies wasn't even buried. Did you want to get caught? I mean, why didn't you at least burn it, or I don't know, something, anything? You are so incredibly smart. You have to explain this to me, because it's killing me on the inside. It's like you didn't even care. Did you think because you had gotten away with it several times already that you were invincible? Obviously, you had no idea that your husband was traveling around the country destroying all the evidence. So, what was your plan? Were you just going to get caught and go to prison for the rest of your life? You were just going to leave me? Leave me all alone, without you? I can't live without you. That's why I was so angry with you. That's why sometimes I couldn't even be around you. How could you just leave me? Did you stop loving me?

I pause again. *So this is why you were so angry with me. You thought I didn't care. You thought I wanted to get caught. You thought I didn't care about you. That's the total opposite, my love. I wanted to keep you out of this. I needed you. I wanted you. I loved you. I love you still. I wanted you to keep loving me. The way you used to. I never wanted to abandon you. Why didn't you talk to me? Now it's too late, you big fool.*

We need to talk, but I just can't find a way. I'm sorry. I need to go find the bodies of the other people on your list. I need to find the evidence and get rid of it. But if you are reading this, it's too late. Damn it, Jo, why did you want to leave me in this world alone? You are my everything. I would die for you, don't you understand? Don't you get it? I need you. I love you more than life itself.

Obviously, this letter was sealed. I trust Justin not to open it. He would never betray me like that. I hope you aren't reading this. I hope

I get to ask for this letter back from Justin and burn it. I hope I can talk to you … I just don't know how. I don't know the right time. I've been cleaning up your mess, but now I feel like I'm at the end. I need to know where the other bodies are. I've done all I can do on my own. I need you now. I need you to help me help us get through this. JoDi, I need you.

Love,

Your best friend, your partner, your forever soulmate,

Yusuff.

I fold the letter and set it on the table in front of me. A combination of grief and regret washes over me. There is nothing I can do now. What's done is done. I imagine him rambling through my things in my office. Anger sets in. Not so much that he is going through my private things, yes, that is irritating, but it's mostly because things shouldn't have ended this way.

Why didn't you tell me you found the ledger sooner? We could have figured this out together. You betrayed my trust. The consequence of this mistake has been death. You fool. You big stupid fool. Now you are gone!

I cover my eyes with the flat of my fingers. The slight vibration comes in waves. Gushing tears fall from my eyes. The enormity of it all surprises me. During his last moments, the time of his death, all I was worried about was how heavy and physically difficult it all would be. Now I realize my emotional distress would be much, much heavier.

Wait … the missing members. The-other-fucking-members. Why are they missing? Why the fuck are the members that I did not kill missing? I don't understand. It has to be a mistake. But, no, it can't be. Yusuff is a police officer in line for detective. He would not mess something like this up. Was Madame Fontenot right? Is this Mike person able to take control of me and do things that I am unaware of? How the fuck would that work? No, that is impossible. If I am a combination of two souls, all that means is that I'm being driven by two passions. I am I. I am me. I am all there is. The twoness that is oneness has always been obvious to me. I have to know. I-need-to-know-why-my-members-are-missing!!!!

It's hard to describe what I am feeling at this moment. I am angry. I am sad. I am anxious. I am curious. I am in a fucking shit hole. I consume the rest of my wine. I set the glass back down next to the letter.

Another issue has just come to mind. I pick up the letter and stare at it. I stare and stare, and stare.

Justin ... did you read this letter and put it in a new sealed envelope?

Trees have wrapped their limbs around my body. I am ONE with the woods always. They are protecting me now as I burn and bleed on the inside.

CHAPTER 44

Justin

Dear Jo,

I have written letters like this to you many times. They started when I first entered the military. I never gave them to you or anyone else. As soon as I learned you were with my brother, I got rid of them. The letters stopped that very moment. This time it's different. Many people that have occupations like the military, police force, firefighters, and other life-threatening occupations will leave letters in case something happens to them. They will leave them for "their person." As it turns out, you are still my person. Yes, I have dated, and yes, I have been in love, but they all ended. My love for you has never ended. It will never end. And so, I leave this letter for you ... just in case. Obviously, I hope you never read it.

I have given this letter to my attorney so that in the event I die, you receive it from him. There is so much I want to tell you. It's almost overwhelming. Maybe I should keep it simple. Maybe that's all you need because I think deep down you still love me, too.

Jo, I will do anything for you. I mean that. I will do absolutely anything for you! You don't know the things I have already done for you. And that's okay.

If you are reading this, it's probably because I am dead, so that last statement will only be relevant if I am a ghost and I could actually do things for you in the afterlife. But right now, I am alive and telling you that you are my world ... that will never change. Your life means more to me than my own life.

I will go to the ends of the earth and back for you. We have a bond that can never be broken, and even though you are married to my brother, that doesn't change this fact. You breathe life into me, Jo. My world means nothing without you in it.

I will stand and watch from a distance. I will watch the way your ears move when you are telling an exciting story. I will watch strands of your hair fall onto your face while you put on your shoes. I will watch as you bite your lower lip while typing on your computer. If, for some reason, I have the opportunity to do more than just watch ... I will. I hope you read this letter when you are ninety years old. After you and I have lived some form of life together, you cannot die before me. I won't allow it.

Love,
Justin

CHAPTER 45

JoDi

I have had a constant feeling like my life, my house, my world, my city, my books, all of it, was on fire, and soon it would all come crashing down. I need a distraction. I need Nicky. I follow her closely, but not too close. I have to keep my mind busy. Her presence will help me. I have been a mess. But yes, I need to stay close this time. There have been many times when I have lost her, but today I have been lucky. I find it highly amusing that Nicky Lee has just parked at a spot on Burnt Hickory RD that is really only known by locals and experienced hikers. It's a rough lot, but not really a lot at all. Locals don't like to give away semi-secret spots like this. Most tourists go to the Kennesaw National Battlefield Museum parking lot, where there are restrooms, a small gift shop, and employees that have an impressive amount of knowledge of not only the history of the battle that occurred there but also the many trails up and around the mountains. But that's not where Nicky has decided to go, and I am loving it.

It's late afternoon, and there's only one other vehicle here, which isn't a problem since the couple is currently putting away their Camelbacks in the trunk. At this point, there will be no one else. It's way too late.

Five minutes have passed, and Nicky is still sitting in her car. Perhaps she's on the phone or stuck searching through Facebook. I open the readers' FB page to see if Nicky has posted anything lately. Sure enough, I see a new post from Nicky. It's a book she has just recently finished. It's a book written by the famous and extremely talented John Marrs. She adds mind-blowing emojis and five stars to *The Marriage Act*, which is very impressive considering it's only available in the UK at the moment. This means she received an ARC copy. I had recently contacted John Marrs, asking him if he was interested in me hosting a book giveaway for him. Giveaways are a big hit in my group. I host them every Sunday. When he told me he would give away a signed ARC copy, my heart fluttered just a bit, being a huge fan myself.

Oh, the things I do for my group, always putting them ahead of my own needs and wants. These countless giveaways, all for them, and never being able to win one myself. The other admins couldn't win either. Just another selfless act to show our appreciation and love for the members, for my second family, for the ones that matter the most. Maybe one day they will know just how much I think about them, how often I am on the page making sure they are treated kindly and respectfully. I am always watching.

After all, the only reason I am in this parking lot is that, at some point, Nicky Lee had done something unforgivable. She had taken it too far. But now, all that has been forgiven … at least for the moment.

This pull, this spell she has over me, will not go away. I love her. There is no denying it at this point. It is a different kind of love. The kind that resembles perhaps a brain tumor. You aren't sure how it got there or why or how it keeps growing. I just know I couldn't live without her. I can't kill her. I can't *not* kill her. Deep down, I don't want to live without her. Feeling her presence is all I can get for now. Observing from a distance is slowly filling the gaping hole created from that first day I laid eyes on her at the bookstore.

Hopefully, things will change soon. Hopefully, one day Nicky will feel the same way I do. My love for her isn't sexual. At least, I don't think it is. Do I desire to make love to her? Yes, yes, I do. But just to be near her, to touch her, to be a part of something in the most intimate way.

I scroll to the top of the readers' page and click on the MANAGE icon in my group. I click on PEOPLE, click on SEE ALL, and search for Nicky Lee, just as I have done so many times. Scrolling through her posts that I have seen and read so many times isn't boring. It's another way to be connected to her. We have the same taste in books, which is also a saving grace for her.

I look up from my phone, and I'm startled to see Nicky walking to the back of her vehicle. It's fascinating how quickly one can get so wrapped up in the reading group ... time becomes irrelevant.

She opens her trunk and pulls out a plastic bag. She stuffs it into her backpack and shuts the trunk. I gather my things, putting my keys and Jade in my fanny pack. After putting my phone in my pocket, I wait. When Nicky steps into the wooded area, I emerge from my car carefully, silently. I am already aware there is really only one main trail from here, and it would be highly unlikely to lose her. In this area, the woods are so dense that it's uncommon for anyone to veer off the main path. Only daredevils and murderers do that sort of thing. No, Nicky is much too elegant for that.

I imagine Nicky finding a smooth boulder overlooking the landscape, perhaps sitting down to eat a quick snack from her plastic bag. She has a book. Of course, she does. I have never seen her without at least one book. Maybe she will rest on a boulder, eat her snack, and read for about an hour. Then perhaps she will return to her car just before the darkness becomes utterly black. Very few people stay in these woods when darkness turns black, when there are no more dancing shadows and warm drafts of wind.

Not once does Nicky turn to look behind her. In all fairness, most people don't turn and look behind them, only the paranoid, only the ones who feel like they should be followed. No, Nicky has no reason to believe she should be followed. She is not plagued with fear. She is not weak and paranoid. Her confidence is matched by no other.

We keep a steady pace, and I am beginning to worry that maybe she is going too far into the woods. When does she plan on heading back? If she waits much longer, it will be too late. Thankfully, I have my headlamp inside my fanny pack. That is something I never travel into the woods without, no matter what time of the day my adventure begins ... one never knows, and one can never be too careful. There are some crazy people out there.

I am astonished that she has taken a hard right off the main trail. What could this possibly mean?

Oh no, Nicky, what are you doing? Have you done this before? This must be a mistake. Don't worry. If you get lost, I will help you. I will reveal myself to you if I have to. I don't want to, though. I'm not ready. But why would you need me? You are strong and so very smart. I will not leave your side. You are not alone.

Revealing myself would certainly mean my face would be etched in her mind. She has seen me once already in the museum. She saw the brick in my hand. She would know this is no coincidence. Has she forgiven me? Even though my current profile picture is not a clear picture of my face, surely Nicky has scrolled through past profile pictures and seen exactly what I look like. Surely many members have clicked on all the admins' profiles to see what we look like. I could be wrong.

Would that be so bad? Would that not be what I really want anyway? Would tonight be the night the veil comes down, the wall comes down, the mystery shattered?

It's getting much harder to keep up with her. The fear of losing her in these dense woods is not a fun game. I can't let anything bad happen to her. I must follow close enough, but not too close. The sounds all around us are changing. The sounds of birds chirping are coming to an eerie halt. The warm breeze has turned cool. I can no long see Nicky. Not because it's pitch dark, but because I left too much distance between us. A panic arises, and I am finding it hard to control my breathing. But these are my woods. This is my realm, my domain. I will not let anxiety take over. I am ONE with nature. I belong to the woods. The woods belong to me.

There is nothing to fear, nothing at all. The forest is where I have offered not only my own blood but the blood of many. I had offered many a glorious death. I had offered wildlife food, soil nourishment, and the forest respect.

I inhale deeply, allowing the organic earthly aromas to fill my lungs. I can taste nature just by the smell. I welcome the scent, the feeling, the calmness that comes over me. As I inch around bushes and fallen branches, I glimpse something moving up ahead. It is my darling Nicky.

She had indeed found a smooth boulder to sit on. It's not perched up high with an amazing view. No, it's in the low, dark valley of a place. A spot where one would rarely find solitude, yet there she is. Her gaze to nowhere and everywhere brings out curiosity and alarm bells. What could she possibly be doing?

I continue to hide behind one of many giant trees. I wait. I wait some more. It is dark. It is pitch black.

"If you deliberately plan on being less than you are capable of being, then I warn you that you'll be unhappy for the rest of your life."

-Abraham Maslow, American Psychologist

CHAPTER 46

Soulmate

"I know you are there," Nicky says. Her voice is so profound in these dense woods. Her voice is piercing. It clashes with the sounds of nature. It's a break in everything normal. There is a muffling sound. I suddenly see a small camping light come on. It's the perfect amount of light. Not too bright, not too dim ... glowing over all the right places. With woods this dense, the moonlight can barely make its presence.

"I've always known you were there." Nicky reaches for her backpack and pulls out what looks like a large gardening shovel. She gets on her knees and begins to dig.

She continues. "From the very beginning, I've known." She pauses and looks up. "JoDi." She says my name as if it were a statement, an accusatory tone laced with arrogance.

The sound of her saying my name plays repeatedly in my head. That voice, those words coming out of her mouth, the enormity of it ... was I repeating it? Or was I in a trance, stuck in the ever presence of shock?

"I've watched you, *watching* me. I've watched you *being* watched." She continues with her project.

A combination of panic, fear, and excitement swirls around in the center of my belly.

"I have to admit. I was greatly flattered to know I was being stalked. It quickly metamorphosed into the best game I have ever played. What are the odds of us two sharing this delightful adventure together? I must say ... you've really put a whole new meaning to the word dismembered."

I am in bondage. I feel like someone has a hand over my mouth like someone had tied my arms against my body. This is what dread feels like. There is no one holding me. There is no one else here with us deep in these woods. We are alone.

Fuuuuuck, just break free! What is wrong with you? Grow a vagina and bust out of this. You are better than this.

Much like a switch of a light ... something dark, menacing, deep from the darkest part of me, my dark friend comes to my rescue, and it begins to arise. The corners of my mouth unwind, and I can feel the beginning of a smile. Yes, it is a smile. One so strong and full of delight that I can hardly contain myself. The shackles burst. The fear melts away like warm butter. I am no longer plagued with fear.

"Don't you want to know what I am burying, JoDi?"

A warmth fills my legs as I step into the open. Can she see the dramatic smirk etched across my face?

"Ah, there she is." Nicky pulls the plastic bag from her backpack and pulls out a shiny object. It's clear at this point that she is wearing gloves. She wipes the small object and reads Yusuff's badge number out loud. When she is done, she tosses it in the deep hole she had just dug.

I inch closer, mesmerized by every detail of this moment. A feeling of euphoria creeps up and swallows all my anxiety.

"Just so you know, I don't appreciate the blow to the head. I actually did have some memory loss, but thanks to Dr. Trudi, or should I say, Madame Fontenot, it all came back. I do forgive you, by the way. I have seen how messy and immature you have been." Nicky continues as if every word isn't unavailing something with the same enormity of a nuclear bomb.

"Not to worry though, all that will change. I will guide you. I will teach you *all* the things." She drags out the word ALL as if there were so very many *things.*

I inch even closer to her until I, too, find a boulder to rest on. I sit. I take every word in as if they were the last words I would ever hear.

"I'm sure it goes without saying that you didn't bury your husband deep enough. Poor man, I'm sure you have realized by now that he was helping you. I thought of giving you a heads-up, but in the end, I realized he would only be in our way. You and I have bigger things ahead of us JoDi. I'm sure he couldn't figure out why the other members on your ledger didn't have coordinates. I'm sure he couldn't find the other members. It's because I am much better at this than you. Don't be angry. Yes, I took pictures of your list. Yes, I helped to carry out the things you couldn't do yourself. Don't worry, though. They will never be found and never bother anyone in your readers' group again. I did that for you, JoDi. I did it for us. My wealth and endless resources come in handy." She continues to fill in the hole.

"Anyhow, back to your husband … that was a scary one. He was a police officer, for Christ's sake. But like I said, I wanted to help you, JoDi."

Again, my name came off her lips like a melody.

"Don't worry. I took care of it. I buried him deeper. I took a few items from him so that you and I could share this moment together. Now, this is our place. Our special place. You know where I have buried items. I know where you have buried items. We can move on to more …" she pauses, "we can move on to grander things. This is where you and I will start our true adventure. No one can take this special place from us.

Don't you agree? Oh, don't answer that just yet. I have so much more to say. Would you like me to tell you a story, JoDi?"

This time Nicky is actually waiting for a response. I hesitate for a moment, but only so I don't seem overly eager. She may be grand, but I, too, have a large presence in this. I, too, have skin in the game. "Yes," I finally say. "There is nothing I want more right now than to hear a story from you, Nicky Lee." My voice is strong.

"Very well." Her response has excitement woven into it. "You see, JoDi, you have been quite sloppy. Not all the time, just here and there. So, after reading your ledger and finding out what exactly you had been up to, I decided to start following you. Obviously, I couldn't follow you everywhere, but here in Georgia, I did. It's hilarious that we were following each other. What a laugh! I'm sure you remember a woman named Lony Gansmann. I believe she had told a member to go suck a dick. She also told the member to go kill herself or something along those lines. I obviously know this from your ledger. Anyhow, you see, after you hit her over the head a few times, she later woke up. I don't know how. She did look dead. I suppose that's what you thought, too, once you saw how much blood she had lost, and the fact that she wasn't moving. I suppose you must have been in a hurry that day. I was surprised you didn't slit her throat. Anyhow, I was worried that you hadn't finished the job, so I stuck around. I'm so very glad I did because she woke up. I watched her drag herself to a creek. I watched her roll around in pain. I thought perhaps she would bleed to death, but she didn't. I had to finish what you started. It wasn't easy, by the way. One day I will tell you all the details. It wasn't easy moving a body from the woods to my property. Not easy at all. But, what's done is done."

"But why? Why would you do this for me?" I ask in astonishment.

"Out of foolishness, I suppose. But really, it turned out good in the end. You see, I needed something like this. After much evaluation, I realized that you might need proof or something to show I am not full of shit. I knew this day would come, and this day would be so full of surprises that I just knew you would need some form of verification. So, I trapped a present for you. She is currently in a tiny little cabin on one of my properties. I'm sure you still want to end her life because of what she has done. But I'm hoping this will be our first lesson. Always, and I mean *always,* make sure they are dead, JoDi."

"Are you going to take me to her?"

"Of course I am. She will be *our* first victim."

The idea of us working together is breathtaking. Endorphins are running wild throughout my body, spreading like ants over a freshly cut finger.

"Our first victim together." The words roll off my tongue like smooth cream. I'm sure she could sense the tremendous amount of euphoria I was experiencing. She knows. She must know. She must know that I need her. That I love her. How did she know I wanted her partnership even before I knew I wanted it? How did we come together? Nicky and I needed only the dark desires of our own uncommon passion.

"Something else needs to be addressed," She continues. "I did plenty of research on Dr. Trudi. I'm going to call her Dr. Trudi from now on because Madame Fontenot is just too much. Anyhow, I found her extensive notes on you. She probably didn't share all of them with you. But no worries, I will. I took pictures of it all. Seems you have two souls—how exhilarating. I will not lie; this is the ultimate reason I chose you. It wasn't so much the idea of you having two souls, my dear. It's that you were clever enough to make a professional believe you have two souls. I happen to believe you indeed have the soul of Mike, and you have built on it, grown it, nurtured it, and developed it, just like we all do. But you, sweet darling, are a murderer through and through. Just not a great one. But that will change." She pauses for a brief moment.

"It does, however, seem odd to me that you have so much sympathy. Most serial killers do not. It's all very puzzling. Who knows, perhaps you *are* cursed with two souls. You fascinate me. I will carry you on my wings. I have never craved the presence of another in my journey of revenge. But you … you JoDi, are special. Or should I say Mike?"

Nicky begins to dust off her pants. "Oh my, I have monopolized this conversation, haven't I? I imagine this is a lot for you to take in. Here is the last thing I have to say for now." She tucks the gardening shovel back into her backpack. "I am aware of your volunteer work. You can't live without it. I see that now. And that's okay. No need to stop that now. I do want to talk about your ledger. I'm sorry, but I read the whole thing. You were stalking me, so I thought it was only fair. I understand now why you can't stand bullies. Your sister was not just a bully, JoDi, she was indeed a psychopath. Perhaps that's why she is dead. Maybe one day you can tell me more about her. Maybe you can tell me why she is dead. Maybe you can tell me how she died."

She had taken little pleasure in my childhood, and I could read her pity like the headline of a breaking story.

She continued. "But for now, let's talk about potentially redirecting your passion somewhere else and finding a new target. Yes, the members are important. They do need you. But have you ever considered killing people who hurt children or animals? Or maybe the elderly? That, my dearest friend, is my specialty. You seem to care about them as well. Again, what are the odds? I'm so tickled by this. You know … I'm not surprised that there are two of us here in Atlanta. I mean, we *are* talking about Atlanta, after all. One of the major crime cities in America. What I am surprised about is that we actually found each other! Without the group, that would have been impossible. It's like the stars aligned for us, JoDi. We have to take advantage of this! They do say we attract like-minded people. That there are forces beyond our control. I suppose this is proof. The dark web still exists, you know. How do you feel about recruiting others from your group?"

Made in the USA
Monee, IL
14 December 2023